WHEN DAWN NEVER COMES

Novel By Kim Carter

When Dawn Never Comes

Published by Raven South Publishing

Atlanta, Georgia 30324, USA

Copyright © 2016 by Kim Carter

Cover Design by www.mariondesigns.com

Editing by CharmaineParker

Interior Design by Lissha Sadler~Writing Royalty Promotions

Library of Congress Control Number: 2018933817

ISBN 10: 978-1947140073 (paperback)

For speaking engagements, interviews, and book copies, please get in touch with Raven South Publishing:info@ravensouthpublishing.com.

Dedication

To Tom and Cheri Carter who first introduced me to Maine's majestic beauty. My love to you both!

And to Martha and Cecil Gaddy who have been on this roller coaster ride with me from the beginning. You've been fabulous friends and we have so many wonderful memories, most of which were made in our flannel pajamas!

Acknowledgments

I continue to be both amazed and humbled by the many people who share selflessly of their time and knowledge to help make my novels come to life. I certainly cannot let their efforts go unnoticed. Many thanks to the following:

John Cross from the Fulton County Medical Examiner's Office (GA). Joanna Macpherson and Lt. Mike Whitlow from the Fayetteville Police Department (GA). Pam Youngblood and Lisa Mobley Putnam for their many hours of edits and ideas amidst love and patience.

Chief Bob Hasch of the Boothbay Harbor Police Department (Maine). Major Donald Colburn, Clayton County Police Department (GA), retired. Keith Saunders, the most amazing cover designer I know. Raven South Publishing - I continue to be so proud to publish under your label.

Charmaine Parker, Trina Richardson, and Lissha Sadler who have worked tirelessly on edits and formatting, and have been my calm amidst many storms! They are all three tremendous talents and such strong, determined women. What a blessing, indeed, to know each of you.

Last, but certainly not least, my husband, Julius, who has supported me all the way.

Note to Readers

I hope you enjoyed reading When Dawn Never Comes. I'd appreciate it if you would post a review on the site you purchased it from, as well as on Amazon and Goodreads. I'm grateful for every one I receive. Feel free to contact me on Facebook and my website if you have any questions or thoughts about the stories. I love hearing from readers.

Very best regards,
Kim

Chapter 1

The waves crashed incessantly against the rocks. The roar was strong, as it was on most evenings, sounding more like a thunderstorm than the tide coming in. Her thin, blonde hair floated lightly on top of the waves, then lay matted on the wet sand. She'd been a beautiful girl although it wasn't visible now.Her eyes were open in a hollow stare, her mouth distorted in a silent scream, mirroring the last moments of fear that had raced through her mind. She bobbed up and down in the water until the sea decided it was time to retreat and finally allow her broken body time to rest. To lie still.

It was two days later when an old man found her there, naked and bloated from the sun. Thankfully, the rugged jetties had kept her body near the beach, and Jake Sims watched as the coroner's office struggled to pull her free.

"Thank you, Mr. Sims. Sorry you had to walk up on this. Any idea who she could be?" Sheriff Murphy asked.

"No, Elias, I don't. Pretty young lady though. Can't imagine anyone wanting to do such a thing. Any idea how she could've died?"

"There are several blows to the head, but they could be from the rocks. Looks like she was strangled, best I can tell."

"Can't imagine this happening in Solomon Cove," Jake said solemnly.

"Me either. Want a lift home? I'm heading your way."

"I'd appreciate that, Sheriff. I think I've walked enough for today."

The two rode in silence, but not an uncomfortable one. They'd known each other far too long for that. It was simply unimaginable... a young woman, murdered in this quiet fishing village on the coast of Maine. The sheriff rarely even wrote a speeding ticket, and if he did, most were to the tourists passing through, not to the locals. The gravel crunched loudly under the cruiser's tires as Sheriff Murphy pulled into Jake's driveway.

"Want to come in for a drink?" Jake asked.

"I need to get back and start on this paperwork. The mayor will be demanding answers long before I can produce them," Elias noted.

"C'mon, Sheriff. One stiff drink never hurt anybody. Besides, I believe we're both due one today."

Nodding in agreement, the sheriff followed him inside. Elias Murphy was surprised to see how neat Jake kept his small cabin. He often wondered why Jake had never married. He was an interesting man, and as far as Elias could tell, he wasn't a bad-looking one either. Jake broke his train of thought to hand him a small snifter of cheap bourbon.

"To better days than this one," Jake said, holding up his glass.

"To better days than this," Elias replied, tapping his glass lightly with Jake's raised one. In one quick swoop, the two men finished off their shots and walked back onto the front porch.

* * * *

Just as the sheriff had expected, Mayor Thomas Blake was sitting restlessly in his office. He never took time for formalities and this time wouldn't be an exception.

"What've you got on the girl? Was it a drowning or homicide?" Thomas demanded.

"Good morning, Mayor," Sheriff Murphy said with little attempt to hide his disdain. "The coroner just retrieved the body. We didn't find any identification on the scene. I'm heading to the morgue now if you'd like to ride along."

"I'll do that," he countered.

Thomas Blake was a distant man, even to those who knew him best. His long, lean body resembled a professional athlete, and although he was beginning to bald—at forty-five—he was a handsome man. Along with running the only law firm in town, he'd been the mayor in Solomon Cove for over ten years. After the accidental death of his wife and son, he had become obsessed with his work, and many times the town felt the wrath of his dedication.

The two men rode the four blocks to the medical examiner's office with little to say to one another. The county morgue was small, rarely holding more than two bodies at any given time. The dead were usually retired residents or an occasional car crash victim. A possible murder was big news for Solomon Cove.

"Good morning, Alexandria," Sheriff Murphy said in a professional tone.

"Good morning, Sheriff," she spoke in the sweet Southern accent she'd spent years trying to conceal. It was obvious the two had something for each other, and everyone in town wanted to ask why they even attempted to disguise it.

"Where is Dr. Chambers, Alex?" Mayor Blake questioned brusquely.

"He's in the back. He told me to bring you two back as soon as you arrived."

She stood up, pressing her skirt down neatly with both hands. She was tall and thin, with striking blue eyes and dark hair. There was a kindness about her that made everyone in town love her. Alex walked to the second examination room, tapped on the door, and walked away. The mayor entered without hesitation, then stopped in his tracks.

It was hard to look at the young body lying on the cold metal table. She looked as if she should be frolicking on a beach with her girlfriends or walking across the green grass of a large college campus. Instead, she lay here, her small, delicate hands and feet wrapped carefully for evidence.

"It never gets easier seeing young people like this," Dr. Chambers said quietly. "It just isn't the way God intended it." He reached for a small Styrofoam cup of water and took two swallows.

"Have you determined the cause of death?" Elias asked.

"More than likely strangulation. Wasn't an easy death. She was raped and beaten before she died. Can't imagine what this world is coming to." Dr. Chambers pulled the thin, crisp sheet back, revealing purple bruising that covered most of her body. "The rocks weren't too kind to her either."

"Could you find any evidence?" Mayor Blake asked, getting tactlessly to the point.

"A couple of fibers under her fingernails and a dark pubic hair. The cold water was the only element that was good to her. Called *adipocere*, it is," he said calmly, trying to turn the situation into a medical lesson rather than the brutal murder before them. "The fatty tissue under the skin begins to saponify."

"Damn it. I give." The mayor rolled his eyes. "What the hell does *saponify* mean?"

"Kind of turns the body into soap, can preserve it for months, sometimes years. The low water temp kept her from the normal changes that come with decomposition."

"Thanks for the gory details, Doc." Thomas turned from the body.

"Do you think you guys could help me bag her up and

get her into the cooler?" Doc asked calmly.

The two men stood silent and motionless.

"I'll take that as a *yes*. I'm getting to be an old man." He handed them each a pair of rubber gloves, which they put on slowly in a meager attempt to delay the inevitable.

The plastic body bag was heavy and dark with a sharp, shiny zipper. They placed her young body in it as tenderly as they could. The three men stood for a moment, their eyes transfixed on her contorted face. Elias felt a sudden urge to scream at her, to plead with her to wake up before the zipper made its way up to her once beautiful face. Instead, he looked away, listening to the cruel sounds of the zipper as it closed her off from view.

Thomas shivered openly and rubbed his hands briskly along his arms. "Let's get out of here," he muttered, relieved to walk out of the refrigerated tomb.

"Any idea who she is?" Elias asked, his eyes moist.

"I had Alex fax her prints over to state police, but she doesn't look like someone that'll have a police record. She was nude, and there weren't any personal belongings anywhere on the shoreline," Doc replied.

"Call us when you hear anything, Doctor Chambers," Mayor Blake ordered.

"I'll be in touch," Elias said.

Chapter 2

Jordan lay in bed listening to the sounds of New York. The constant clamor of tourists and businessmen, and the screeching of tires from the traffic. She was amazed she no longer consciously heard the cries of the sirens.

It'd taken her two years to sleep through the night, but now New York was in her blood. It was going to be hard to leave but would've been even harder to stay. Her freelance articles weren't bringing in enough money to cover expenses, and she refused to move to a worse neighborhood than she was already in.

She studied the copy of the will again, only keener this time.

James Maxwell does hereby bequeath all material belongings to his great-niece, Jordan Tae Maxwell. The stated shall include the estate located at:

815 Alden Drive Solomon Cove, Maine 04538

All furniture and possessions therein, and $950,000.00.

She'd met him once. So long ago, it strained her memory to recall it. He'd been sixty and Jordan only five years old.

She remembered his gnarled hands, reflecting the burden of years of arthritis. He'd frightened her, and as she looked back on it as an adult, she could understand why.

His mansion had been dark and dusty and smelled of mildew. Large framed portraits of solemn faces hung along the walls, while quiet butlers and maids served coffee and tea.

Jordan had sensed her parents felt uncomfortable too as their visits were always brief and noncommittal. She wished they were alive to talk to about this whole situation. How did she inherit the estate; why did she inherit it? Jordan had been told that James Maxwell's only son had spent years in an asylum and she'd wondered what had become of him. She made a mental note to question the attorney about it the following morning.

The ring of the phone startled her.

"Still in the bed, sleepyhead?"

Jordan smiled as she thought of Eric. He'd probably been in the office for a couple of hours by now. She could picture him with a pen behind his ear and one in his hand as he peered over the mountain of paperwork piled high on his desk.

"What's the story of the day?" Jordan asked inquisitively. She always enjoyed hearing about his work as a journalist for *The New York Times*. Eric covered a great deal of the local homicides. Sometimes his stories were so gruesome Jordan found herself dreaming about them; others were so mysterious she would ponder over their motives for weeks. Others were senseless acts of random violence. Regardless of the situation, Eric would put his heart into not only reporting them but in solving them as well. The NYPD valued his opinion, which got him closer to most stories than other journalists.

"A drive-by shooting in Bedford-Stuyvesant. Perp missed his target, killing a four-year-old girl. Cute thing, lots of pigtails. Sometimes I think I have to be sick to enjoy this job. What have you got planned for today?"

"I really need to get up and start organizing this packing mission. Are you coming over tonight to help? I'll order Chinese. I only have a few more chances to eat L'ings."

"I wouldn't want to deprive you of more takeout from L'ings. He's going to have to shut the place down when you move. I think you're his only business." With that, Eric laughed and Jordan thought of his smile. He was gorgeous, and she loved everything about him. It was hard to put leaving him out of her mind.

"Oh, that's real funny, smart-ass. Try to be here before 8:00 if you can." With that, she hung up the phone, no "good-bye," no "I love you." Sometimes that is what it took for him to realize she was serious. Otherwise, she would be calling him at the office around 9:30 threatening him to put down a story.

She rolled back over in bed, covering her head with an overstuffed pillow.

"I've got to get up and get at it," she said out loud. It was something her mother used to say when she'd try to sleep late as a teenager. Jordan lifted the pillow, glimpsing around the small, crowded room. Heavy boxes in need of assembling lay everywhere, while stacks of dishes sat in the middle of the floor, waiting to be wrapped in newspaper.

The studio apartment had never been large enough. The heavy antique bed took up far too much room, but it came with childhood memories, and she couldn't bear to part with it. Jordan closed her eyes and remembered all the nights her parents had read her to sleep. Her father had been much more animated than her mother. Their laughter could be heard all over the house, while her mother read softly and intently. Jordan would lie against her breast and fall asleep. Good memories.

She had many of those. She only needed to close her eyes to relive them over and over again. Other than the bed, the apartment wasn't very homey. The small kitchenette had been adequate, but only because she rarely cooked meals there. It had sufficed for preparing her famous boxed macaroni and cheese and peanut butter sandwiches.

There hadn't been room for a kitchen table, but that'd been fine since she didn't have one anyway. There was, however, a dingy gray sofa, which she had inherited from her college roommate, and a scarred coffee table that held both her computer monitor and printer. *Home Sweet Home,* she thought.

Rummaging around in the debris, Jordan couldn't imagine what she'd possibly miss about this place.

Maybe it's just that it's been home for the past three years, she thought, then realized quickly it'd never actually been home.

Be honest with yourself. She sighed. It's not New York you'll miss; it's Eric.

The two met at Berkeley when they'd both been journalism students. There had been an instant attraction, but their relationship had been adversarial. They constantly competed against each other's work, and it wasn't until they connected in New York that they realized their shared talents were beneficial. The rest had been history.

It was Eric who had been there for her when her parents had been killed in the house fire and Eric who'd encouraged her writing. Even when she hadn't felt like pushing herself to do it anymore, he'd been her determination. Eric couldn't understand why Jordan wanted to leave, all but pleading with her not to, but her mind was made up. She needed the change, her career needed the change, and Jordan was convinced a change of scenery would do her work some good.

Most of all, Jordan wanted desperately to be near family. Even though she'd not known her great-uncle well, at least this house had belonged in her family—a house her parents had visited, if only a handful times. Her plans were to leave in a week, but the movers would be picking up her belongings in two days. After that, she'd spend the remaining few days at Eric's place.

At twenty-seven Jordan was an eye-catching beauty. She was tall, with a willowy body that seemed to dance across the floor as she walked. Sauntering toward the bathroom, she slowly undressed, and looked at her naked body in the mirror. Critiquing her figure, she examined her long lean legs up to her trim torso and large, firm breasts. Her forearms and biceps were easy clues she spent a great deal of time in the gym.

She took the rubber band out of her hair, letting her golden locks flow around her shoulders. She'd taken after her mother: fair skin, and light-blonde hair. Her eyes were green, sometimes looking hazel. More than once she'd longed for her father's dark skin and hair, but he'd always told her she was more fortunate to resemble her mother.

Opening the shower curtain, Jordan stepped into the steamy water. Closing her eyes, she put her head under the faucet letting the hot mist cover her face. She lathered her hair and body, then stood under the water until it ran cold. That was one of the pleasures of living alone, she often told herself, never having to save hot water for someone else.

After taking an hour to dress in jeans and a T-shirt, she pulled her hair back into a ponytail and finally began the task of boxing up her possessions. Before she knew it, the day passed her by. The clock, about the only thing left hanging on the wall, displayed 7:30. Jordan grabbed the phone and dialed L'ings.

"Hello, Johnny. This is Jordan. I'll have an order of beef and broccoli and Moo Goo Gai Pan. Throw in four egg rolls with that, please."

"It'll be ready in twenty minutes," Johnny said. He'd worked takeout for the L'ings since Jordan had been in New York. She often wondered what his story was. Tall and lanky, he looked to be the age of a college student but had never shared anything with her about how he spent his off time. Jordan often spotted him riding his bike through the streets with L'ings deliveries strapped to the back. *Yes, she would miss Johnny too.*

Placing the phone back on its receiver, she went into the kitchen to mix up a batch of strong margaritas. Tonight, they'd be strawberry because of the few fresh ones left in the fridge. The whirl of the blender drowned out the radio, but a faint scream could still be heard. At times, Jordan forgot she lived in the big city. Without a second thought, she flung her door open and discovered her neighbor Anna lying bloodied on the floor.

She saw movement from the corner of her eye—the back of a large-framed male, dressed in dark clothing, and running down the hallway. Jordan's heart was racing as she bent down to gently brush Anna's hair from her face. It was difficult to pinpoint the exact source of the profuse bleeding. Using her shirttail, she began wiping the blood away from Anna's face.

"Someone *help* me, please!" Jordan screamed, her voice

resonating loudly throughout the building. "Somebody *come* quickly!"

Jordan didn't know many of her neighbors and had only spoken to Anna on occasion. So, it came as no surprise when no one answered her plea for help.

Struggling with the weight, she managed to drag Anna into her apartment, leaving her briefly to retrieve some towels. With one swipe, Jordan grabbed the cordless phone and dialed 9-1-1 as she rushed over with the towels and a pillow.

"Anna, it's me, Jordan. You're okay now, I've got you."

Anna's eyes reflected confusion and pain as she slowly opened her mouth. "Help. Help me."

"Don't try to talk; the ambulance is on its way. Where do you hurt the most?"

Anna moved her finger up, indicating her abdomen was the source of the pain. Jordan hadn't even noticed there were other sources of bleeding. She'd been so shocked by the amount of blood on her face.

I should've assessed the whole situation, she thought. How many times have I taken first aid?

"Don't touch it, Anna." Jordan felt a sudden wave of nausea as she assessed the wound on her round, pudgy belly. It had to be a knife wound. It was so deep she couldn't see where it ended.

Jordan knew enough to keep direct pressure on it until EMTs arrived. Thankfully, it didn't seem to cause Anna any additional pain.

"Who did this to you, Anna? What happened?"

Anna's words were measured and deliberate. "Followed me. Followed from the parking deck," she said weakly before starting to gurgle. "I–I–tried-to-run-fast."

Jordan felt the bile rising in her throat as she laid Anna's head down and ran to the kitchen sink. She was there vomiting when the paramedics arrived. Stationing themselves at Anna's side, they talked calmly and patiently to her.

"What's her name, Ma'am?" one of them blurted to Jordan.

"Anna, Anna Stephens. She lives next door." She turned to heave into the sink.

"We're gonna need a chopper; she's critical," one of them said into a static-filled radio. "Check with the Super to confirm it can land on the roof, stat."

They were busy inserting an IV as Jordan finally pulled herself together enough to walk over and sit beside her on the floor. Stroking Anna's blood-soaked hair, she heard her own voice sobbing despite efforts to silence it. Anna was fading in and out; her breathing was becoming labored.

"You're strong, Anna," Jordan whispered, suddenly wishing she'd gotten to know her better. She didn't know why she hadn't.

Anna had been friendly enough, with a contagious and sincere smile. The voice on the radio interrupted the group, startling Jordan.

"Super gave permission for roof landing. ETA is less than five. We're heading to Mt. Sinai Medical. Vitals are falling. Stab wounds to the abdomen and chest area. Blunt force trauma to the head." They lifted her broken body onto the gurney and were gone within seconds.

Johnny walked in just as Jordan fell to the floor, breaking into sobs. She was hugging a bloody towel close to her face, giving the appearance that she was the one injured. He dropped the brown bag on the end table and ran to her side. Jordan fell over onto his shoulder and she could feel his panicked breathing on the nape of her neck.

"Oh my God, oh my God. Someone stabbed her, someone from the parking deck. She's going to die; she just can't make it."

"Are you hurt, Ms. Maxwell? Are you okay? Please tell me you're okay."

"I'm sorry," she said, surprised at how calm she sounded. "There was an accident. An attack, actually, on Anna Stephens. She was screaming in the hall; it was terrible."

"Let me help you up to the sofa," he said, gently pulling her up by her elbow. "Where do you keep your towels?"

"In the closet in the hall."

Johnny left her and was gone only a few seconds before returning with a couple of wet towels. He wiped her hands until all of the blood was gone, then put a warm bath cloth over her face.

"What's going on here, Jordan? Are you all right?" Eric demanded as he entered the apartment. He was standing above her, his face flushed.

"I'm okay. It's Anna across the hall. Someone attacked her. I'm so afraid." The sobs came again, only harder this time. Eric held her in his arms while kissing the top of her head.

"The takeout is on the end table. I'll go now. Let me know if I can do anything."

"Thanks, Johnny," Eric said, reaching for his wallet.

"No, Sir, there won't be any charge tonight. I hope you sleep well, Ms. Maxwell."

Eric pulled an old quilt out of the closet and wrapped it around her, then handed her a large glass filled with the thawed margarita. Her hands were trembling uncontrollably, so he held the glass for her to take a sip.

"My God, Jordan, thank God it wasn't you. I saw the helicopter and the police and it scared the hell out of me. I'm actually glad now that you're leaving this place."

Chapter 3

The little town of Solomon Cove was already abuzz with the news of the young woman's murder. Much to everyone's surprise, she'd been identified through the bureau's fingerprint files.

Sheriff Murphy was sitting down, tapping his pencil loudly on his desk calendar. He looked up briefly as the mayor entered. Elias heaved an exasperated sigh. "You know, Thomas, even a sheriff would appreciate a knock every now and then."

The comment went unnoticed or more likely than not, it went unacknowledged. "Rachel called and said you got some prints back on the girl."

"An OUI came back from two years ago. She was a college student at Radcliffe. Probably drank a little too much and drove home from a sorority party. Her name was Jennifer Flemming. Comes from money, bright girl, graduated two years ago. She just finished teaching her first year of elementary school—first grade, I believe. She taught over in Somergrove."

"Any suspects yet?"

Elias looked at the mayor, refusing to answer for a few seconds. He paused just long enough to let him know he was disgruntled.

"I'm working on that as we speak. I spoke with the school principal. She was well-liked on the job, but not many close friends nearby, with it being her first year and all. She was seen dating a young man by her landlord, but he never slept over. Figured it couldn't have been all that serious."

"Have you contacted the family?"

"Her family lives in a small town in Massachusetts. I called the local sheriff there and requested he send a deputy and clergyman over to the house. He hasn't phoned me back."

"What about college friends, roommates, boyfriends?"

"It's been a day and a half, Mayor. I'm working on it," Elias said blandly.

"Don't take it personally, Sheriff; we all have jobs to do. As you know, murders have to be solved in a timely manner or they become cold case files. We don't want any of those in Solomon Cove."

With that, the mayor stood up, stretched a little, and walked condescendingly out of the office.

"Prick," the Sheriff said under his breath. "Rachel," he said over the speakerphone, "call Doctor Chambers and tell him I'm on my way over. I need to see the body again."

"Will do, Sheriff."

Rachel was a sweet girl, and Elias never took the time to tell her how much he appreciated her. At the tender age of twenty-one, she'd already worked for him for three years. She'd married right out of high school and came to work for the department. In all honesty, Rachel actually ran the place. She was the secretary, the dispatcher, the recordkeeper, and the payroll clerk.

I've got to tell her thank you one of these days, he thought, as he grabbed his coat off the back of the door.

"Don't forget your radio," Rachel yelled as she chased him to his car.

"What would I do without you?" he asked.

* * * *

Doctor Chambers was sitting up front, drinking a cup of steaming coffee with Alex.

"Don't you two realize tax-paying dollars are paying your salaries?" Elias laughed, more to himself than to his audience. If he had a dime for every time he'd heard that insulting comment through the years, he could retire.

"Now, Sheriff, you know everyone is due a coffee break." Doctor Chambers laughed. "I think that's covered by the law; maybe you could check on it."

"Hello, Alex," Elias said. "Do you have to put up with this smart-ass all day or does he give you a break every now and then?"

"Now, boys, let's play nice," she scoffed. "Can I get you some coffee, Sheriff?"

"That'd be great. Black, please."

"I don't know why, Doc, but I just need to see the girl again," Elias said as Alex handed him a cup of the steaming brew.

"Come on back," Doctor Chambers said, standing and motioning down the hall. "I expect the family to be here to identify her sometime today. Won't be easy. Hopefully, it won't be the mother. No mother should have to see her child like this."

Jennifer was lying on the table, still zipped up in the dark tarp. It seemed even sadder now that she had an identity. Elias wasn't sure what he was looking for. Maybe he just wanted to remember everything about her, so he'd never stop looking for her killer.

"Have you got photos of everything, Doc?"

"I had a special I.D. unit come down from Anderson. Did a real thorough job. Took both Polaroids and digitals. Those boys know what they're doing. The Polaroids are in a file up front; we should have the others in a few days. I could probably expedite it if I need to."

"Thanks, Rusty."

Elias instantly felt awkward. No one ever called the doctor by his first name. It was either Dr. Chambers or just plain Doc. Elias pulled the zipper back to look at her wrists again. Swollen and blue, but they didn't appear to have been bound at any point. Neither did her ankles.

"She must've come willingly. Do you think she knew her attacker?" Elias asked.

"Could be. She didn't have any skin under her fingernails, so she must have been unconscious during the rape. Did find a few fibers though, hopefully from the killer's clothing and not hers. They're at the state crime lab. No offense, Sheriff, but something of this magnitude needs to be handled by folks who deal with it on a regular basis," Doctor Chambers said, diverting his eyes from Elias.

"No offense taken, Doc, you should know that by now. This woman deserves justice, no matter who gives it to her."

Elias put on a pair of rubber gloves and felt around her head softly, almost as though he was afraid he might hurt her.

"Major contusions to the head," Doc said. "Hard to tell the difference, but it appears one may be something like a baseball bat, whereas the others are more likely from the rocks. She died ultimately from strangulation. Rope. I got a few fibers from it and you can see from the ligature marks on her neck, it was almost certainly rope."

Doctor Chambers reached over to the cardboard box and pulled out a pair of latex gloves for himself. He quickly slipped his hands into them and reached carefully for Jennifer's head. Turning her face to the side, he pointed to dark bruises behind her ears. "This is certainly characteristic of a strangulation," he said, shaking his head in disbelief.

"But the nail in the coffin is the petechiae in the eyes," he continued as he lifted her eyelids, displaying the red dots of blood in her eyes. "Dead giveaway of any asphyxiation."

"Any semen?"

"I don't know if it'll be identifiable. The current was pretty strong. I'm sure the water diluted any chance of DNA evidence."

"Let me know when the family gets here. I'll need to see them," Elias said.

* * * *

Alex was facing the filing cabinet with her back to Elias. He stopped for a minute to admire her just as she was turning around. He fumbled with his keys and felt his ears burning as they had when he was embarrassed as a teenager. Elias hadn't dated much and at thirty-one, his social life was more than inadequate; it was nonexistent.

"It looks like you'll be busy for a while," she drawled.

Damn, she's beautiful, he thought.

"Sheriff, are you all right?" she continued.

"Just a lot on my mind, sorry. Listen, Alex, I got a couple of tickets to a play in Anderson for Friday night. Someone sent them to me; I'm not sure if it'll be any good." He felt himself droning on and on, his voice ranging from light to heavy. "It probably won't be any good; most free tickets aren't you know."

"If you're asking me to go, I'd love to."

"Great, I'll pick you up at 8:00," he stammered. With that, he rushed out the door almost hitting the frame. "I need a haircut," he mumbled to himself.

* * * *

Elias was walking into the station as Rachel motioned for him. "Doc Chambers is on your line and Sam called in sick. His back is bothering him again."

"Great," Elias muttered, knowing he'd have to cover for him if there were any problems.

He threw his coat on the nearest chair and sat down heavily at his desk. Feeling the beginnings of a headache, he rubbed his temples in a circular motion for a few seconds before picking up the phone.

"What's going on, Doc? I just left you," Elias stammered into the phone, forgoing any pleasantries.

"The girl's parents and brother will be here in a couple of hours. They have a funeral home scheduled to pick her up at 5:00. I don't see a problem with it. We've gotten all we can, just wanted to check with you first."

"Let them take their daughter home. Let's not hold it up; they're going through enough already. I'm going to grab some lunch and make a couple of calls. Call Rachel when they arrive. She'll reach me by radio if I'm not in the office."

"Will do."

Elias looked at the small mountain of messages on his desk: calls from residents curious about the murder, a complaint about a small pothole on Elder Street, and a request for an interview from the local paper. He pushed the speakerphone and asked Rachel to come in.

"I need you to return the calls concerning the murder. Just tell them I'm busy working on it, and they shouldn't fear for their safety. Call it an *isolated incident*. Don't give out her name although none of them would know her. She's a Harvard grad, and we don't have many alumni around here.

Forward the pothole complaint over to Public Works and tell them to fix the damn thing. It's been four weeks now; the natives are getting restless. The citizens want my job, and I tell ya, it doesn't sound like such a bad deal right about now. Call Regina at the *Solomon Gazette*. Tell her I can talk with her tomorrow at noon. You'll have to remind me about it in the morning though," Elias said, leaning back in his aging desk chair.

"I'll do that. Want me to call Evan in to work tonight? It's his day off, but I hear he could use the overtime." Rachel jotted notes on a memo pad.

"The mayor is bitching about overtime, but call Evan in anyway. If he doesn't want to work, ask Trent if he'd like to pull a double. Otherwise, I'll be on call."

"I'll let you know either way, Sheriff."

Rachel got up to leave, but Elias stopped her before she reached the door.

"You know you're my better half, don't you?" he asked sincerely.

"Yes, I do," she answered sternly.

"I've been talking to the mayor about a raise for you. If you ever left us, it'd take five people to replace you. Thanks, Rachel, for all you do. I never stop to tell you, but we all appreciate you."

"Thanks, I needed that."

"How's Hank doing? Is business going well?" Elias felt guilty for not asking her about her personal life more often.

"The plumbing business is like being a doctor; he's always on call. It's going okay though. We bought a couple of acres on Helmer Road. We hope to build soon."

"That's great," he responded, feeling left out that Rachel hadn't shared it before now. "I know you'll be happy to get out of the apartment."

"Oh, how right you are," she agreed, clearly pleased with the prospect of a new home.

"I'm going to get some lunch, then I'll be at the morgue most of the afternoon questioning the family. My radio's on; call me if you need me."

Elias walked the two blocks to the Corner Café and grabbed a small booth in the back. Not that it would matter, of course, because he was never able to eat a meal in peace. He hadn't had an appetite since the murder, but his stomach had that undeniable queasy feeling of someone who needed to fill their belly.

Food would probably help this headache, too, he thought. Elias didn't bother to pick up the menu; he'd known it by heart for years now. The only thing different would be the daily special.

"Good afternoon, Sheriff," Lacy said. She'd worked at the diner since Elias was a boy. "What sounds good to you today?"

"Hi, Lacy, what's the special?"

"Meatloaf, mashed potatoes, green beans, and apple pie."

"Who could turn that down? That'll be fine. I'll take the usual iced tea; hold the lemon."

"Be right back."

Elias watched Lacy walk across the diner speaking to everyone by name as she passed. That's what he loved about this place. As aggravating as it could be at times, everyone knew everyone else, and that's what made it home. He thought back to his college days, recalling how he'd been the only one who wanted to return to his hometown. It never seemed right living anywhere else. Lacy returned and motioned for him to slide over as she squeezed her plump behind next to him in the booth.

"We've all heard about the girl. Horrible, horrible tragedy. Heard she was a pretty thing. Do you think Solomon Cove is still safe or are we turning into one of those big cities with muggings and murder? Suppose we'll be seeing gangs next."

She looked so innocent that Elias had to force back a laugh. "Ms. Lacy, I don't think we have anything to worry about. This was an isolated incident. Someone just dropped her off here. No, Ma'am, we're far from the big city and I intend to keep it that way."

Lacy seemed satisfied with his reply and wiggled herself out of the booth.

"Your mama would be proud of you, dear; just quit that smoking, you hear?"

Lacy placed his steaming food in front of him, but Elias didn't feel like eating it. His stomach was in turmoil as he thought about the girl's parents. He hated for them to have to see her like that.Elias listened intently as Lacy scolded him for not cleaning his plate before downing the remainder of his iced tea.

He pulled two dollars from his wallet and laid them carefully on the table before carrying his ticket to the cash register. The sheriff knew his meals were on the house, but he refused the gesture. Lacy told him he must have "more money than sense," but he couldn't bring himself to accept the slightest gift. It brought back memories of his criminal justice professor at the University of New England.

"Accepting so much as a free soda is the first step toward being on the take," he'd continually said. It'd rung in Elias's ears through the years, even though he allowed his deputies to accept any discounts the town businesses offered.

They were underpaid, and he knew it, so he never made an issue of it. The knot in Sheriff Elias Murphy's gut continued to grow as he struggled to keep his mind off the murder. It wasn't going to happen, so he decided to ride by the crime scene before going over to the morgue. He had plenty of time and wanted to insure he asked all the pertinent questions of the family. The rocks where the body had been discovered might help him to think of those.

Elias made the fifteen-minute drive out of town in less than ten. Traffic was nonexistent, so he drove a little faster than he would've at any other time of day. There was no denying Solomon Cove was a beautiful place. The combination of beautiful, snowy winters, and summers spent by the water kept him devoted to his home.

His car slowed as he pulled to the side of the road. He reached into the back seat and grabbed a pair of fishing waders. Elias stumbled over the rocks and across the sand to where the strips of yellow crime scene tape still floated atop the water. The area was deserted now. The only sounds were of the waves crashing against the rocks.

Why would someone dump her here in the water? he thought. They'd have to know she would wash up to the shore.

Fluorescent markings painted on some of the rocks got his attention. He climbed over to them, conscious of the fact he was getting wet. About forty feet out, the waves were coming down hard against the rocks, spewing foam high into the air. He was grateful she hadn't looked any worse than she did.

Looking down the coast, Elias saw the roof of the old Maxwell mansion. He'd always been afraid of it for some reason. Maybe because it sat so close to the cliff leading to the water's edge, or maybe it was simply the sheer enormity of it. When he was a little boy, his friends had often called it *haunted*. Mr. Maxwell had recently died, and Elias wondered who would move into the place. Rumor around town was that a great-niece had inherited it. Regardless of who moved in, they'd have to be more pleasant than James Maxwell. Lucky for the town, he rarely left the old place. He'd made his fortune in the paper mill business.

He'd been buried him on the mansion's property and Elias heard there were only twelve people in attendance, most of whom he'd employed to run the household. Elias's body shivered as he turned his attention back to the water.

We don't know her here, he thought. So why would we need to find her? Maybe the killer was someone who had cared about her and didn't want her body rotting away somewhere without a proper burial. That was a possibility, but why Solomon Cove? It wasn't exactly on a main thoroughfare.

"Or it could be there's no damn reasoning at all," he said to himself, to the ocean, and the rocks, and anything else that might hear him.

Elias walked back and sat down in the police car, his feet dangling out as he struggled to get his waders off. He could hear the static fuzz over the radio followed by Rachel's voice.

"Sheriff Murphy, Doctor Chambers is ready for you."

"Ten-four, Rachel. My ETA is less than ten."

Elias disregarded the beautiful scenery on the return trip into town. His body was filled with dread, reminding him of the night he'd gone to tell Thomas Blake about his wife and son.

They had died on this same roadway on a stormy night. Lauren had been speeding, her blood alcohol level well over the legal limit. She'd driven off the cliff, falling 175 feet to her death, killing her son along with her.

It'd been a horrific sight, in fact, Elias found himself still dreaming about it. Thomas had sworn Lauren hadn't been drinking and that someone had cut her brake lines. There was never any truth to it, but Blake had almost lost his mind over the whole ordeal. Elias and Thomas were never close after that.

It was as though Thomas blamed everyone he could set his eyes on. Elias hated the thought of another family having the life sucked out of them.

Elias pulled his car in front of the building, noticing the sleek, black Mercedes. *They will already know by now,* he thought. Nodding to Alex as he walked by, he noticed her face was damp with tears. He could hear the wails coming from Dr. Chamber's office as he slowly walked down the hall, wishing this were another one of his nightmares.

Elias tapped lightly on the door before letting himself in. He held his breath, aware the scene would hit him with the full force of a blow. The mother was hysterical, looking as though she may need medical attention. Doc was trying to soothe her and encourage her to take a Valium. The father reflected the stone face men often wear when they're trying to hold it together. The younger brother was hovered over a trashcan waiting for the next wave of vomit to surface.

"Mr. Flemming?" Elias asked, extending his hand hesitantly.

"Yes?" he said, looking up as his voice cracked.

"I'm Sheriff Murphy and I'm terribly sorry for your loss. I understand this is not a good time for questions, but I need to speak with you."

"Sheriff, I just want to get my little girl home. I just want to get her home." He said it as if he believed she'd somehow come back to life when he got her there.

"I understand, Sir," Elias said softly. "Really, I do. But I want to find your daughter's killer and I need your help." The silence that followed was deafening as Elias ran his tongue across his parched lips.

"We're staying at the Bayside Inn tonight," Mr. Flemming said, clearing his throat. "The doctor is giving my wife a sedative to help her sleep. I'm going to have a stiff drink. Meet me in the bar at 9:00." He turned, putting his arm around his wife's shoulder, and began to sob along with her.

Elias didn't reply. He stood, nodded to Dr. Chambers, and let himself out. He didn't look at Alex this time when he walked by. He didn't want her to see the tears rolling down his own cheeks.

Chapter 4

Sheriff Murphy spotted Mr. Flemming, slumped over the far side of the bar, looking into his drink with dull, lifeless eyes. He suddenly felt terribly thoughtless for bringing his memo pad and pen. Sliding onto the barstool beside him, Elias ordered a Dewar's scotch on the rocks. "Is your wife sleeping?"

"Finally. She sobbed herself to sleep. My son's taking it just as hard. I never imagined losing one of my children, especially not this way."

Elias didn't pretend to know how he felt; he wouldn't have dreamed of insulting him. He slugged his scotch, holding up his glass and two fingers to the bartender.

"I'm sorry to bother you at a time like this, but it's important to get all the information I can. Do you know anyone who would want to harm her?"

"No," Mr. Flemming answered quickly, adding emphatically, "no one." The rims around his eyes were red from crying, and his eyelids were starting to swell. It appeared to Elias he'd aged several years since their meeting earlier in the day.

"Tell me about her friends. Did she have any from her job or her apartment complex?"

"Jennifer mentioned she dated another teacher a few times. His name was Justin, I believe. They liked each other, but it was more of a friendship than anything. She wanted to find someone special. She would've told us if she had."

"Any friends other than work?"

"Jenny made friends everywhere she went," he said. "I'm sure she was well-liked, but she never mentioned anyone in particular."

Elias decided to give it a rest for a few minutes. The two sat quietly sipping their drinks. The bartender slid a bowl of pretzels in front of them, and they ate until they were gone. He motioned for another round, even though he was already feeling the effects of the first two. Elias was anxious for anything that would deaden the pain of the evening.

"Did she have any enemies back home, anyone that could've been jealous of her?"

"No one at all."

"Any close friends?"

"She had two best friends, Amy and Debbie, both she's known since grammar school. They'll be devastated." He stopped talking and Elias realized he was envisioning telling them about Jenny's death.

"Jenny was a popular girl," Mr. Flemming started again. "She was a cheerleader and the prom queen. I can't imagine it being anyone she knows." He reached into his back pocket, pulling out his leather wallet. His hands shook, either from the effects of the alcohol or the strain of the day, as he handed Elias a photo of Jennifer.

"This is my daughter. She was special; she lit up the world. Keep this to remember her by in the upcoming weeks and months as you search for her killer. Please don't stop until you have found them."

Elias took the picture, looking at it before he commented. She was much more beautiful than he'd thought. "I give you my word, Mr. Flemming," he said devoutly. "I won't stop until I find the heartless bastard."

Chapter 5

Jordan opened her eyes and noticed the bright stream of light coming through the windows. She sat up quickly on the bed, in a panic, as she recalled what'd happened the night before.

"It's okay, honey," Eric said. He was sitting on the couch wrapping the dishes in newspaper.

"How could I have slept through all of this? Tell me it was a dream, Eric, please."

"Don't get upset again, Jordan. I called the hospital; Anna's still alive. They have her listed in critical, but she's holding her own. Apparently, someone tried to rob her last night, and she resisted."

"Oh God, I hope she makes it. She looked really bad."

"Why don't you take a hot shower? I'll make us some breakfast."

"Maybe that'll make me feel better. It's such a shock," Jordan said.

"I'm taking the next two days off. I don't want you here

alone anymore."

"I love you, Eric."

"You too, Jordan."

The shower did help to brighten her spirits. The breakfast didn't hurt much either. "I really don't know why we're packing all this stuff. The house will have everything I need. Maybe I should just pack my clothes and a few sentimental things. The dishes were originally hand-me-downs anyway. I should pass them on to the local thrift store."

"It's your call. Do what makes you feel comfortable."

"It's weird, Eric. Moving into a house, that's now, *technically* my house, and I don't even remember what it looks like. I think its sort of spooky, actually. We'd taken a trip up there and scoped things out," Jordan said nervously.

"I'll be up to see you in six weeks. You should almost be settled in by then. Maybe you'll have even found another L'ings," Eric said jokingly.

"Cute, real cute."

Jordan put a call in to the thrift store to pick up her furniture and dishes. She decided to pack her computer, photographs, the two quilts her mother had made, and her clothes. She even conceded to leaving her bed behind. It was time for a fresh start.

"I guess I can buy anything else when I get there."

"Don't worry. Everything will work out," Eric said.

"Famous last words. I almost forgot about the meeting at the attorney's office. It's in an hour. I'm glad you're going with me. Maybe we could stop by the hospital and see how Anna's doing."

"Are you sure you want to do that, Jordan?" Eric asked.

"I can't leave without at least checking on her."

Eric pulled the roll of tape across the top of the last box and stood with satisfaction. "Why do we always put things off until the last minute?"

"I guess this time it's because I'm not anxious to move away from you."

Eric wrapped his arms around Jordan and pulled her to his chest, breathing in the sweet smell of the peach shampoo she'd used since he'd met her.

"Let's not talk about that today," he whispered. "I'm so grateful it wasn't you who was hurt last night. I don't know what I'd do without you."

A hard knock at the door startled them both. Jordan looked through the peephole to discover two policemen and a suited detective. She slid the chain lock to the right, opening the door.

"Ms. Maxwell," the detective started, "we're with the New York City Police Department. Can we speak with you for a few minutes?"

"Yes, please come in. Is Anna still alive?"

"The last we heard, yes." He reached his hand out to Eric. "Detective Oxford and you are?"

"Eric Riley. I'm Jordan's boyfriend." He gestured toward her.

"Do you mind if we sit down, Ms. Maxwell?"

"No, of course not. As you can see, I'm packing to move, so you'll just have to find a spot."

"Tell us what you saw last night, in as much detail as you can recall," Detective Oxford stated firmly.

"I heard a scream and ran to the door. When I opened it, I saw Anna laying on the ground bleeding. God, she was bleeding so much."

Jordan paused for a moment, running her fingers through her hair, closing her eyes as though to erase the memory. Detective Oxford did little to hide his impatience.

"I saw a large man running down the hallway. He exited through the stairwell," Jordan continued.

"Could you distinguish his race?"

"No, his clothing was dark. I just remember he was fairly tall with broad shoulders. It all happened so quickly. I was more concerned about Anna. He was obviously running away and didn't seem to pose a threat to us."

"Did he have on a hat? Could you see the color of his hair?" the detective asked.

"I'm sorry. Detective Oxford, is it?"

"Yes."

"I really only saw movement. He could've had on a dark cap or had dark hair; I'm just not sure."

"So, it didn't appear Anna knew her attacker?"

"She said someone was chasing her and tried to rob her in the parking deck. Anna said she ran as fast as she could, but he must have caught her in the hallway."

"We don't have many robbers that will chase their victims up a couple flights of stairs to their apartments," he mumbled sarcastically. "It's usually a quick transaction like grabbing a purse or jewelry. The perpetrator must've wanted more than that. You're a lucky woman, Ms. Maxwell. It appears to have been a random attack. It could just as well have been you," Detective Oxford said.

"Do you have any leads?" Eric interjected.

"Not yet. We'll be fingerprinting her vehicle and apartment today, but otherwise, we don't have much to go on. Here's my card, Ms. Maxwell. Call me should you think of anything else. Will there be any way for us to reach you in the following weeks?"

"Yes, let me write down my new address. It's in Maine. I can't think of anything else to tell you though."

"Just a formality, Ms. Maxwell. Thank you for your time."

Detective Oxford and his two mute officers nodded their heads and walked out. They paused at Anna's apartment leaning forward to look inside. Jordan shut the door as a shiver ran up her spine.

"Think of all the times I've walked up that stairwell at night, Eric," Jordan said nervously.

"Let's try not to think about it. As much brutality as I see on my job, you'd think I would be more careful, at least with you. Crime is the downside of every major city. At least we won't have to worry about that where you're going. This move couldn't have happened at a better time," Eric concluded.

Chapter 6

The attorney was waiting for them in his office when they arrived. "Come in, Ms. Maxwell," he said, motioning for her to sit down. "Ben Callahan," he continued, reaching his hand out to Eric.

"Eric Riley, Jordan's friend. Do you mind if I come in?"

"I don't have any objection if she doesn't."

Eric did a mental comparison of his own desk and Mr. Callahan's. He'd always believed that a clean desk was the sign of a sick mind. The office was immaculate, furnished with a mahogany desk and matching bookshelves. There was a photo of what appeared to be his wife with a German shepherd and another of a small child. There were two plants on their last leg of life and a shiny, leather briefcase.

He must not have many clients, Eric thought.

The attorney pulled out a dark tan file, opening it slowly as he paused to collect his thoughts.

"First things first, Ms. Maxwell. Here's a check for $950,000. It may seem like a lot now, but the upkeep of that home has to be phenomenal. There's also $250,000 in an account specified for repairs and additions only. That will be under your name at the local bank in Solomon Cove. Your great-uncle employed a staff of six, all of whom have been there for numerous years. They're still on the payroll until you decide if you want to retain them or not. There are two gardeners who live on the grounds, a Mr. Fix It, and three maids who reside off the premises. They were each left $25,000, so don't feel guilty should you decide their services are no longer necessary. Any questions so far?" Mr. Callahan asked.

"Has there not been anyone to contest the will? Doesn't he have a son?" Jordan asked.

"Yes, he does have a son. The boy's mother died when he was eight and he never seemed to get over it. I think he's eighteen now. Apparently, his father hadn't seen him in years. His care is paid for in full until his death. Young Mr. Maxwell has been told his father has passed away, but he has made no attempt to contact the estate."

"How sad. Is that all you know about the story?" Jordan questioned further.

"Yes, it is. Any other questions?"

"No, I can't think of any."

"Well, here is a set of keys to the house and a skeleton key that will open any of the outside buildings. There's a copy of the deed in this folder. The original is in a safe deposit box at the bank in Solomon Cove. If you think of anything else, just give me a call," Ben Callahan said as he handed over the items.

* * * *

"This is just too weird," Jordan said as soon as they got into the car. "It gives me the creeps, like a bad horror movie."

"Oh Jordan, don't be silly. Count your blessings. How many twenty-seven-year-old women have an estate with six full-time employees and a banking account that's not too shabby either?" Eric asked.

"Like I said, it's too weird."

"Do you still want to go by and check on Anna?"

"Yes, if you'll go in with me."

Anna was in the Intensive Care Unit where only immediate family members were allowed. However, the nurses were more than happy to allow them a visit.

"Anna doesn't appear to have any family, at least that we've been able to locate," the nurse said, her voice catching. "Her boss came by, but other than that, no visitors. Her condition is still grave, so don't stay very long. If she's asleep, don't wake her. Second door to the left."

The two walked at a snail's pace down the hall, scared of what they might find at the other end. Anna's chest was rising and falling with the labored breaths of the respirator. Her face and hair had been cleaned, but she was terribly swollen. There were only a couple of scratches on her face, and Jordan noticed a few patches that'd been shaved on her head where she had been stitched. They stood over her as she twisted in a fitful sleep.

"Oh Eric," Jordan whispered. "How awful, and she's so alone."

"Shh," he whispered back, placing his finger on his lips.

They stood there for what seemed like an eternity with Jordan swaying uncomfortably back and forth. As they turned to leave, they could hear the rustle of the sheets. Anna's eyes were opening and despite everything that'd happened to her, they were clear and coherent.

"Hi, Anna. It's me, Jordan, your neighbor."

Anna shook her head in slow, methodical movements.

"I'm so sorry this happened to you. I wish I could've done something to help."

Anna's swollen hand opened and reached for Jordan. She squeezed so lightly that Jordan wasn't sure if she'd even squeezed at all. She was struggling to speak but was unable to with the respirator in her throat.

"Don't try to talk. You'll be okay. I'll have moved when you get out. I'm going to Maine, but I'll try to phone you when you get out of the hospital. I'll leave my new address with the nurse. Call and let me know how you're doing." Jordan leaned down and kissed Anna lightly on the forehead. "I'm so sorry."

Chapter 7

Elias left the bar and Mr. Flemming with a sadness he'd never felt before, like a child that'd suddenly lost his innocence. The fog was so thick he was forced to drive at a slower rate of speed. The scotches, along with the murder, were causing his mind to race.

The sheriff wasn't sure why, but as he passed Mayor Blake's house, he decided to pull in. The mayor would be anxious to hear any news and Elias wasn't ready to go home alone.

Two full minutes after he rang the bell, Thomas opened the door. He had a bourbon in his hand and his eyes were red from crying. He didn't offer a greeting, only motioned for him to come in. Thomas led him back to the den pouring another drink for himself and one for Elias.

"What brings you out on a night like this, Sheriff?" he asked.

"I just met with Mr. Flemming over at the Inn. They're pretty torn up."

"I can say I know how they feel. It's been over nine years

now, Elias, and still feels like yesterday. It was almost all I could bear to see that young girl."

Elias was surprised to hear Thomas referring to his own tragedy. It had been so long since he'd actually heard him say more than a few words at one time, much less share some of his feelings.

"I was going to talk to them, try to tell them I know how it feels, but I just couldn't do it. Guess it wouldn't have made me feel better if someone had said it to me back then," Thomas said, diverting his eyes from Elias.

Elias sat there quietly for a few moments, not sure if he should continue to listen or say something. "She was a popular girl with no known enemies. She dated another teacher a few times, nothing serious. Two best friends that she'd known since childhood. Young, beautiful, no record except for a drunk driving ticket coming back from a sorority party. I don't know, Mayor, we're not equipped for a major investigation. What do you say we have the police department in her hometown question any known friends and enemies?" Elias asked.

"That'd be good but stay close to the case. We want to know how Solomon Cove ties into this."

Thomas poured himself another bourbon and raised the bottle toward Elias.

"No thanks, man. I've already overdone it."

"Yeah, me too, so how's everything at the station?" he asked, obviously anxious to both change the subject and keep his visitor there a little while longer.

For the first time in years, Elias felt sorry for Thomas Blake. He looked so empty and lonely, almost pitiful.

"Pretty good, just the same old thing. Say, have you had a chance to talk with the city council about that raise for Rachel Kelley? She's doing a hell of a job."

"My memory is about as long as a toothpick, Elias, sorry. I'll recommend a couple more bucks an hour next week at the meeting. Shouldn't be a problem."

"I appreciate that. Just want to keep good help."

"I understand."

They sat in silence for a few more minutes until Elias stood up. "Got an early day tomorrow."

Thomas stood and walked him to the door. "Listen, Elias, thanks."

"For what?"

"For coming by. I'm not sure why you did, but I appreciate it. I know I'm difficult to get along with. It's just…after I lost Lauren and Connor, I didn't want to live anymore. In a way, I still don't." Elias gave him a hard pat on the shoulder and walked to his car.

Chapter 8

Elias woke up surprised he'd been able to sleep. Maybe it'd been the scotch or perhaps sheer exhaustion. Either way, he wasn't complaining. The clock radio read 6:00 a.m. He woke at the same time no matter the day.

He showered and dressed in khaki pants and a burgundy polo shirt. His uniform was only worn when he had a council meeting or some other form of official business. Elias tried to sketch out his day, which was difficult without the aid of Rachel. Surprisingly, he remembered the meeting with Regina.

At least I don't have to go back to the morgue, he thought. I don't think I could take it today.

Sheriff Murphy stopped by the diner and grabbed a sausage and egg biscuit to go. Rachel had his coffee brewing as he walked through the door.

"God, I need that. It smells great," Elias said.

"One large coffee coming up," Rachel said.

He walked into the breakroom to eat his breakfast, not

anxious to see all of the messages piled high on his desk.

"Here you go, strong and black. Don't forget Regina at noon. I told her it'd be easier for her to come here."

"Good, that'll help."

"Your voicemail is full. They've been rolling over to mine. Looks like you're in for an exciting day. I passed the general calls to Sam, Evan, and Trent. They'll return them for you on their cell phones when they're not busy. Andy at Public Works said they've fixed that pothole four times this year, but the road needs repaving. He wants you to help him advocate for funds at the next council meeting. You'd better speak up for my raise first though," Rachel insisted.

"Can I go back home now?" Elias laughed.

"Not a chance. We need to set up a tip line for the Jennifer Flemming case. There's at least twenty calls on the voicemail concerning it. I'll forward them all via fax to her hometown police. What is it, Dekalb, Massachusetts?"

"Something like that. I'll have to look up our contact and get back with you."

"Sheriff Tucker and Detective Arrington," Rachel spouted off.

"Damn, you're good. We do need you more than we need newly paved streets."

"Duty calls. I'll be up front if you need me."

Elias grinned to himself wondering what time she had to get to work to be so on top of things. He finished his biscuit and walked grudgingly to his office. Rachel had been right;

the messages were unending. He put his first call into the Dekalb Police. Surprisingly, he was patched straight through to the sheriff.

"Good morning, Sheriff Murphy, Sheriff Tucker here."

"Good morning to you, Sir."

"I've got two detectives out questioning family and friends right now; that's all I could spare. I'll have them report to you at least once a day," the Massachusetts sheriff said.

"We appreciate it, Sheriff. We're an extremely small department. We'd have to fold up here if I had to do the investigation myself. Any luck there?" Elias asked.

"None at all. She's just what they said, an all-American girl. It has the community pretty broken up. I'll keep in touch."

"Thanks again," Elias reiterated.

He placed the phone on the receiver and thought about whom to send out to Somergrove Elementary to question the employees. Sending uniformed officers never worked well; they were too intimidating. They also weren't detectives. He silently scolded himself for not training a detective before now. He thought about sending Rachel. She had what it took, but he couldn't spare her.

Elias put a call in to the principal and set up a meeting with the staff for the following afternoon. *Lord, please let them be cooperative,* he thought.

It was 11:45 before he looked up from his desk again.

Rachel was there with a soda and a bag of chips.

"Lunch will be later than noon today. Regina will be walking through the door any minute," Rachel said as she handed over his snack.

"Send her back when she gets here," the sheriff sighed.

****

The interview went as grueling as Elias had predicted. Everyone wanted answers, and he simply didn't have any to give.

"That should do it, Sheriff, thanks for your time."

"Anytime, Regina. Just try not to send the town into a panic. We're not equipped to handle it."

"I'll see what I can do, but this is a small town. We don't see murdered girls floating up on the beach very often," Regina said flatly.

"Oh, how delicately you put that," Elias said, trying not to unleash the distaste he had for journalists.

Chapter 9

The interview with the school's staff went as expected. They were all shocked and dismayed and hardly looked like a bunch of rapists and murderers. Justin, the boyfriend, was a young redhead in his first year of teaching. He was about as *apple pie* as Jennifer had been. Elias felt no need to question him any further than the others.

Elias returned to his car and dug through his unorganized notes to find the address to Jennifer's apartment. The officers in Somergrove would've inevitably combed through it by now, but it wouldn't hurt to stop and take a look.

The complex was a new one, and although the apartment was of modest size, it was neatly decorated. It helped to give him a feel of what she'd been like. The living space was bright and airy with new furniture and lots of magazines, all stacked neatly in a cabinet beside the television. A newspaper was spread across the small kitchen table next to a half-empty bottle of soda. Photos covered the fridge, all reflecting good times, most likely during her college years.

Sheriff Murphy walked back down the narrow hallway

and looked into the bathroom. Nothing out of the ordinary—makeup, perfumes, facial creams, and lotions. A towel lay piled in the corner, most likely from her last shower.

Jennifer's bedroom was equally as neat and clean with a thick, chenille bedspread, and several throw pillows on her bed. A stack of books sat on her nightstand.

It was a quaint apartment only one step above a dorm room for a young college grad. Elias found no indication a struggle had taken place.

The ride back to Solomon Cove wasn't a disappointing one. Elias had never believed he'd find anything at the school. This was a brutal crime, and as far as he knew, it could have been committed by anyone. *God, don't let it be a serial killer,* he prayed.

It was after five when Elias got into town. He stopped at Knox's grocery and bought a six-pack of beer. The mayor was still at his office, so he took his package in and sat down. He opened two beers putting his feet up on the desk.

"We don't have shit on this case and I don't foresee us having shit on this case," Elias said indignantly.

"Forgoing the pleasantries, I see," the mayor said with a chuckle.

"Well, if that isn't the pot calling the kettle black."

Thomas had to laugh at the old saying. "You sound like my grandmother."

"I'm just frustrated."

"Don't take it to heart, Elias. You're doing the best you can with what you've got. Do you know how many murders go unsolved each year? We're covering all the bases."

Elias pulled the picture of Jennifer out of his wallet just as a father would. "She's counting on me," he said, sliding the photo across the mayor's desk.

"You didn't kill her, Elias. You can't let yourself go mad over this. I didn't sleep for two nights after I saw her. It broke my heart to see another life cut short like Lauren's and Connor's, but we're left here. We have to do the best we can and accept the lot we're given."

"Damn, what's come over you?" Elias asked.

"I guess it's years of grief. Grief that almost ate away my soul. Hey, pass me another beer. Next time, buy some expensive stuff."

"Some of us are paid more than others." Elias laughed. "Speaking of pay, what about Rachel?"

"Damn, are you screwing her or something? She's got the raise already," Thomas scoffed.

"Just looking out for the *little guy,* that's all."

Chapter 10

Jordan drove the old, tattered Honda along the stretch of highway leading into Solomon Cove as butterflies danced in her stomach. She wished she'd allowed Eric to ride along, but knew he was far too busy at work.

"I can wait a month and a half, Eric," she'd said, trying to sound convincing, although she'd felt like a small child leaving home for her first sleepover.

Jordan decided to drive around town for a while before heading to the house. She would need a few items and wasn't quite ready to settle in yet. Solomon Cove was a quaint old town, small, but delightfully full of hustle and bustle. The squeal of the brakes as she slowed to park at the Corner Café reminded her of one more thing that needed repairing on the old monstrosity. She self-consciously looked around, but no one had seemed to notice.

Sucking in a deep breath, Jordan stepped out of the car and walked into the diner. She felt instantly at ease with the small-town atmosphere as the cashier handed her a sticky menu and motioned toward a small booth.

"Thanks," the cashier mouthed, continuing with her phone call, and ringing up a customer.

"Sorry about that," she said, making her way to the booth. "Today is just one of those days. What can I get you to drink?"

"Water will be fine, with a lemon, please," Jordan said.

"Be right back," she said as she rushed over to take another order.

"Today's special is pot roast, English peas, mashed potatoes, and a biscuit," she spouted off as she set down the water.

"That sounds good to me, thanks."

Jordan looked around at the crowd as she waited for her meal. They were so different from the normal lunch crowd in New York. None of them looked hurried or preoccupied, and they were all casually dressed.

Looks like I can say good-bye to the mad rush, she thought.

"Service with a smile," the young waitress said as she set the plate in front of Jordan. "I haven't seen you in here before," she said, her eyes pleasant. "Do you live nearby or just traveling through?" The waitress knew she would've remembered someone with such striking looks.

"Well, actually, I'm moving here. I've just arrived in town. I inherited a house on the outskirts of town. It's on the edge of the water. I haven't seen it since I was a little girl," Jordan said.

The young girl's expression changed so quickly that she turned red with embarrassment. "I-I'm-sorry," she said. "It's just you're not who I pictured to inherit the old Maxwell place. You are so—so pleasant."

Jordan couldn't stifle her laughter. "Well, thank you, I guess. I don't remember my great-uncle very well, but from your expression and my recollections, he must not have been a very pleasant man."

"Oh, forgive me, Ms. …Ms."

"Jordan Maxwell. And you?"

"I'm Olivia Yates. My mother has worked for Mr. Maxwell for over twenty-five years. She and the other staff are waiting to hear if you'll still need them. It is a rather large place."

"What's your mother's name, Olivia?" Jordan asked.

"Myra, Myra Yates. They're expecting you today. She'll be up at the house when you arrive. They wanted to have it ready for you. She'll be so pleased to meet you, Ma'am."

"Ma'am?" Jordan laughed. "I hardly qualify as a *ma'am*. I'm only a few years older than you."

Olivia smiled sweetly turning to answer the impatient requests of her other diners.

The meal was delicious, reminding Jordan of Sunday dinners with her grandmother. *Seeing how I don't cook, this place just may be my sustenance,* she thought.

She left a generous tip for Olivia, then paid at the cash register. Olivia waved good-bye from the other side of the diner.

Jordan spotted a small grocery store across the street and headed over to pick up a few items. Crates of fresh fruit and produce lined the front walk, flanked by a cart of fresh flowers. She picked up a few pieces of fruit, some bottled water, bread, cheese, milk, peanut butter, and a nice Merlot.

That's surprising, she thought. I wouldn't have expected such a vast wine collection. I should fit in well.

A young boy, probably less than eight years old, carried her bags to the car. Jordan handed him a dollar causing him to smile broadly, displaying his missing front tooth.

"Wow, a missing tooth!" Jordan bragged, acting very impressed. "Did the tooth fairy come to your house?"

"I'm eight years old, Ma'am," he said proudly, "and eight-year-olds no longer believe in the tooth fairy."

"Oh." She smiled. "I see."

"Afternoon, Ma'am," said a plump gentleman wearing a crisp, clean apron. "Is Ryan here holding you up?"

"Oh no, not at all. We were just discussing that missing tooth."

"Ralph Knox. I own the store, and this here's my son, Ryan," he said, extending his meaty hand.

"Very nice to meet you. I'm Jordan Maxwell."

"So you're the great-niece who inherited the old Maxwell place."

"Yes, I am. I haven't seen it in over twenty years."

"Big place, she is."

"I'm looking forward to seeing it. I just had to grab a few groceries before I got there."

"Let me know if we can ever get anything for ya. We order special for folks if they need it. We're the closest grocers within thirty miles. Meats cut to order too. My wife, Diane, does the accounting end of things, but you'll see her from time to time if you shop with us often."

"I'm sure I will be. Thanks again, and Ryan, take care."

So far, so good, Jordan thought as she got into the car. *Maybe this could feel like home. Maybe now I'll be able to write.* It had been over six months since she'd had anything published, and Jordan was beginning to think she had lost her touch.

I'm a little concerned about meeting Uncle James's employees, she thought, wondering if she had enough money to keep them all on board. Jordan wasn't sure how she felt about six people working for her, especially when she'd never even been able to afford a "mini maid" service for her apartment. She'd lived alone since college, and the thought of having people around made her a little uncomfortable.

The ride to Uncle James's house was a beautiful one. She rode right along the water's edge, watching the waves crash up on large mountains of rocks. The road winded along like a ribbon, and if it weren't for worrying about the condition of her car, it would've been the most relaxing twenty minutes of her life. Jordan was mesmerized by the dark water slamming against the rocks and turning to foam.

God's country, she thought. No more stabbings or murders or muggings. No more traffic and congestion and sirens to interrupt my sleep.

Jordan edged around the next curve and saw it sitting there, high upon the cliff, like a beacon. It reminded her of the Nancy Drew books she'd read as a child.

"The Haunted Inn," she said eerily to herself. She pulled into the drive and noticed how immaculately the grounds were manicured. *The gardeners have certainly been earning their keep,* she thought. *I hope the rest of the house is in good condition.*

As she wound her way around the drive, the mansion came into view. If it hadn't had such a perilous and haunting appearance, it would've made a nice postcard. The setting was captivating. The house was made of worn red bricks and stretched across the cliffs like a dark, unnerving castle. The stone structure looked weathered but had the appearance of a place that'd been looked after since its inception.

Jordan noticed several small buildings surrounding the main house and a large octagonal tower. *Home Sweet Home,* she thought to herself, as she pulled up to the front of the residence.

She had only turned for an instant to unlock her door when a large Hispanic man opened it for her.

"Good Afternoon, Ms. Maxwell. My name is Quincy Velez. I am one of your gardeners. We glad you found us." His English was broken and practiced, but his eyes were sincere.

"Very nice to meet you, Mr. Velez. I'm happy to be here."

Jordan was embarrassed to have this type of reception when she'd driven up in an overheating clunker. She reached for one of her suitcases when Quincy quickly interjected, "No, Ma'am. I get for you. Ms. Myra will show you the house."

With that, the front door opened and a short, stout woman came barreling out. She wasn't the refined help Jordan would've expected from her great-uncle. She was bubbly and happy and smiled just as her daughter had at the café.

"Good Afternoon, Ms. Maxwell." She grinned. "So happy to see you. My name's Myra Yates. Olivia, my daughter from the diner, has already phoned to tell me you were on your way."

"Yes." Jordan smiled. "She's a sweet girl."

"Come in," she continued. "Quincy will take care of the car and its contents. I'll help you get settled in." Myra led her through a huge foyer which sparkled from years of cleaning and waxing. They took the first right into an enormous parlor that Jordan found dark and forbidding. She found herself wanting to walk out of it as soon as the doors were opened. Above the fireplace was a portrait of her late great-uncle, James Maxwell. The deep burgundy furniture obscured the rest of the room, but there in the middle was a dim light that illuminated his portrait, almost—in some strange way—bringing it to life.

Her childhood recollection of him had been right on target. His eyes were small slits that sat amid a ruddy, wrinkled face. There was no kindness there, not even a slight hint of compassion. Wisps of white hair concealed much of his wrinkled forehead, and there, wrapped around the cane, were the gnarled hands Jordan had remembered most. It made a chill go up her spine and she struggled to stop her body from shivering.

"Your great-uncle had that portrait done two years ago. A striking likeness of him," Myra said, nodding and pretending not to notice Jordan's reaction.

"I didn't know him very well," Jordan started, "I-I didn't know him at all, actually. This whole thing is strange to me. I only met him a couple of times during my childhood. My parents have both passed away, and I'm not really sure why he left this place to me."

"He must have wanted you to have it, dear," she said kindly. "So, you enjoy it." Myra stood silent for a few moments as she watched Jordan stare at the painting. "Don't be frightened, child. It's a marvelous home. This is where he had tea every day at noon and bourbon at night before he retired."

"I remember this room as a child. It…it frightened me," Jordan said, feeling both embarrassed and ashamed of the comment. Myra didn't respond; it wasn't her place.

"Let's go back to the kitchen and see what they're preparing for tonight's meal," she suggested. "We didn't know what you preferred, so we made an educated guess. Mr. Maxwell always enjoyed prime rib and lobster, with new potatoes, and asparagus. Does that sound all right?"

"My goodness, I never expected for someone to prepare dinner for me. That isn't necessary."

"That's what we're accustomed to, Ms. Maxwell. I don't mean to be forward, but I hope you'll still need our services."

Jordan reached for the kind woman's hand and held it in her own. "I don't know how long this whole lifestyle will play out for me, but we'll all go through it together. It's only fair for everyone to keep their jobs. Besides, there's no way I could possibly maintain this place myself."

"You couldn't know how relieved that makes me," she said, her whole face smiling. "Would you mind if I passed that on to the others?"

"Not at all, please do," Jordan encouraged her.

The kitchen was exquisite. Jordan smiled to herself as she thought of how her whole apartment in New York would fit in the corner of it.

"The estate has seven bedrooms and nine baths," Myra said, sounding like a practiced tour guide. "Of course, you can choose which bedroom suits you best," she continued as they walked up the spiral staircase. "I'll show them to you and you can freshen up and relax for a few minutes before dinner."

The thought of resting for a while sounded delightful to Jordan. "This was your great-uncle's room," she said, opening the large mahogany door. The room was large and dark, similar to the parlor she'd left earlier. Myra didn't offer to walk in, and Jordan stood firmly in the hallway. Taking her cue, Myra lightly closed the doors. Jordan chose the last bedroom she was shown.

Myra had to know I would choose this one, she thought. *It's perfect.* It had a large oak bed covered in white eyelet, reminding her of her childhood bedroom. There were French doors opening onto a large balcony with a phenomenal view of the water. Antique pots overflowed with red geraniums, and white rockers sat patiently as if waiting for someone to join them.

Thin white sheers hung over the doors and windows. The bathroom was spacious and delicately decorated. It smelled of jasmine and vanilla making Jordan anxious for Myra to leave her alone. As if reading her thoughts, she turned to let herself out.

"Dinner will be served in the main dining room in an hour. I'll let you settle in now. You can use the intercom on the wall should you need any of us. Someone is always nearby and there's a phone by the bed. I'll have Quincy bring your luggage up."

"Thank you," Jordan said, sounding like an overwhelmed child. Looking around the room, she realized her fears were suddenly gone. Relief washed over her as she took in the rest of the room. There was a vanity with an antique stool and mirror. Several bottles of the latest perfumes, all of which she liked but could never afford, had been placed on top.

There was also a hair brush, a hand mirror with ivory handles, and a cameo music box. Jordan carefully lifted the lid as though she feared getting caught touching it. It played "Evergreen," one of her favorites. She sang softly with the music ...*one love that is shared by two, I have found with you...*

A light tapping on the door caused her to quickly close the box.

"It's Quincy, Ma'am. I got your luggage."

"Oh, thank you. I'm not used to the royal treatment, Quincy."

He looked as if he wanted to smile but was hesitant to do so. "Would you like by the closet?"

"That would be fine," Jordan assured him. He set them down and promptly left the room.

The walk-in closet was the size of a decent-sized bedroom. Satin hangers hung on the rods and empty shelves awaited her shoes. Jordan started to unpack her things, then considered how silly her clothes would look here. This was a closet meant for elegant gowns and Dior dresses. She hung her jeans and sweaters, her three dresses, and the four skirts she'd brought with her. She laughed as she looked down at her two pairs of sneakers, a pair of brown and a pair of black flats, and one pair of heels. She put her panties, bras, T-shirts, and socks in the chest of drawers, stopping to smell each of the sachets placed there.

Jordan lay across the bed before reaching for the phone. She dialed Eric's number, expecting to get the answering machine, but was surprised when he picked up.

"Hey there, it's me," she said excitedly. "I've already unpacked and I'm lying in the biggest bed I've ever seen. I wish you were here."

"Me too. So, does it feel like home?" Eric asked.

"I haven't even seen it all yet. It's huge. I have a beautiful balcony off my bedroom with a view of the Atlantic. I can definitely see myself writing here."

"That's good to hear. It'll feel like home before you know it. I need to run by my apartment and change clothes. I'm having dinner with Mr. Harris tonight."

"Mr. Harris?"

"One of the editors, remember?"

"Oh yeah, I guess I'll talk to you later. Call me tonight?" Jordan asked.

"Will do. Hey, Anna's showing some improvement. I called the hospital earlier. They updated her condition from critical to serious."

"That's good to hear. Eric?"

"Yeah?"

"I love you."

"You too, baby."

* * * *

Dinner was excellent. Jordan felt more than a little foolish sitting in the dining room by herself, but the food had been delectable. She finished her second glass of Merlot before standing up to carry her plate into the kitchen. As if on cue, an older lady in a starched apron opened the door.

"No, Ms. Maxwell. I'll get that for you. Can I bring you a slice of pie? I made it this morning; it's blueberry."

"That sounds great. Would you have a slice with me?"

"I–I…"

"Oh, please. I'm not used to eating such a good meal alone. Are any of the staff still here or have they left for the day?"

"They're all here, Ma'am. No one ever leaves before 7:00 p.m."

"Would you ask them to join me?" Jordan asked. "I haven't met all of them and they haven't met me either."

"I'll call them right away."

"Is there enough pie for everyone?"

"Yes, Ma'am."

Jordan poured the last of the Merlot in her wine glass as the staff started entering the dining room. Their faces all wore the same expression, nervousness amid distrust.

"Please sit down," she said as she motioned. "I'm Jordan Maxwell. This is all new, so please bear with me. As you know, I've inherited this house from my great-uncle. It was quite a shock to me, and to be honest, the reality of it still has not fully sunk in."

They smiled politely but remained quiet.

"Mr. Maxwell left money for the house to be maintained. I hope all of you will consider staying. I know very little about the house; in fact, I haven't even seen it all. But I really wanted to meet all of you. Maybe you can fill me in on this place."

She sensed their relief to still be employed. Myra spoke first. "We've already met, but I'm Myra Yates. I take care of any visitors to the estate and I spend a lot of my time cleaning. If you need to order anything for the estate or need any errands run, you can ask me. I'll see that it's taken care of." She turned to the older woman who had brought in two blueberry pies.

"My name's Grace Courtland. I'm the cook. Meals are served at the same times daily unless you should specify otherwise. Breakfast is at eight, lunch at noon, and dinner at six p.m." She took a quick breath while smoothing her apron gently with her hands. She was a tiny woman with a kind face. Jordan estimated her to be in her early seventies.

"I can prepare any meals you request, but I prefer to do my own shopping. I've been doing it here for over thirty years." She looked up at Jordan before continuing. "If you're expecting visitors, let me know and I'll prepare tea, coffee, and sweets. It's not proper for folks to come calling and not get some refreshments out of it." Jordan strained to contain a smile and nodded her head in agreement. "Mr.

Maxwell always kept a running tab at Knox's Grocery, and I took in a check once a month to cover it. It worked out well since Mr. Knox will order what I need and deliver if necessary." Grace paused so Jordan took her cue.

"Well, I don't want to change any policy that's already working. Let's stick with that if it's okay with you, Ms. Courtland," Jordan said.

"Please, call me Grace. I feel old enough as it is," she said without smiling. "It's fine with me to leave things be." She obviously was satisfied with Jordan's answer. "Ms. Maxwell wants us to have a slice of pie with her, so I'll cut you all a piece," she said authoritatively.

"Name's Cyrus Hames," a short, skinny, balding man spoke up. "Been gardnin' round this place since I can remember. Me and Quincy that is. We each have a small cottage round back. I get started early before the heat of the day rolls in and then generally rest during the middle of the day. Usually work on into the night til I decide to turn in," he said.

Cyrus appeared to be in his late sixties. He was terribly thin and Jordan surmised he might *favor the bottle a little* as her grandmother used to say.

"I don't pick up supplies," he continued. "Quincy takes care of all of the important stuff. I don't drive into town neither. I just drive Mr. Maxwell's old truck around the grounds. Just do as I'm told."

"Very nice to meet you, Cyrus. The grounds are lovely.

They were the first thing I noticed when I drove up." He smiled, obviously pleased. "So, Quincy, you garden as well?" Jordan asked, turning to make eye contact with him.

Quincy stood up as though he was about to formally deliver a book report. "I do little bit of everything, Ms. Maxwell. I like gardening most. I'll need list of flowers you like right away." He paused briefly to make sure Jordan had heard him.

"I'll do that in the morning, Quincy," she answered kindly.

"I drive to Anderson and do yard business. It cheaper and they have more than Solomon Cove. If you need help, let me know. Cottage out back." Quincy sat down relieved his turn was over. It was comforting that he and Cyrus would be nearby. She wouldn't run into them in the house, but they'd be close enough if she really needed them.

"I'm Zeke Mullis," a young black man, probably in his late twenties, said. He was tall, about six-two, and broad-shouldered. He was built much like Quincy but was several years younger. "I've been working for Mr. Maxwell for eight years now. I got my girl pregnant in high school and needed a job. Mr. Maxwell gave me one. I do repair work, change the light bulbs in the high fixtures, and anything else they need me to do.

I leave early on Tuesdays and Thursdays to go to technical school in Somergrove. Mr. Maxwell paid me anyhow because he said I was learning something that'd help me to do my job better. I'm working on my air conditioning and heating certificate. I've got four months left." He paused for a minute, obviously embarrassed at all he'd said. Jordan was touched by his candidness.

"How old is your child?" Jordan asked.

He grinned, appearing pleased she'd asked. "I got three now. Ruth's nine, Taylor's six, and Danny's two. My wife isn't doing too good these days. She's been sick most of her life. Sickle cell hasn't been kind to her." Zeke paused for a minute and cleared his throat. "I don't know what I would've done without the people at this table. They've brought us food and watched after the kids for us to go to the doctor. Fine people."

The table sat silent until a young girl, not more than twenty, spoke up.

"My name's Emma, Emma Jones. I haven't been here as long as everyone else, probably close to a year now. I help Myra clean and Grace cook if she ever needs me to." She had bright-red hair, pale skin, and an abundance of freckles. She blushed as she spoke. "I live in the apartment off of the kitchen. My father used to do some work for Mr. Maxwell. He died a little over a year ago. I didn't have anyone else, so Mr. Maxwell offered me a job. I'm learning a lot from Grace and Myra."

"I'm sure you do a fine job," Jordan replied.

She looked around the table at all the people who played a part in this place. They looked at her with suspicious eyes and Jordan realized how much they needed her. "I look forward to getting to know all of you and appreciate the fact you're willing to stay on." They seemed to like the idea that Jordan Maxwell thought they had options and that was exactly how she'd wanted them to feel. "I expect everything to remain the same," she continued. "Salaries and paydays, etcetera. Let's stop talking business now and enjoy our pie."

The mood appeared to relax a little and they talked casually until they'd finished.

"We will all wish you a good night, Ms. Maxwell. You've been kind to all of us," Grace said.

"Oh, could you call me Jordan?"

"No, Ma'am. It just wouldn't be proper," Grace answered sternly.

Everyone nodded in agreement and dispersed quickly leaving Jordan suddenly alone. She could see faint streams of light throughout the hallways, left on for her to find her way. She decided to look around a little before turning in, walking past the foyer and on down the marbled hallway.

There were several large portraits detailing the lineage of the family through the years. Jordan didn't know any of them and thought of how odd it was for her to live in a house filled with paintings of people she didn't recognize. The hallway led to a huge room filled with ostentatious, velvet furniture. It was so formal that Jordan couldn't even imagine having friends over for a visit. The pieces were antique and had more than likely been handed down through the years. *Maybe I'll get used to it,* she prayed.

Continuing down the hallway, she turned left down a darkened corridor with dark-cherry beams overhead. On the left was an arched entranceway leading into the most incredible library Jordan had ever seen. Mahogany shelves lined each of the walls and stretched from the floor to the ceiling. There were so many books she didn't know where to start. There were leather-bound classics, mysteries, history books, and reference guides. It was overwhelming.

"There's even one of those ladders you can push around," she whispered to herself. "I've died and gone to heaven. This is too good to be true."

There were also worn leather chairs and a couch, along with several floor lamps. Another archway led her to the far side of the room. Jordan followed it into a den, not as big as the other rooms in the house, but sizeable. The walls were covered in varnished pine paneling, and inside was a claw-footed desk with a computer and printer, two soft-leather lounge chairs, and a television set.

"I can work here," she blurted out loud. "This is perfect!"

Jordan continued to look around in shock. This was not what she'd expected to find. Especially in this house that was so far from anything she felt comfortable with. She ran her hands along the top of the desk before sitting down in one of the cozy chairs.

It was early the next morning when Jordan awakened. Someone had come along and covered her with a blanket.

As the sun shone in, she was delighted to discover the two rooms still existed in the daylight.

She was walking back down the hallway when she ran into Emma.

"Good morning," Jordan said with an embarrassed smile. "Was it you who covered me up last night?"

"Actually, Ms. Maxwell, it was more like this morning. I didn't see you until I got up around six. I was surprised to see you there," Emma answered.

"Myra hasn't shown me the whole house yet. I love the library."

"It's nice. I'm just not used to seeing anyone in there. Grace is ready to serve your breakfast."

The two walked side by side until they reached the dining room where Jordan could sense Emma was anxious to leave her. As she entered the dining room, Jordan saw Grace standing over a steaming plate of food. Her apron was heavily starched; her white blouse buttoned all the way to her throat. She had her gray hair pulled tightly into a bun and her hands were angrily attached to each hip.

"Good morning, Grace." Jordan smiled, keenly aware she was about to be scolded.

"It is ten minutes after eight, Ms. Maxwell. That's not how I do business. My meals are not done justice when they're cold."

"I-I'm terribly sorry; I fell asleep in the library and…"

"So, I hear. Mr. Maxwell would've never approved. Every

young woman should be asleep in her bed when the sun comes up." Grace softened a little as she pointed to the front page of the paper. Jordan saw the face of a beautiful young girl under the headlines, *Killer Still Not Found in Solomon Cove Murder.*

"*That,*" said Grace, "is the reason why every young woman should be home at night. It startled me when I didn't find you in your bed this morning."

Jordan realized the scolding was not about cold food, but rather Grace's concern for her.

How kind, Jordan thought. It's been so long since I've had someone to worry about my comings and goings.

"It won't happen again, Grace, I promise," Jordan said sincerely.

The strain eased from Grace's face and her eyes hinted of a smile. "Enjoy your breakfast, dear."

Although she was late to breakfast, Jordan could tell Grace had just put her plate on the table. There were hot pancakes with cinnamon apples on top and two sausage links. A china cup held coffee and a crystal wine goblet was filled with orange juice. *My God, I haven't even missed L'ings,* she thought, reaching for the paper. She read the article about young Jennifer Flemming and chills ran up her spine. *That's great,* she thought. *The first murder in ten years and it has to be now.*

Jordan folded the paper, placing it under her arm as she walked up to her room. She decided to fax the article to Eric and see what he could make of it.

He'll really find this ironic, she thought. *I left the murders to come to a safer place, and this is my greeting.* Jordan got out a pair of shorts and a T-shirt and threw them on the bed, then undressed and took a long hot shower.

This whole thing was like waking up and feeling like you're still in Oz, she thought. She dressed, pulled her hair into a ponytail, put on a light coat of lipstick, and slipped into her sneakers. Jordan knew she had to take a trip into town to go to the bank, but she wanted to walk around the grounds first. It was a beautiful day and although it was only August, the weather was already becoming a little brisk.

As she walked down the staircase, she spotted Zeke with an arm full of light bulbs.

"Good morning, Zeke. Where are you headed?"

"Mornin', Ms. Maxwell," he said bashfully. "Ms. Myra said you were a little spooked by the parlor, so I thought I'd put more light in there."

Jordan felt like laughing at herself. Now that it was daylight, she felt foolish.

"Why thank you. You must think I'm acting like a frightened child."

"Oh, no, Ma'am. Can't say my feelings are much different about the place. I'm not sure why that is though."

Jordan smiled. "Do you have a few minutes to show me around the grounds? I was headed outside, but I could use a guide."

"Sure, not a problem. Let me tell Ms. Myra where I'll be."

He was gone for a couple of minutes and came back with an oversized sweatshirt. "You may get a chill, Ms. Maxwell. This is mine. I know it'll be too big, but it's clean and will do the job."

"Thanks, Zeke. I like a man who thinks of everything."

"I guess it comes from having little ones," he said proudly. "You start thinking about somebody other than yourself."

"I suppose you're right," Jordan said, envying him for a moment. "Maybe one day I'll have a family. I just can't imagine myself with children."

"That's what I said," Zeke responded. "Then God decided to trust me with three of 'em."

They walked along silently until they reached the back of the house. Jordan caught her breath when she saw how close they were to the edge of the cliffs that led to the water's edge. The grounds were blanketed with trees and the view was splendid, but Jordan remained fervently aware of the dangerous rocky site the estate was nestled on.

"I hope I don't ever sleepwalk," she said nervously. "I'd hate to wake up in the Atlantic."

"She's awfully close to the side, isn't she?" Zeke replied. "Mr. Maxwell had a time getting workers to flatten this area for construction. At least, that's what I've been told. I enjoy hearing the history of the place."

Jordan was surprised at his interest and wondered about

his relationship with her great-uncle. Zeke seemed to have been close to him. They took a step closer and she could almost feel the ocean spray as it licked its way above the rocks. Even before Zeke spoke, Jordan could tell he, too, was frightened of the cliffs.

"There's something mystical about this place," he said, sounding far more philosophical than he'd intended. "Something that I can't explain."

"I know what you mean. I'm not anxious to get near the side. What's around that way?" She pointed.

"Oh, you've got to see this," he said, motioning for her to walk ahead. They followed the sodden grass around the edge of the cliff until they came to a tower. "It's seventy-five feet high," Zeke continued. "It's Mr. Maxwell's own lighthouse. He loved it out here, although I was never quite sure why. It's an empty, sort of lonely place."

They walked up to the octagonal-shaped tower and Jordan noticed it did look more deserted than the rest of the estate. Ivy ran up the side of the building and wrapped its fingers around its center until it reached the cage that encompassed the light itself.

The door looked as if it was rotting, and it took Zeke several tries before he could push it open.

The door creaked and moaned before opening, so the two could look inside. It was empty except for a spiral, metal staircase that led to the top. "After you," Jordan suggested, hoping Zeke would lead the way.

He reached out and parted the cobwebs standing in their way as they trampled loudly up to the top. By the time they reached their destination, Jordan had long since pulled off the sweatshirt and tied it around her waist.

"I was hoping there would be a pitcher of lemonade waiting for us at the top." She laughed.

"Not my kind of luck."

Jordan took a deep breath as she took her last two steps. The top was worth the effort. There was a large bench with a plush cushion and a telescope. The view was phenomenal. Zeke could sense her surprise and walked over to take in the view for himself.

"Maybe there's more to this place than I gave it credit for. Cyrus turns the light on every night at eight and off in the morning at six. You can see it long before you reach the house."

Jordan realized she was holding him up from his chores, so she started back down the stairs. They walked around the grounds, stopping briefly at Cyrus's cottage and Quincy's small place. They both seemed like adequate living quarters. She imagined the two would probably stay for as long as their jobs allowed. They passed the flower gardens and fountains before returning to the main house.

Chapter 11

"Ms. Grace?" Jordan called as she stepped into the kitchen.

"Yes, dear?"

"I'm heading into town. I need to go to the bank. Can I get you anything?"

"Not today. Everything's covered so far. I'll put lunch off until 1:30 since you'll be away."

"I won't be late," she assured her.

Jordan grabbed her purse, slung it over her shoulder, and looked around for her keys. She thought perhaps she should change into something a little more appropriate but decided shorts would have to do. Before she could inquire about her keys, Cyrus walked into the house.

"Have you seen my keys?" Jordan asked.

"Yes, Ma'am, Ms. Maxwell. Quincy has them down in the garage. I'll walk you down there," Cyrus answered. "He's not very happy with you. Says the brakes were damn near gone on that thing."

They reached the garage just as Quincy was washing the

grease off of his hands.

"Mornin', Ma'am," he said firmly. "Your car in bad shape. It not safe to ride 'round the roads with no brakes. It is okay now. Went into Anderson and got new ones," he continued in his broken English. "I charged to house account. Myra will take care of it."

"Why thank you, Quincy," Jordan said, genuinely pleased. "I didn't expect you to do that. I could've taken it into town to get it fixed."

He looked at her stubbornly. "It my job to fix things for you. Garage in town cost too much money."

Jordan was aware she had offended him, which was the last thing she'd meant to do.

"I'm not used to this kind of treatment. Thank you again. I'm going into town and I'm not sure I would have made it without your repairs."

"Ladies don't take chances with cars. It is dangerous. Now, we don't have to worry," Quincy said proudly, handing her the keys. "Maybe soon you can look for new car. These roads are curvy. They wear cars out."

"Point taken, Quincy." Jordan smiled, "I will take that into consideration."

She slid into the driver's seat, cranked the car, backed slowly out of the garage, and started down the winding driveway. Jordan enjoyed the ride into town as much as she had the night before.

The bank wasn't difficult to find. It sat right in the middle of town next to the city hall. Ryan waved at her from across the street as he carried someone's groceries to their car. She waved back as she walked into the bank. Jordan approached the closest teller and asked for someone to assist her. She had copies of the two accounts and her checkbook but wanted to discuss them.

"Mr. Crane can help you. I'll take you to his office." Jordan could feel the eyes on her back as she made her way around the bank. "Here you go," she said politely.

"Good morning or afternoon is it? I'm Billy Crane, the bank president. Can't say that I know you," he said kindly as he reached out his hand to meet hers.

"Hello, I'm Jordan Maxwell," she said.

"Oh yes, Ms. Maxwell. We've been waiting for you to come into town. Please, have a seat," he said, motioning as he sat down behind his desk.

"I wanted to check on these accounts and make sure everything's in place."

"Yes, let me pull those up," he responded as he punched on his computer. "Let's see. There are three accounts. The first is a personal account for you, $950,000. I'd recommend you invest in mutual funds or CDs. You're losing money by keeping all of that in a checking account." He handed her some financial packets and told her to confer with the bank's vice president. "He'll be more than happy to help you, but try to get with him soon. Time is money, you know."

"Yes, so they say." Jordan smiled.

"I see you have the checks there," Billy Crane said. "I mailed them to Ben Callahan in case you needed some money for moving expenses."

"Thank you. Yes, I have them here. I appreciate you thinking of that."

"The other account is for operating expenses. It has both your name and Myra Yates on it. That's the way Mr. Maxwell wanted it. It seems she takes care of the expenses incurred by the household, so either of you can sign the check. There is $10,000,000 in trust. You're allowed to spend five percent annually. That's, uh, $500,000. It can be used for anything pertaining to the household: food, repairs, salaries, etcetera."

"*What?*" Jordan asked, sure she'd misunderstood him. "I wasn't aware of that account. I knew there was $250,000 set aside for repairs, but I didn't know there was that kind of money left for operating expenses."

"I guess that's good news then. Mr. Maxwell wouldn't have let the place go down. There's an account for repairs and additions. I'm not sure why he has that one. You're the only one on it, but $250,000 wouldn't go very far with that place. It would hardly put a roof on her. I don't quite understand that one myself."

"I can keep the employees on for as long as I need them now. Thank you for your time," Jordan said.

"Anytime you need me, just give me a call," he said,

handing her his business card. "It's no secret the Maxwell accounts make up most of this bank."

"Well," Jordan said honestly, "this is new for me. I'm not used to having any money left over at the end of the month."

They both shared a laugh as Jordan stood up.

"It's nice to have a new face in Solomon Cove," he said. "I've lived here all my life. I'm sure you'll be happy. You have some fine people working for you. My wife is big in the garden club, so I'm sure she'll be calling you soon. Her name is Sara. Maybe we can all have you to dinner soon."

"I'd like that. It was nice to have met you, Mr. Crane."

"Billy, please. Thanks for coming by. I suggest you get with Myra on that house account. Take care."

Jordan walked out of the bank stunned beyond belief.

My God, I'm rich, Jordan thought. She was almost to the car when she heard a deep voice. "Hello there, you must be Ms. Jordan Maxwell." She turned to face a tall, handsome man in a three-piece suit.

"Yes, I am."

"Hello. I'm Thomas Blake, the mayor here in Solomon Cove. I knew your great-uncle."

"Nice to meet you, Mayor Blake. You have a quaint town here. I'm anxious to get settled in," Jordan said.

"Glad to hear it. Let me know if I can be of any help. It's a small town where everybody knows everybody." Thomas Blake smiled at her as he opened her car door. "I'll see you around town, Ms. Maxwell."

Jordan glanced at her watch and realized she had just enough time to get back for lunch. She backed out of the parking space at the bank and headed toward the estate. The sky was starting to cloud over, and she hoped to make it back before the rain. Quincy met her as she pulled up to the house and opened her door, obviously relieved she'd made it back safely. He strained to get his large body into the Honda, then pulled it over to the garage. Myra opened the front doors before Jordan reached them.

"How was your trip to town?" she chirped.

"Good. It's a nice place to call home. I'll need to meet with you sometime soon about the checking account," Jordan said.

"How's after lunch?"

"Fine with me."

"I'll meet you in the dining room in about forty-five minutes."

Jordan looked at her watch and smiled when she realized she had four minutes to spare. She was walking into the dining room as Grace was coming out of the kitchen. It reminded her of a scene from *Hazel* as she watched her swing the door open with her hip and place the dishes on the table.

"Glad to see you made it back," Grace said.

Jordan looked down at her plate and back up at Grace.

"You know this really isn't necessary. I hate to see you go

to all of this trouble."

"Wouldn't know what to do without my job," she said and winked.

Jordan sat down and ate a stuffed pork chop, wild rice, and green beans. She was finishing her glass of tea when Grace came in with a piece of lemon meringue pie. "I'm going to be as big as a barn." Jordan laughed. "Please grab a piece and sit with me."

"Okay, dear."

"Would you bring an extra piece? Myra's supposed to meet with me too."

"Yes, Ma'am, I will. I'll call her on the intercom."

Myra was back when Grace returned with the two slices of pie. They sat down together while Jordan started talking about Solomon Cove.

"I met with Mr. Crane at the bank today. I also met the mayor. You had to attend a parade in New York just to see the mayor pass by," Jordan exclaimed.

"It's a small town," Myra said, "but you still need to make your place in it. Mr. Maxwell was an important man and you'll be important as well. I think it'd be fitting for you to host a party and invite some of the leaders of Solomon Cove. What do you think, Grace?"

"What a marvelous idea!" Grace was genuinely excited. "I could make up a menu right away."

"I hate to disappoint you two, but I know very little about entertaining. Besides, I wouldn't know *what* to say to those people."

"Leave it all to us," Myra said. "We'll take care of everything. You're a Maxwell; let them worry about what they're going to say to *you*."

The three laughed and finished their pie. "I'll excuse myself, ladies," Grace replied. "There are dishes to be done."

She walked spryly out of the dining room with all of the dishes resting on her hands and forearms.

"Myra, I was surprised today at the large amount of funds in the operating account. I wasn't expecting that."

"Yes, Mr. Maxwell was a wealthy man."

"How'd you manage the account with Uncle James? I don't want to change things."

"I write a monthly check to Knox's Grocery and the hardware store in Anderson. I also write the utility bills for both the estate and the cottages and do the payroll. Anything else that comes up, I send checks as well. I rarely checked with Mr. Maxwell on small purchases, but I can set up a policy with you. We reviewed the bank statement at the end of each month together."

"It sounds good to me. You seem to have an awful lot of responsibility, Myra."

"It's my job. I'm flattered you trust me enough to allow me to continue."

"How are we on payroll? Does everyone draw a decent salary?"

"We do for Solomon Cove. Everyone seems content. Quincy, Cyrus, and Emma draw less because they live here, but they're doing okay."

"Would it be reasonable to raise everyone by $300 per month?"

"I don't see why not."

"Do Cyrus, Quincy, and Emma have any money allotted for food?"

"No, Ma'am. That's been their responsibility."

"Let them know we can give them $200 a month on the Knox account in town."

"That's very generous of you, Ms. Maxwell."

"No, that's generous of Uncle James Maxwell. I've struggled all of my life and there's no reason for everyone here to struggle to make ends meet. Can I ask you about something?"

"Certainly, what can I help you with?"

"I just wanted to know about Chandler."

Myra's face grew flushed as she looked down and fumbled with her hands. "It's a sad story, really. Maybe you'd rather not hear it."

"No, Myra. Please, tell me. None of it makes sense."

"Mr. Maxwell was a very lonely man. Many people disliked him because they thought he wasn't sociable. He was a hermit, rarely going into town or traveling at all. He was a kind man, Jordan," Myra said, feeling the need to call her by her first name.

"So that's why everyone was afraid of him, because he never went out anywhere?"

"Basically. That and the fact he was so riddled with arthritis, even as a younger man. He never dreamed he'd marry, but he met a beautiful young woman named Elizabeth. They fell deeply in love. For many years, we all wondered if she'd married him for his money, but she truly loved him. The place was alive then."

She smiled, but it was mixed with sorrow. "Young Chandler was born, and the three of them were very happy. When the boy was eight, Elizabeth was murdered in front of him.

Chandler never spoke another word. Poor Mr. Maxwell couldn't forgive him for not telling who the murderer was, so they grew further and further apart. Chandler finally had to be admitted to a state hospital for the insane. Mr. Maxwell never visited him and spent his last days racked with grief over it.

Quincy and Cyrus visit him on occasion, but the rest of us prefer to remember him as the rambunctious little boy who brought life to this place."

"How terribly sad," Jordan said.

"Yes, dear, it is, but don't spend any time fretting over it. Mr. Maxwell saw to it his medical bills would be taken care of for many years to come."

"I just wish I knew where I fit into this picture."

"Jordan, you're the only relative left. It was fitting that

you have the place. Now cheer up, we have a party to plan."

Chapter 12

Dorian Keller ran her hands through her shoulder-length black hair as she tried for the fourth time to balance her till. She was finding it more and more difficult to concentrate on her job at the bank since her parents had decided to divorce. It'd been a difficult year with her father losing his job, but she had hoped that somehow, they'd work it out.

What was waiting for her every night after work was too much for her to stomach. The horrible, endless fighting, with slanderous words being so mercilessly flung at her mother, had become a nightly occurrence. Dorian had rented the basement room from the Knoxes for the past three weeks and was enjoying the solitude. If only she could concentrate on her job.

The other girls had long since clocked out and she felt the tears starting to well up in her eyes.

"Are you okay, Dorian?"

"Yes, Mr. Crane," she managed to lie. "Just a little headache, I'm almost finished."

"Is everything all right, Dorian? You seem preoccupied,"

he asked again.

"I'm sorry, Mr. Crane. I can't keep my focus."

The tears started to fall. Billy could sense the young girl was terribly embarrassed and troubled.

"Things have a way of working themselves out," he said soothingly.

"I know," she stammered.

He'd heard about her moving in with the Knoxes but didn't want to question her about it. If she wanted him to know, she'd share it. Dorian had worked for him for almost three years now, and she'd been a dedicated employee. She'd started right out of high school and had been a quick learner. Billy knew Dorian needed to talk to someone, but he wasn't going to push her. He passed her a tissue and sat down on a stool beside her.

"My parents are getting a divorce." *There. She'd said it and she felt better.* "I know it shouldn't hit me so hard, but it's killing me."

Billy smiled at her. "It's never easy when a family separates, Dorian. I don't think age really has anything to do with it. No matter how old we get, we're still our parents' children." He took her thin hand in his and patted it. "Let's work out this till, shall we?"

Dorian forced a smile, dabbed her eyes with the tissue, and the two spent the next fifteen minutes balancing her daily transactions.

"Lucky for us, it's Friday," Billy said. "Why don't you

98

come over and have dinner with Sara and me? She'd love to have you and you two could have some *girl* talk."

"Oh, that's okay, Mr. Crane. I wouldn't want to intrude."

"Won't take no for an answer. I'll give you a lift."

"I'll drive over; I need to run a few errands first," Dorian said.

"Let's say seven. We'll expect you then."

"Thank you," she said, still dabbing at her eyes with the damp tissue.

Mr. Crane set the alarm and turned the lock as he closed the bank for the weekend. He knew Sara would be happy for Dorian to be their guest. She was always willing to help anyone, especially their employees.

Dorian waved half-heartedly as she backed her red Hyundai out of the employee parking lot. She had a couple of bills to mail and thought she'd pick up some wine for dinner. She pulled into the grocery store just as Mr. Knox was bringing in the fruit carts.

"Thank God it's Friday," he yelled across the sidewalk.

"You're right. I'm going to pick up a bottle of wine. I'm eating with the Cranes tonight. I shouldn't be late."

Ralph Knox waved at her in recognition and turned back to his work. He and his wife thought a lot of the young woman. Even though she was only a renter, they considered her part of their family. Dorian was always considerate, even letting them know where she'd be if plans were going to keep her out later than usual. *Too bad about her folks,* he thought.

****

As Billy expected, Sara was delighted to have Dorian for dinner. She'd been outside working in the garden most of the day, so she came in to take a quick shower.

"I put a pork roast in the oven earlier. It should be ready by seven," she said. The two sat with a glass of wine discussing their day. Their home was a happy one, and anyone who visited felt welcomed. It was comfortable, filled with pictures of friends and family, and bursting with bright bouquets of Sara's flowers in various vases. Billy loved her and he loved what they had made together.

"Time to set the table, Mr. Crane," she said teasingly.

Sara called him that so he'd call her Mrs. Crane, and after fifteen years of marriage, it still thrilled him to say it.

"I'll get right on that, Mrs. Crane."

Sara had already lit two candles on the table, so he took his cue and brought out the china. That was one of the many qualities he loved about his wife. She enjoyed using her finer things, not saving them for some big occasion.

Sara started slicing cantaloupe and honeydew melon, then pulled the roast pork and potatoes out of the oven.

"Smells delicious, dear," Billy yelled from the dining room.

"Only the best for you, dear," Sara said teasingly. The clock dinged seven just as everything was placed on the table.

"Dorian said she had to run some errands. I'm sure she'll be right along. Want to sit down and have another glass of wine?"

"Sure, let me put some foil over the roast," Sara said as she walked back into the kitchen.

The glass of wine turned into two more. When the clock dinged 7:30, they were both deeply worried.

"It's not like her to be late, and certainly not like her not to call if she's going to be," Billy said. His forehead wrinkled into a frown. Sara knew he had cause for concern.

"She's not answering her cell. I'll call Ralph and Diane," Sara said finally. "Maybe she's still at the house."

"That's a good idea." Sara walked into the kitchen to look up the Knoxes' number in her address book. The phone rang five times and just as she was about to hang up, Ralph answered.

"Hello, Ralph. This is Sara Crane. How are you?"

"Just fine, Sara, and you?"

"I'm all right, I guess. Dorian was supposed to eat dinner with us tonight at seven and still hasn't arrived. Have you seen her?"

"Yes, I saw her earlier this evening. She was picking up some wine and said she was headed to your place. She never came back by here."

"That's odd. I hope she hasn't broken down somewhere. Maybe she stopped by her parents. Billy said she's been very upset over the divorce."

"That's a possibility. Dorian's very sensitive, poor girl. Let me get their phone number. It's worth a try."

Ralph came back a couple of minutes later apologizing for the wait. "I can't find anything around this place when Diane isn't home. It's 207-555-0572. Let me know if she doesn't show up soon."

Sara walked back into the den and told Billy about her conversation with Ralph. "Do you think I should call her folks? I sure hate to worry them."

"It's 7:45 now; I'll give them a call." When there was no answer there, Billy decided to go out and look for her. "I'll retrace her steps from the bank to here. Will you please call Elias? Something isn't sitting right with me."

An hour later, Billy pulled back into the driveway. Elias was there deep in conversation with Sara.

"Any luck?" they both asked in unison.

"I don't understand. I retraced her route two times and went by her parents' place. They were sitting out on the front porch and hadn't heard from her either. It's just not like her."

"I reached Sam and Trent on the radio. They're looking for her too," Elias said. "I'm sure everything is fine, Billy. I'll call you when I hear something."

The two shook hands and walked toward the door. They'd been friends for many years and trusted each other. Elias knew if Billy Crane felt there was cause for concern, there was a damn good reason for it.

Just as they stepped onto the front porch, the static of the radio blared.

"Sheriff," Trent said, "do you read me?"

"That's a Ten-Four, Trent. Got anything?"

"I think you'd better call me on a landline."

Elias felt his stomach begin to churn. He knew it wasn't good. They only used the phone when they didn't want anyone to overhear their radio traffic.

"Stand by," he heard himself say.

Elias placed the phone carefully back onto its receiver. His face had gone pale and his hands were shaking so badly, he had to put them in his pockets.

"Oh, my God, Elias," Sara said, almost screaming. "What is it, what the hell is it?"

His voice was barely above a whisper. "Dorian's dead. She's been murdered; her body is behind the bank."

Billy felt weak and stumbled toward a chair. Sara was in hysterics and Elias was trying hard to comfort her. He put his arm around her and kissed her lightly on the cheek. "I'm sorry, Sara. I've got to go."

"Not without me!" Billy demanded.

The two rode into town and were greeted by the faint light of blue and red from the two deputies' cars. Doctor Chambers was there too with a van from the morgue. Trent met them at the car with a tear-stained face.

"It's bad, Sheriff. I just can't believe someone could do

this. She's such a sweet girl," he said, before correcting himself. "She was."

Her body lay sprawled across the dark asphalt of the parking lot with only her top half covered. There wasn't any blood, only her twisted, misshapen neck with a telephone cord still wrapped around it. Her arms lay spread out beside her, forming the shape of a crucifix, and her eyes looked up at them in horror.

"Oh, dear God!" Billy screamed as he knelt beside her. "This can't be happening. Poor, poor child."

"Trent," Elias said, "please get him. I've got to call the state to come in for photographs." He turned away hiding his face in his hands. "Sam, go tell her family, and for God's sakes, don't let them come over here."

The sheriff made his calls to the crime lab and walked over to where Doctor Chambers stood. "What do you think?"

"Strangulation. No sign of rape or molestation. I'm not sure why she's not clothed from the waist down. Maybe he got scared away."

"Damn it, not soon enough. What the hell is going on here? Do you think this is tied to the Jennifer Flemming case?"

"We won't know until we get more evidence. It's awfully odd to have two murders so close together."

It was well after two in the morning before they could transport her body to the morgue. Elias wanted the forensics team to take as much time as they needed. As he walked into the morgue, he realized, for the first time, he was supposed to pick Alex up for the show. He'd been dressed and almost ready to go when Sara had called. "Damn," he said. "I didn't even call her. I guess it's too late now."

Doctor Chambers walked by. "If you're talking about Alex, I called her for you. She was excited about tonight, but I'm sure you'll be forgiven."

"I suppose I do have an excuse, but I should've called," Elias said. "Please tell me you have coffee. I haven't called the mayor yet and he's going to be furious."

"I'll put a fresh pot on," he said, "but you'd better make that call. He'll be ready to string us both up."

Just as Elias wrapped his fingers around the steaming cup of brew, he heard a door slam.

"Mayor's here," he said. "Protect me, Doc. I just couldn't deal with him at the scene."

"Know what you mean, Sheriff."

Mayor Blake rounded the corner with a red face and clenched fists. "What in the hell's going on here, Sheriff? Why the hell haven't you called me? Are you aware I'm the mayor in this town?"

"Yes, Sir, I am. We were busy at the crime scene."

"And when did you decide you were solely responsible for a murder scene?"

Elias was beginning to feel as tired as he looked. He

rubbed his hands through his short hair and turned to the mayor. "Listen, Thomas, I'm sorry. Really, I am. This whole thing has just come as a shock. I should've phoned you."

"You're damn right you should have. You haven't heard the end of this." His face had turned a dark crimson and for a minute, Elias thought he might have a heart attack. "What happened here?" the mayor demanded.

"It's the Keller girl. Dorian Keller, the one who works at the bank."

"Yes, I know her."

"She was murdered behind the bank tonight. She was supposed to eat with the Cranes, but never showed up. They called me, so we started looking for her. Thought she might have broken down but no such luck."

"Did you talk to her family?" Thomas seethed.

"I sent Sam. The forensics team from the state police was in route and I wanted to be there to supervise them."

"At least you had the forethought to do that. Can I see her, Doc?" Thomas asked.

"Are you sure you want to?" Doc Chambers asked.

"Yes, I'm sure," he said as he made his way to the back.

Doc had her covered up with a white sheet. Her arms were back by her side, but her neck was so horribly distorted, and the swelling had gotten worse.

"Thank God he closed her eyes," Elias said out loud.

Thomas glanced down at her face, but before he could react, he passed out, landing with a thud onto the floor.

Doctor Chambers knelt beside him and placed his head in his lap. "Get a wet rag, Elias, hurry."

He handed it to the doctor and stood above the two men helplessly.

"Mayor, Mayor!" Doc said loudly over and over again. After a couple of minutes, he began to stir and attempted to open his eyes. "You're all right, Mayor," Doc continued. "You passed out. Don't try to get up yet."

"What the hell?" Thomas said, openly embarrassed.

"Elias, grab one arm. Help me get him to a chair," Doc ordered.

Thomas fell back into the chair putting his face in his hands. "What's going on in this town, Sheriff?"

"I don't know, but I intend to find out." Elias knelt beside him and patted his knee. "We'll get a break soon, Mayor, I'm sure of it."

"Let's hope we get it before someone else dies."

"It's after four now," Dr. Chambers said. "I think we'll be better equipped to handle this situation on a few hours of sleep."

Elias suddenly felt the weight of the exhaustion he'd carried throughout the night. "You're right, Doc. Come on, Mayor, I'll drop you off at home."

"I'm not stubborn enough to turn down a ride when I need one."

"Wise man," Elias replied. "I'll have Sam and Trent drop your car off later. You just get some rest."

* * * *

Elias stumbled into his own bed and fell asleep on top of the covers without getting out of his clothes. He slept fitfully with reoccurring dreams of Dorian screaming out for him and his deputies. He awoke a little after 9:00 a.m. and went into the bathroom to splash cold water on his face. It seemed to help, but as he was rubbing the towel across his damp face, the doorbell rang.

Who the hell could that be? Isn't there any rest for the weary?

"Who goes there?" Elias asked, not sounding very inviting.

"It's me, Sheriff," he heard Rachel say. "Can I come in?"

He opened the door motioning for her to come inside. She headed back to the kitchen and opened the brown paper sack she'd brought in.

"I knew you wouldn't eat this morning, so I stopped by the café. There are two sausage biscuits and a strong black coffee. Sit down and eat," Rachel ordered.

Elias smiled at her and realized she'd been good friends with Dorian Keller. "I'm so sorry about Dorian," he started. "I wish we could've done something."

"Me too," Rachel said, almost coming to tears, before catching herself. "There wasn't anything anybody could do. The important thing now is to find her killer. We *need* you for that."

Elias ate in silence, surprising himself by eating both

biscuits.

"I needed that, Rachel. You're right, I wouldn't have eaten. This is something I never thought we'd see around here. The mayor's taking it pretty hard too."

"I heard. Sam and Trent told me this morning when they got back from taking his car home. We really need you two to be strong for all of us."

She sounded like an old woman who had been through years and years of sorrow, not like the young girl he knew so well.

"I've got to get back to the station," Rachel stated in a professional voice. "The phones are crazy. When do you think you'll be in?"

"I'm going to take a hot shower. I'll see you in about forty-five minutes. Try to keep everyone at bay; we don't need a wild panic on our hands."

She looked over and spoke to him as if he were a young child, "Take care, Sheriff."

Chapter 13

Jordan woke up to a dreary, gray sky and lay snuggled under her down comforter. She was beginning to settle in to her new life. She rolled over to look at the clock and realized it was 7:30. She jumped out of bed and into the shower before getting dressed for the day, rounding the corner for breakfast in just the nick of time.

"Good morning, Grace," she said, feeling much more comfortable every day. There was silence for a minute as Grace looked up with tears in her eyes.

"Morning, dear," she said, placing her hot breakfast in front of her. She turned to walk back into the kitchen when Jordan stopped her.

"Grace, are you okay, what's wrong?"

Grace stopped but didn't turn around. She kept her head bowed. "There's been a tragedy. Something awful has happened."

"What? What are you talking about?" Jordan said, feeling the uneasiness that accompanied panic.

"Dorian Keller, a young girl at the bank, she's been

murdered, left dead outside the bank."

"Oh, my God! When did this happen?" Jordan asked frantically.

"Last night. She was supposed to eat dinner with the Cranes, but never showed up. She was a sweet child, not quite twenty-two years old." Grace's voice cracked with emotion.

"I can't believe it. Could it be related to the other murder, the young girl in the water?"

"No one knows yet. The whole town is devastated. It's putting fear into a place that's never had to fear before. It's a shame."

Grace walked back into the kitchen, having never turned around to face Jordan. Her breakfast suddenly didn't look as appetizing, but she knew not to hurt Grace any further by refusing to eat it. Jordan reached for the paper, but news of the murder had not yet hit.

This was a small city and the town paper didn't include anything happening after dinnertime the night before. Jordan thought of Eric and realized she hadn't talked to him in two days. She'd been so busy that she had honestly forgotten.

Pushing her plate toward the center of the table, she reached for the cordless phone that laid nearby. He answered his office phone on the second ring, sounding genuinely relieved to hear from her. "You give new meaning to *out of sight, out of mind*," Eric said teasingly.

"I'm sorry, sweetheart. I've been settling in. How's New York?" Jordan asked.

"You haven't missed much. Same old thing. So, are you missing me yet?" Eric asked playfully.

"You've got to be kidding. I missed you the second I left. Did you get my fax about the murdered girl?"

"Sure did. It seems like tragedy is following you these days," he said jokingly.

"That's not funny, Eric. This is serious. Her body was found not far from the estate and last night another girl was murdered in town."

"Damn, what's going on up there?" Eric asked, his tone quickly turning serious.

"I'm not sure, but I'd like to find out. Will you look into it for me? Just see if anything rings a bell with you or offers any clues."

"Yeah, I'll look at the article again and see what I can pull up on the town. But in the meantime, don't panic. I'm sure the crimes aren't related," Eric assured her.

"You're probably right. Have you heard from Anna Stephens?" Jordan asked.

"I checked on her this morning, as a matter-of-fact. She's doing well, just afraid of getting out of the hospital and having to go back to her apartment. Unfortunately, it looks like she'll have to in a couple of days."

"I should call her today," Jordan said, then changed the subject. "The staff thinks I should host a party for some of the locals, just to get to know them, kind of thing. I thought I'd have it when you're in town. Am I still on your agenda?"

"Yes, Ma'am. I can drive up on Friday and stay until Tuesday if that jibes with your schedule," Eric said.

"What schedule?" Jordan laughed. "I can't wait for you to see this place. It's great. I miss you, Eric, really I do."

"Miss you too. I better get back to work now. I'll call you this afternoon if I come up with anything."

Jordan hung up the phone and sat at the table for a few more minutes. Her thoughts were on Anna and how bad she felt for her. It was bad enough to have all that happen to her, but not to have anyone there for her was infinitely worse.

Myra walked in and pulled out a chair across the table from Jordan. Her face didn't mirror her usual perkiness. "I guess you've heard about the murder in town?" she asked quietly.

"Grace told me this morning. I'm so sorry. Do they have any suspects?"

"Not that I've heard. The funeral will be tomorrow. I wanted to know if it would be all right for everyone to take off around two. It's a small town and only fitting we all show our respects."

"Oh certainly. That's fine," Jordan assured her.

"Thank you, Ms. Maxwell."

Chapter 14

When Elias finally got to the office, it was a madhouse, taking all three deputies to calm the crowd. He was practically mobbed when he got out of his car.

"What's going on, Sheriff?" he heard someone yell from across the street.

"Have you caught the murderer yet?" someone else screamed.

Elias wound his way through the crowd without saying a word, closing his office door behind him. His head was pounding again as he swallowed four Tylenol.

"Rachel," he said through the intercom, "could you come in, please?"

She squeezed her little body through the small opening she'd made for herself and heaved a sigh of relief.

"It's crazy out there. Regina Collins is waiting in the lobby. She won't take no for an answer and has apparently set up camp until you talk with her," Rachel said.

"Give me about thirty minutes, then I'll see her. She's persistent as hell and can definitely wait for me. Have you talked to the mayor today?" Elias asked.

"He's on his way over." Rachel handed him a slip of paper with a phone number on it. "That's the crime lab. They called about five minutes ago. I assured them you'd call as soon as you got here."

"I'll do that now. Anything else?"

"Not that I can think of."

"Thanks, Rachel. Try to get this place cleared out if you can. I'm under enough pressure as it is."

Elias was holding for the director of the crime lab when the mayor walked in. He held the phone to his ear motioning for him to sit down across from the desk.

"Good Morning, this is Sheriff Murphy from Solomon Cove. I got a message you called. Do you have anything for us?"

"The only prints on the phone cord belonged to Dorian Keller. We got a couple of dark-blue fibers. That's about it. There was a blow to the head that occurred before the strangulation. Can't make out what she was hit with though, still working on that."

"Did you do any comparisons of the fibers from the Flemming girl?" Elias asked as he held his breath for the answer.

"I've got someone on it now. I'll let you know. Keep your eyes peeled for anything that could've been used for blunt force trauma. I'll be in touch."

"Thanks a lot." Elias hung up, feeling like he needed four

more Tylenol. He turned to the mayor who, for once, was waiting patiently. "That was the state crime lab. They didn't get any prints, but they did get a few fibers. They're going to compare the DNA with the ones found on Jennifer Flemming."

"Do you feel like they're doing all they can?" the mayor asked.

Elias was surprised he'd ask for his opinion. "Yes, Sir, I do. I'll stay in close touch with them."

"I want every deputy at the funeral home viewing, as well as the funeral. They say most killers show up there, so they won't be suspected," the mayor said.

"I've heard that theory too and we'll be watching. I have a meeting with Regina Collins in a few minutes. I was going to ask if the paper would show up and take pictures. Figured we could review them with the family and see if there's anyone there that doesn't sit right with them," Elias said.

"Sounds like a good idea, just keep an eye out for Regina. I don't trust journalists."

Elias feigned a laugh before nodding in agreement. "Are you all right, man?"

"Yeah. I'm okay. I decided I needed to pull myself together. I'm supposed to be this town's leader."

"Good to hear. You look like you need some sleep," Elias said.

Thomas nodded before excusing himself. Elias decided not to prolong the inevitable and told Rachel to send Regina on back.

She walked in and plopped down hard in one of his leather chairs.

"Make yourself at home, Ms. Collins. What can I do for you?" Elias asked.

"Cut the bullshit, Sheriff. You know what you can do for me. Tell me what's going on. This town looks to me for answers. They're getting understandably impatient," Regina stated flatly.

Elias was pleased with himself for not allowing her to anger him. "You'll be one of the first to know when we have anything to share. Right now, we're working in conjunction with the State Bureau of Investigation. All evidence is being processed at this time."

"What was she doing at the bank after closing?" Regina asked.

"We have witnesses that put her at other places after leaving work for the day. We're looking into that," Elias answered without emotion.

"Does she have a boyfriend?"

"We're looking into everyone as a suspect, Ms. Collins," he said flatly.

"So, what you're saying is there aren't any leads on this case," she said, giving him a skeptical look.

"What I'm *saying* is, we're taking everything into consideration. If you want to know who the murderer is, then I don't have an answer for you." He felt his face growing red. Elias wasn't sure how much longer he could contain his frustration. He was aware Regina was doing her job. She was good at what she did, and he couldn't blame her for probing. It had gotten her far through the years.

She would make one hell of a detective, he thought. She's so damn persistent.

"Is this latest murder related, in any way, to the Jennifer Flemming murder?"

"We're comparing fibers at this time."

"Would that mean a serial killer is on the loose in our small town, Sheriff?"

"For God's sakes, Regina, don't print that! You're well aware of the unnecessary panic that'd cause!"

"Yes, I am, Sheriff, but the town needs to prepare itself for what's really going on here."

Elias ignored her last comment, instead changing the direction of their conversation. "We could use your help," he said, hating like hell to ask for it. "We need someone to take photographs of the funeral and visitation."

"Oh, that's tasteful," she said sourly.

"Regina, I'm serious. We think the murderer may show up at one or both places. People won't be suspicious of a photographer from the *Gazette*. If it's related to the Flemming murder, we can have both families review the pictures. Maybe, we'll hit on something."

"I suppose you have a point there. I just hope this isn't the main focus of your investigation or we're screwed,"

Regina said.

"Just looking for that needle in a haystack," Elias stated.

"I hope that you have a little more confidence than that, Sheriff."

Regina thought she'd pushed him enough for one day, so she let herself out. Elias was a good man and she was one of the first to admit it. He knew his job well, but he wasn't faced with this type of dilemma every day. He was in over his head, and she realized he was terribly aware of it.

* * * *

Most of the town showed up to view the body. Many were saddened, many were afraid, and many were simply nosey. Dorian's family had her dressed in a turtleneck to cover the strangulation marks, and the funeral home had done an excellent job of preparing her. She was still a little swollen, but you couldn't detect the horror that'd occurred less than three days earlier.

Relatives and friends surrounded her mother while her father sat in the corner trying to conceal that he was intoxicated.

It was a sad scene. Elias and his men had to mask their sadness and keep an eye on the crowd that was coming and going. There were several people Elias didn't know by name, but he could place their faces from around town. There were a number of young people, and he could tell from their grief she'd had many good friends.

Regina's photographer was inconspicuous, which came as a relief to Elias. *The last thing we need is to make this a circus,* he thought. As he turned to walk outside for a breath of fresh air, he ran into Alex.

"Hi there," he said. "I'm sorry about the other night."

"I understand, Elias. I know how much you care about this community," Alex said softly.

"Well, it's going to hell in a handbasket right now, and I'm not doing much to stop it," Elias said.

"Stop," she said calmly. "You're doing all you can. I just walked over to see if I could have you over for a drink tonight. You look like you could use one."

"You don't know how true that is. I'd love to. It'll probably be an hour before I can finish here."

"That's fine. I'll be waiting."

Under other circumstances, the opportunity would've thrilled Elias, but it was hard for him to get excited over anything, especially when he was standing amid so much grief.

The rest of the viewing was uneventful. Elias stayed after everyone had left to close up with the funeral home's owner.

"I feel as though I'm betraying Dorian by leaving her here alone," Elias said, turning to Jeffrey Todd, the owner.

"She'll be fine, Sheriff," he answered kindly. "No one can hurt her anymore."

"She was just so damn young. The murder scene was bad, but seeing Dorian in that casket, it was…"

"So… final. I know, Elias," Jeffrey said softly. "We have to believe in the hereafter. She's in a better place now."

"Do you ever get used to death?" Elias asked.

"No, Sheriff, even in this business, you never become accustomed to it. Especially, when it's a tragedy or a young person. This one was a double blow."

"Yep, you're right, Jeffrey. Hope this is the last young person we have to bury."

* * * *

The ride to Alex's house was short, and he stretched as he got out of the car.

"I think I'm old beyond my years," he said to himself.

Alex answered the door before Elias could reach the doorbell.

"I'm glad you could make it," she said.

"Me too. This has been a crazy couple of weeks."

She led Elias through the apartment into a small den decorated with beige furniture. "Have a seat," she said. "What can I get you to drink?"

"How about a scotch?"

"Will do."

Alex walked back in with his drink and sat down beside him with a glass of Chablis. She smelled of expensive perfume, and he wanted desperately to breathe in her scent.

"It was so horrible about the Flemming girl, now Dorian. Do you think the two are related?" she asked.

"I doubt it, but it's hard to tell yet. Let's not talk about it tonight."

"I'm sorry. I know you're exhausted." She walked out of the room returning with a tray of cheese and crackers. "I bet you haven't even eaten dinner."

"You guessed right, but I can't say that I'm hungry."

His eyes darkened. She knew not to probe any further. She held the tray in front of him and he picked up a couple of pieces of cheese, then downed his scotch.

"This is a nice place. How long have you lived here?"

"About four years. I'm hoping to be in a house real soon."

Elias sat back on the couch and laid his head against the wall. He took a deep breath before turning to Alex. "You're so beautiful," he said, no longer embarrassed about his feelings.

She set her glass of wine on the coffee table and leaned over to kiss him. Elias gasped as her mouth touched his. He'd waited so long for this moment. Her breath was sweet as her soft lips lightly touched his. They teased each other's mouths for a few seconds, then he grabbed her in his arms and held her close to him, pressing his mouth hard against hers.

He kissed her cheek, her neck, and then her ear. Elias could feel her nipples grow erect against his chest as he longed to touch one of them, but he didn't want to scare her away. He loved her. He'd known it for a long time, and he simply wanted to enjoy this moment. He wanted to enjoy her sweet kisses. She put her head on his chest and they sat there, quiet and peaceful.

"I've been waiting on that for a long time," Elias admitted.

"Me too, I was beginning to think it'd never happen," Alex teased.

She got up and took his glass in the kitchen for a refill. Elias took a couple of small sips, then swallowed the rest.

"You look so tired," she said as she went into the kitchen to bring the bottle of scotch back into the den. Alex finished off her wine and changed over to scotch herself. They toasted each other, then nursed the bottle of scotch until it was gone.

It was five o'clock in the morning when Elias opened his eyes. Alex was lying in his arms. He could smell the shampoo in her hair. She looked so peaceful as she slept. He slowly nudged his way out from under her, laying her head carefully on the pillow. Covering her with a blanket he'd found on her bed, he let himself out the front door.

The rain was coming down in sheets. Pulling his jacket up over his head, he ran for the car, drove the five miles to his house, and jumped into the shower. It was early, but he knew if he went back to sleep, it'd be hours before he awoke again. The storm was growing louder as he dressed in his uniform, wondering if it'd lighten up before the funeral.

* * * *

The office was dark and quiet as Elias opened up. It'd been a couple of years since he'd been the first one in the office. The percolator seemed to sputter louder than usual as it brewed coffee. He sat behind his desk and thought hard about the past couple of days. Elias couldn't point the murder in any single direction. It was like the Flemming case.

No one would've wanted to hurt the girls; it didn't make sense. He was deep in thought, his eyes closed, as he heard the door open. It was 6:30 in the morning, so he reached for his weapon without hesitation. Elias squatted behind the desk, then felt foolish when he heard Rachel's voice from the front room.

"Good morning, Sheriff. It's me. What brings you in so early?"

He peered around the office door. "I should ask you the same thing. What're you doing opening up this place so early?"

"We open this early every morning. Sam will be in any minute."

"I realized the deputies came in, but I never knew you got here this early," Elias said.

"Well, now you know. Are you all right?" she asked. "You look a little tired."

"Yeah. I'm just thinking about things. None of it adds up. Neither one of the girls had any enemies."

"Let's hope the murders had nothing to do with one

another," Rachel said grimly.

"Let me fix you a cup of coffee for a change," Elias said, getting up from his desk.

"Not today, Sheriff. I feel sick to my stomach. I brought a ginger ale from home."

"You're just afraid to try my coffee." Elias laughed as he walked toward the coffeepot. "You really need to be careful about opening up this building by yourself."

"I'm fine, Sheriff; we haven't determined there's a serial killer on the loose yet," Rachel said.

"Knock on wood," he said. "Don't let Regina Collins hear you talk like that. That's just what she wants to hear."

They heard the front door open again followed by Sam's voice. "Is that the sheriff's car I see out there?" he asked jokingly. "I must be dreaming."

"Oh, that's funny, Sam. Real funny," Elias responded.

"Just messing with you, Sheriff. Any news on the murder?"

"None yet. I haven't heard from the forensics team this morning. Can you cover things here for a few minutes? I thought I might take Rachel to breakfast. I owe her one."

"Not a problem at all. She hasn't felt good lately, so if you can get some food down her, then more power to you," Sam agreed.

"You heard the man, Rachel. Let's blow this joint and get breakfast with real coffee."

"Can't say I've ever turned that down." Rachel looked

pale and a little squeamish.

They were waiting outside when Lacy pulled up to the diner in her old, wood-paneled station wagon. "Well, ain't this a sight for sore eyes." Lacy grinned. "How'd you get him out of bed this early, Rachel?"

"He beat me into work today. Miracles never cease," she answered teasingly.

"Okay, okay, I get the point," Elias said, sounding stern and aggravated, but the two women didn't buy it. "Can you seat us toward the back so we can eat without any murder inquiries?" the sheriff asked.

"Guess that's my cue not to ask either," Lacy said, walking them to the back of the restaurant. "I'll try to cut your fans off at the pass."

"Much obliged, Ma'am. Could you bring us two breakfast platters with a little of everything? I've got to fatten up my better half here; she's been kind of puny."

Rachel looked tired and definitely not hungry, but she forced a smile.

"You're scaring me, Sheriff," she said. "Am I about to get fired or something?"

"Nope. Just a little celebration for that new raise of yours. Believe it or not, I got $2.50 an hour out of the mayor. Scary, huh?" Elias said with a chuckle.

They both laughed as Lacy brought their breakfasts.

"Today's going to be a long day with the funeral and all," Elias told her. "We'll close the office for the service."

"I was going to ask about that. I'm glad I'll be able to make it," Rachel commented sadly.

Elias looked at her, realizing she'd held it together much better than he had, and Dorian had been her friend.

"Are you sleeping all right, Rachel? You look worn out."

"Yes, I'm sleeping, but I just stay so tired. I'll be fine."

"I think I'm overworking you. Take some time off. Come in later if you want."

"Stop it. I'm fine, really."

They ate in silence, the food making Elias feel like a new man.

"I needed that," he said, rubbing his flat belly. "Did Dorian have a boyfriend?" he asked Rachel.

"She dated Tanner Phelps for a while, but I'm not sure if they were still seeing each other. He works at the hardware store in Anderson. Pretty nice guy, I guess."

"Can you think of anyone that'd want to hurt her?" Elias asked.

"Not Dorian. She was a sweet girl. Everyone liked her. She didn't have a big social life, just work and church that I'm aware of." Lacy handed him the bill as they got up to head back to work. Elias's headache was back. He swallowed his usual four Tylenol as they walked back to the station.

Trent met them both at the door with a concerned look on his face. "Dorian's father is in your office. We couldn't keep him out. He insisted on waiting for you."

"Thanks, Trent. I'll be fine," Elias assured him.

Elias walked into his office, and his heart instantly ached for Mr. Keller. It was obvious he hadn't slept the night before and his breath reeked of stale alcohol. His eyes were bloodshot; his hair was a mess.

"Hello, Mr. Keller," Elias said as gently as he could.

"Sheriff," he said, acknowledging Elias with a slight nod. "What're we gonna do about my daughter?"

"We're doing all we can, Sir," Elias responded. "We're going to question everyone who knew her. We'll need your help too, as painful as that may be. Can you think of anyone that'd want to harm your daughter?"

"Not Dorian. She was a good girl; the best thing I ever done was having her. She worked at the bank and went to church every Sunday. She was taking it hard about her mamma and me," he said as tears slid slowly down his weathered face. "Just can't get that off my mind," Mr. Keller added sadly.

"Try not to think about it, Mr. Keller. We can't control a lot of things, and I'm sure that was one of them."

"Can't help but feel guilty though," he said as he put his face in his hands.

"Why don't you go home and try to get a little rest before the funeral? Be there for Dorian's mother now. You two need each other."

"I supposen' you're right, Sheriff." Mr. Keller walked out with his head down.

Elias called in his deputies and asked them all to bring a pad and pencil.

"We have a lot to do in the next few days," he told them. "We'll need to interview all of Dorian Keller's friends and the people who saw her the night she was killed. Trent, you can start with the bank employees and follow any leads from there. Sam, you talk to her parents and find out any high school friends or close relatives. Evan, you talk to her pastor and the Knoxes at the grocery. They may know a few people who have visited her recently. I know it will be hectic, but the mayor has approved all overtime, so please, work as much as you can. I know all of you will be at the funeral today. Keep your eyes peeled for anything fishy. We'll review the pictures from the *Gazette* photographer together and with her family. Thank you, guys, in advance for your efforts on this." Elias sat back in his chair and laced his fingers behind his head. "Do any of you have any questions?"

"We're anxious to know if it was the same killer from the Flemming case," Sam said, already looking worn from the stress of it all.

"I'm not sure yet. We're waiting on the lab to confirm any match between the fibers found at both crime scenes. Let's hope not because we'll be looking at one hell of a mess. I don't want to overreact, and I certainly don't want you to share this with the general public, but we just may have a serial killer on our hands. And I don't know of any who've stopped at two victims."

Chapter 15

The old church on Nevels Road was beginning to show its age. The roof was sagging, and the building was in dire need of a fresh coat of paint. It had long since lost most of its membership to the new Episcopal church in town and with that had gone the tithes that'd aided in keeping her up. Dorian Keller hadn't defected though. She'd grown up in the little church and would never have considered leaving her.

The whole town was present, attempting to cram themselves into the few available pews. The air conditioning, which had long since given out, was openly missed. Her wooden coffin sat in the front of the church, a grim reminder of why everyone was there. Only a side profile of her face was visible, along with a few wisps of her dark hair. The smooth pink satin lining of the casket made Elias openly shiver. He hated funerals, and he hated the thought of this young girl being closed up in that casket for eternity. Looking away, Elias made his way around to his deputies, trying to bypass any questions the public was biting at the bit to ask. When inquiring citizens approached, he simply held up his hand insisting it was neither the time nor the place.

The hum of the old organ began. Those with seats sat down; everyone else squeezed in the back inside the vestibule. Pastor Livingston stood up in his black robe trying desperately to make sense of the horrible tragedy. He failed miserably. Even a God-fearing man like the pastor couldn't change the deep-seeded grief that came with losing someone way before their time.

The rains came down hard just as he was giving his final prayer. It didn't, however, stop anyone from attending the graveside service. Rachel was exhausted by the time it ended. Elias had to lead her to the car by her elbow. By the time they reached her vehicle, he was practically holding her up, and as he helped her into the car, she collapsed.

"Trent, Trent! Get over here!" Elias screamed, barely audible over the torrential downpour.

"What is it, Sheriff?" he asked, looking down at Rachel. "Is she all right?" he said, panic setting in his voice.

"I'm taking her to the emergency room," Elias said, trying to keep it together. "Help me get her to my car and then get in touch with Hank. Have him meet us there!"

With that, he sped off with Rachel, who was just beginning to come to. She was flushed and confused, but more embarrassed than anything.

"What happened?" she asked wearily.

"You passed out on us. I'm taking you to Metro General. Just lay back and relax now."

"Don't do that. I'm sure I'm fine. It must be a bug or something because I haven't felt good in a while."

"Well, we're getting to the bottom of it today! You scared the hell out of me. Not to mention poor Trent."

Elias wheeled into the emergency room driveway designated for ambulances. His sirens blared as two curious nurses met him at the door with a wheelchair.

"What's going on, Sheriff, are you hurt?" the blonde asked.

"It's not me; it's my secretary, Rachel. She passed out. We need someone to see her right away." He helped them get her into the wheelchair, then stepped back. "I'll be in the waiting room. Her husband is on his way."

As quickly as they'd arrived, they were gone, and his body went limp from the excitement of it all. Elias loved that little girl. He didn't know what he'd do if something were to happen to her.

Two hours later, a nurse came out and woke him from one of the deepest sleeps he'd had lately.

"Excuse me, Sheriff," she said, "I have some good news."

Elias looked around to find the three worried faces of his deputies flanking him.

"Is she going to be okay?" he asked.

"I think I'll let her tell you." She smiled. "She wants you

to come on back. I'm sure she meant the deputies too."

They all jumped up in unison and walked quickly behind the nurse. Rachel was lying on the bed, looking pallid and weak, but a huge smile spread across her face. Hank stood beside her with the same silly grin.

"Guess what?" she said excitedly. "You're all going to be uncles. We're having a baby!"

Trent, Sam, and Evan bent down and hugged her, but all Elias could do was heave a big sigh of relief.

"You scared the hell out of me, little girl. Lucky for you, you're with child or I'd make you work overtime without extra pay."

His face was stern, but Rachel knew she'd really frightened him. It just proved to her why she worked so hard for this man; Elias cared for her.

Thank God we are finally having a new life join us. I can't take any more death, he thought.

Chapter 16

Jordan sat on the balcony off of her room with a book from the library. She was watching the storm roll in over the water and enjoying the gentle breeze on her face. She opened the book slowly and looked at the embossed emblem on the cover page. *This book belongs to Chandler Maxwell.* Jordan rubbed her finger across the seal imagining what he'd been like. *Maybe* The Red Badge of Courage *had been one of his favorites too.*

She wondered how her great-uncle could've left him in an institution and never so much as visited him. *What a waste of two lives,* Jordan thought. Chandler would be eighteen now, a young man, no longer a little boy. She wondered if he missed this place, or if it made him think of his mother's murder.

The storm was close enough to touch, so she walked back into her room. The house was quiet with everyone gone to the funeral. She laid the book on the bed and walked down the hall stopping to look at some of the portraits on the wall. Jordan didn't see one that could've been Chandler.

There have to be some reminders of him, she thought.

She returned to the library and looked at its few framed photographs. None were of a young boy. She tried to open the desk drawer, but it was locked. Her great-uncle's desk had to contain something that'd answer some questions, but she didn't have the key. *I'll have to ask Myra about it this afternoon.*

Jordan listened to the thunder as it clapped loudly, and the torrents of rain as it lashed against the windowpanes. She didn't want to go, but she felt her body leading her to her great-uncle's room. She opened the door, standing behind it like a frightened child.

"Is this like one of those cheap horror movies or what?" she said aloud to herself. The room was massive with a hand-carved bed, and matching fireplace mantle. *What talent that had to take,* Jordan thought, taking time to look closer now. The dark, heavy drapes completely covered the windows, making the room extremely gloomy. She pulled back one side of the curtain, pausing to look out. It was a breathtaking view, even with the rains blurring her vision.

Jordan walked over to the sitting area, pausing to turn on a small floor lamp. It gave off little light, adding to the mystery of the place. She sat down and looked up at the portrait above the fireplace for the first time. It must have been Elizabeth Chandler. Myra was right; she was beautiful. She looked like a princess worthy of the lifestyle she'd led. Her hair was almost golden, draped like a thick, shiny mane over her shoulders. Her eyes were deep-blue and reflected kindness and contentment, a sharp contrast to her great-uncle's portrait.

Who would have killed such a beautiful woman and why? Jordan turned to look at the matching vanity and desk that sat to each side of the fireplace. She walked over and sat down on the satin cushion that covered the vanity's seat. She gasped as she saw her reflection in the mirror.

"Okay, I'm being a little melodramatic." Jordan laughed.

The vanity was wiped clean and shone bright from recent contact with furniture polish. On it lay some of the things that must've belonged to Elizabeth. There was a silver brush and comb set, a bottle of Chanel, and two small silver frames. One contained a picture of her and Uncle James sitting out in the flower garden. He looked so happy, so different from what she'd remembered. It was a side view of him and he was watching her tenderly and smiling.

Smiling, that was something Jordan had never seen. She longed to know about that part of his life. The other frame contained Elizabeth with a small baby wrapped in a thick blue blanket. You could only see the top part of the baby's face; his nose was red from the cold. His eyes were the same electric-blue as his mother's and his hair was a wisp of blonde.

That has to be Chandler, she thought.

Jordan reached down and touched the ivory handles on the center drawer. She started to pull it out, then stopped herself. *What am I doing?* she thought. *This is not my stuff; this is not my room; this is not even my house!* She stood up quickly and started for the door but turned around before reaching it.

The desk was sitting there like an ugly gargoyle waiting for her to return. Shivers were running up her spine as her feet carried her unwillingly toward it. Her hands were visibly shaking as she reached out to touch it, halfway expecting it to burn her fingers. As soon as she touched it, her fingerprints became visible on the heavy coat of furniture polish. There was an expensive ink pen laying on an empty piece of clean paper as if someone were preparing to write a letter. There were two silver frames matching those on the vanity, each containing pictures of Elizabeth.

There was also a picture of a small baby girl wrapped tightly in an afghan and lying in a small oak crib. Jordan recognized the crib immediately as one she'd seen in pictures of herself when she was an infant. The picture wasn't very clear, but she could tell without any doubt, it was her. There was also a cheap paperweight with a small replica of the Statue of Liberty inside, hardly fitting of her Uncle James's expensive taste. Jordan picked it up and rolled it around in her hand, then placed it lightly back onto the desk again.

Jordan noticed a lock on the desk drawer and tried to slide it open, but it wouldn't give. *Curiosity killed the cat,* her mother had always said. But Jordan was more than curious—she wanted some answers; she wanted to know more about her new life. She wanted to visit Chandler.

It was the first time the thought of visiting him had crossed her mind and she shook her head in confusion. Then, as quickly as she'd thought it, Jordan believed it was something she had to do. Closing the door quietly behind her, she was relieved to be out of the room. It was like stepping from darkness into day. Jordan heard the kitchen door open and the slow shuffle of feet. She walked down the long winding staircase to find Grace sitting at the small table in the kitchen, her head bowed and resting in her hands.

"Hello, Grace," Jordan said gently. She could tell how hard they'd all taken the death.

"Hello, dear," she almost whispered. "How was your afternoon?"

"Quiet here. I'm sorry it rained for the funeral."

"Me too. Just seemed to make a sad event even sadder if that's possible. Can I get you a snack?" Grace asked.

"No thanks, how about a cup of tea?"

Grace nodded and as she started to get up, Jordan motioned for her to stay seated.

"Let me," Jordan said, starting a kettle of water on the stove.

She returned to the table, questioning Grace, "Have they heard anything about the killer?"

"It's still hush-hush."

The two sat in silence until the whistle of the kettle

interrupted their thoughts. Jordan poured two cups of hot tea and handed one to Grace.

"Where is everyone else?" Jordan asked.

"They're on their way back. With the weather so bad, it was hard for everyone to get out of the cemetery. I rode with Myra. She stopped by the greenhouse to cut some roses."

"Speak of the devil," Jordan said, as Myra walked through the door with a wet paper towel wrapped around a bunch of white roses.

"Afternoon, Ms. Maxwell," Myra said, shedding her wet rain bonnet. Her eyes were red and puffy from the tears that had accompanied the young girl's funeral.

Jordan was determined not to talk about the Keller girl anymore. "It's been quiet today. This is a big place, especially when you're alone."

"Oh, it's not so bad once you get used to it," Myra said.

"Grace and I were just having tea; would you like a cup?"

"I believe I would; maybe it'll warm me up."

Myra placed the roses in a tall vase and took them into the dining room, setting them in the center of the table. Jordan had her tea ready when she returned.

"I noticed you're spending a great deal of time in the library," Myra said. "Do you enjoy reading?"

"Oh yes, I do." Jordan used the subject as her cue to lead into her visiting with Chandler. "I picked out a book today that belonged to Chandler. He must've liked to read too."

140

Jordan noticed Grace and Myra glance at one another quickly before looking away. They sat in silence until Jordan spoke up again, "Did he like the library too?"

Neither of the women responded until Myra finally did. "Yes, I think he did. By the way, we have a party to plan, Ms. Maxwell, and I think that's exactly what this town may need right now."

Jordan took their hint, dropping the conversation about Chandler, but only until another day. "My boyfriend Eric is coming in next Friday. Is it too soon to get something together by then?"

Myra and Grace both leaned forward, obviously excited with the thought of planning an event.

"My goodness, dear," Grace said, for the first time of the day sounding more like herself. "We'll need to rush around here. I'll have to get with Ralph Knox about ordering the groceries. Oh my, we'll need a menu."

"Would you prefer dinner or hors d'oeuvres?" Myra asked. "That would be a good start."

"Let me be honest." Jordan was a little embarrassed. "I've never thrown a party before, especially one inviting leaders of the town. I'm going to need your guidance, and frankly, I'm game for whatever you two decide."

Jordan sat back in her chair feeling her face blush. Myra noticed the embarrassment but refused to acknowledge it. She looked kindly at Jordan. "Let's look at our options. A dinner is more formal; hors d'oeuvres would make it possible for everyone to mingle at their leisure. That may be easier for everyone this go-round."

Jordan returned the kind smile, nodding her head in agreement. "Sounds good to me. Who should we invite?"

Grace got up to open a drawer in the buffet, pulling out a tablet and a pen.

"Let's start with the business owners in town, the Knoxes, the Cranes, the Kendalls that own the boutique, Ms. Lillian from the florist, Doctor Chambers, he's from the morgue; but everyone in town knows him; Doctor Samuel, Pastor Livingston, Mayor Blake, Sheriff Murphy; might as well invite all of the deputies, that never hurts, especially these days, and," she said, stopping for a deep breath. Jordan realized it was the most she'd heard her say at one time.

"Oh, who else, Myra?" Grace asked as she scribbled names quickly onto her pad.

Myra came up with another ten people to invite before they started putting their heads together for food and drink.

"I'll call the printers in Anderson. They can have the invitations ready in the morning. It's amazing how quickly things can get done if you are willing to pay for it." Myra laughed. "How is seven o'clock?"

"That's fine." Jordan was amazed they'd planned the party so quickly. "What should I wear?" she asked casually.

"Oh, my heavens, child," Grace answered. "You must get a new dress. I'll call my friend who works at the new boutique in Anderson. She'll be happy to help you find something. You must go in the next couple of days!"

Jordan laughed when she saw the dreadful expression on Grace's face and the look of urgency she wore. "I'll do that, Grace. What else do I need to do?"

"You just walk down those stairs at seven o'clock. We'll take care of everything else," Myra said.

Chapter 17

Elias sat behind his desk with a dull expression on his face. It'd been two days since the funeral, and Regina had finally dropped off the pictures. He forced himself not to complain, knowing she'd taken over 400 shots and printed them on *The Gazette's* budget.

"Did you see anything suspicious?" Elias asked Regina, not wanting her to know he valued her opinion.

"Nope, not a thing," she said nonchalantly. "Same people we see every day."

"Well, thanks for the pictures. We'll get right on them," he responded, standing up and walking her to the door.

She left, but not willingly. Regina Collins clearly had a great deal more to say. Elias leaned back, as far as his desk chair would allow, and stared up at the ceiling. He never dreamed things could get this crazy in Solomon Cove. Elias had demanded Rachel take a week off to rest, and now he felt like kicking himself in the ass. The mayor had sent over a temp from city hall to answer the phones, and needless to say, she was no Rachel Kelly.

"Sheriff," he heard the temp calling through the door, "you have a call on line three from the forensics team."

"Thanks, Lisa," he said, cringing. She just couldn't grasp how to use the intercom. A couple more days of this, and he'd throw her out himself. He reached for the phone, saying a silent prayer before answering it. *Please, Lord, don't let these be connected. I just don't have the manpower to deal with it.*

"Mornin'," Elias said, trying to conceal his fears.

"Good morning, Sheriff. This is Harold Penn from the crime lab. How are you today?"

"Well, can't complain, it wouldn't help anyway."

"Know what you mean," he said, his voice rough and raspy. "Listen, got some news for you about those fibers. Seems they match up with the ones found on the Flemming girl. Appears to be a type of commercial carpeting. It's short and coarse, and coated with a stain-resistant solution, more than likely Scotchgard. My guess, it's from an automobile trunk. It's not consistent with carpeting found in homes or businesses. Most of those have a little more height to them. At any rate, it's blue."

Elias suddenly felt sick, and for a minute, thought he might pass out. He sat up in his chair and pulled the trash can over between his feet should the need to vomit surface quickly.

"Damn it," he said, not able to hide his contempt. "That's the last thing we were prepared to hear."

"I'm with you, Sir," he said, sounding a little less stiff.

"We're here at your disposal, so call me anytime. I guess I'll be your point of contact now. My direct line is extension 2545 at the bureau. Keep in touch."

Elias hung up unaware he hadn't said good-bye. Perspiration was dripping down his forehead and he could feel the stickiness forming under his armpits. Knowing what he had to do next, Elias phoned the mayor.

They both were aware it was only a matter of time before the public found out. Actually, it was probably best they did. The sheriff didn't want them to hide behind the façade that their little town was safe anymore.

Elias called his men in again and told them the latest news.

"It's imperative we all go through these pictures. I've seen them, but I don't see anything out of the ordinary. When you're finished looking over them, I need you, Evan, to take them by the Kellers'. Encourage them to take their time. Sam, I hate to do it, but I'll need you to take a couple of days to drive into Massachusetts to show them to the Flemming family as well. It's a long shot, but maybe they'll know somebody from the pictures."

Rubbing his eyes, he reached for the bottle of Tylenol. "I'm sorry, guys, but we're going to need some help. Anderson has agreed to send me a couple of guys from their department to assist in general patrol. That'll free us up for the investigation."

It was clear none of them wanted to share their territory.

Elias knew the three of them were all fine men. He respected and trusted each one, but they weren't trained for this.

Elias picked up the phone again and dialed the mayor's number. "Want to have dinner? I need to talk to you."

"Sounds fine. Where do you want to meet?" Mayor Blake asked.

"Hell, come to think of it, let's not go out in public. We won't be able to talk without everyone blaming us for this godforsaken mess. I'll grab a couple of steaks from Ralph's, you bring the scotch, and we'll cook at my house. Be there at seven."

"See you then," he said.

* * * *

True to form, Thomas Blake was right on time.

You can definitely set your clock by that man, Elias thought. "First things first," he said, holding out two empty glasses.

Thomas filled them both to capacity and sat down at the kitchen table. "What do you make of it all?" he asked, sounding a little more patient, and a little calmer than he had in weeks.

Elias pulled up a chair, turning it backward before straddling it. "I've been trying to think of anything that might tie these cases together. I just can't put my finger on it. Jennifer was a college girl from a wealthy family and Dorian was a high school graduate from a poor, dysfunctional family. Dorian stayed in Solomon Cove, so I couldn't see where the two women would've crossed paths. If they were friends, nobody knew about it. On the other hand, if it's a serial killer, he would pick his victims at random, and they're usually prostitutes or street people who wouldn't be missed. Both girls had families, jobs, and people that would look for them. Besides, it's obvious he wants us to find his victims. Neither Jennifer nor Dorian were the type to get into the car with a stranger. Somergrove and Solomon Cove are both small enough towns that someone would notice a drifter."

"Not bad for a small-town sheriff," Thomas said.

"I try," Elias said.

"I can't seem to find the connection either. Could the connection be Solomon Cove? Why was Jennifer's body brought here and dumped? I mean Somergrove is over an hour away," Thomas added.

"We've both lived here all our lives, Thomas. I don't know of any dark secrets about this place. How could it be tied to murder? The last thing that happened here was the Maxwell murder, and that's been over ten years ago."

Neither man spoke until their glasses were empty.

"Hit me, will you?" Elias asked, pushing his glass across the table. "We need help, Thomas. Will you agree to have some of Anderson's deputies come down and patrol, at least until we can stop this madness?"

"I'm giving you carte blanche on this whole operation.

I've known you a long time, Elias. I trust you to do the right thing. Just keep me in the loop, that's all I ask."

"I was hoping you'd say that," Elias said, feeling as though some of the pressure was lifted from him now.

Chapter 18

Jordan was so excited about Eric coming to visit that she hadn't put much thought into her party. Everyone around the house, even the men, appeared excited at the prospect of a celebration. The last party at the estate had been when Elizabeth was alive.

Maybe, just maybe, this will bring some life back to this place, she thought.

Anna had phoned her two nights before, and they'd talked for over three hours. She was doing much better except for returning to the apartment. Before Jordan hung up the phone, the two had made plans for her to ride up with Eric on Friday. Even though they weren't close friends, Jordan had a lot of space and a beautiful place for someone to recuperate. It was the least she could do.

"I don't feel right about this," Anna had said.

"Please come," Jordan had argued. "Eric is only staying three days, and I could use some company. You can stay as long as you'd like."

They had left it an open-ended invitation, and although

Jordan knew she was doing the right thing, she couldn't help but second-guess herself.

Jordan had spent the week preparing rooms for Anna and Eric. She was sure he'd stay with her, but she was a Maxwell and needed to be proper, or at least *appear* that way.

Zeke had been working hard on the lighthouse. He'd cleared away the ivy and cobwebs and even painted the inside.

Jordan noticed Zeke was a quiet man, always deep in thought, and a hard worker. She contributed it to his sick wife and wondered how he managed with the kids. She sensed he'd been closer to her great-uncle than perhaps anyone, judging by how much he spoke of him.

Jordan walked out to the lighthouse with a book under her arm and saw him sitting on one of the benches near the edge of the cliff. "How are you today, Zeke?"

"Oh, hi, Ms. Maxwell. Just fine and you?"

"I'm fine, too. Mind if I sit for a few minutes?"

"Not at all, Ma'am." He slid over, giving her the large section of the bench.

"This is a beautiful spot. I can't say that I've even noticed it before."

"Oh, it's one of my favorites. Mr. Maxwell even sat out here with me sometimes."

"Tell me about him, Zeke. I only met him two, maybe three times, when I was a child."

Zeke sat back making himself comfortable, appearing

pleased Jordan had asked.

"Mr. Maxwell was a good man. A lot of people didn't like him because they thought he was mean-spirited, especially when it came to Chandler, but he wasn't." Zeke looked down for a few seconds, then scanned the horizon over the water. "I guess we kind of had a connection with my wife being sick most of the time, and with him losing Mrs. Maxwell. He was real nice to my family and me, sometimes getting Myra to buy the little ones clothes or toys."

The sadness in his eyes was genuine, and it touched Jordan. She was hesitant to ask any more questions.

"I miss him," Zeke added, more to himself than to her.

"What was Mrs. Maxwell like?"

His face broke in to a broad smile. "She was a lovely person. Bright and cheery, and well, very beautiful. Everyone liked her and the boy."

Jordan found herself desperately wanting to ask about the murder, Chandler, and so many more things, but she could see Zeke had enough on his mind right now.

"How's your wife doing?" Jordan asked.

"Not so good. Her mother has been staying with us since she got home from the hospital. I was thinking the other day that I've never known Cassie when she wasn't sick, but she's so alive. I loved her long before she even knew my name." Zeke laughed aloud and turned to Jordan. "Do you have anyone special in your life?"

"My boyfriend, Eric. He's coming up tomorrow for the

party. He's a journalist for *The New York Times*."

"Another writer, huh? Maybe he'll like the lighthouse, too."

"It looks great, by the way. I've been meaning to tell you how much better it looks."

"Thank you, Ma'am. Just doing my job."

"Well, I guess I'll walk up to the top now. I enjoyed talking with you. I hope your wife is better soon."

Jordan stood up and took a couple of steps before turning back. "Can I ask you one more thing, Zeke? Did my great-uncle ever mention me?"

Zeke sat motionless and silent for a moment. "Yeah, a couple of times."

* * * *

Eric and Anna arrived earlier than expected, and Jordan was delighted. It'd seemed like years since she'd seen Eric, and Anna felt like an old friend.

They were both astounded by the estate. Eric shook his head as he whispered quietly in her ear, "I feel a little intimidated. Remind me never to take you to my dump in New York."

Jordan laughed and kissed him full on the mouth. It felt so comfortable having him here with her. She found herself already dreading when he'd leave.

She let them both settle into their rooms, making them promise to be downstairs in an hour. Jordan had already made arrangements with Grace that they'd eat lunch at the café in town. It'd give her a chance to show them around, and also give the kitchen workers time to prepare for the night's party.

With Eric coming to visit, Jordan hadn't given much thought to the party, and now she felt the butterflies circulating throughout her stomach.

"What was I thinking, Myra?" she asked. "I don't know any of these people."

"Dear," she said quickly, aware that she had far more to do than coddle Jordan, "everything will be fine. Now clear out of the way and enjoy your company. Just look beautiful at seven tonight, and we'll handle the rest." Jordan flashed her an unconvincing smile as she walked back up to her room. She put on a little lipstick, brushed through her hair, and went back downstairs to meet Eric and Anna. They were both standing around with their mouths gaped open and their eyes wide.

"My God, Jordan," Eric said, "this place is huge. Aren't you afraid of being here alone?"

"Not much anymore. Just certain parts of the house kind of creep me out. Emma lives off the kitchen and Quincy and Cyrus live out back. Besides, I figure I'm much safer now with the two of you here."

Quincy brought Jordan's car up from the garage muttering under his breath about the rattle of the engine.

"Thank you, Quincy," Jordan mouthed as he handed her

the keys. She hurriedly jumped in before she could get her lecture about the outdated machine. Eric climbed in back and Anna eased slowly into the front seat. She was still a bit unsteady from her injuries but seemed happy to be in Maine. Jordan realized just how much she'd enjoy having a friend around.

As they circled down the driveway and made their way into town, the three talked nonstop. They talked about the scenery, the estate, their bedrooms, and the party.

"I'm glad you two will be here tonight," Jordan said with deepest sincerity. "I won't know any of these people. The whole town is coming, the mayor, the sheriff, and the owners of the town businesses. I never thought I'd have this to worry about," she said, laughing nervously. "On a brighter note, I can't wait for you to try out this diner. It has the best home-cooked food. You'll love it." With that, she pulled up in front of the Corner Café and parked.

"Looks like it has character and ambiance." Eric laughed.

"I'm glad the food is good; I'm starving!" Anna was a cute young woman and very vivacious, perhaps a little less now after the attack, but still upbeat. Her face and belly were pudgy, almost like baby fat that never went away, but it took little away from her. Jordan watched as she walked into the restaurant, realizing they'd quickly become fast friends.

Olivia walked out of the kitchen blowing a bubble with her chewing gum. She covered her face with her hands when she saw Jordan and her friends. "Excuse me." She grinned. "That was so rude of me. Please don't tell my mother. I'll get the old *you're way too old for gum* talk."

They all laughed as Jordan said, "You can count on me not to tell."

Olivia grabbed three menus and walked them back to their table. "Welcome to Solomon Cove," she said. "I'm Olivia Yates."

"These are two of my friends from New York," Jordan said. "My boyfriend, Eric, and my friend Anna Stephens."

"Nice to meet you both," she said, eying Eric with obvious approval. "Our special today is meatloaf, mashed potatoes, green beans, and apple pie. That comes with a drink and it's $8.79. You can also order from the menu." She took their drink orders while they all agreed the special would be fine.

As they devoured their meal, Jordan explained to them Olivia was the daughter of Myra, one of the estate's employees. Eric reached for the ticket as they ate, but Jordan insisted on getting it. "I'm finally in a situation where I can buy lunch or dinner and it won't break into the budget. I insist, Eric."

"You may be financially able, Jordan," Eric said firmly, "but I'm still your boyfriend. I will not let the people in this town think you're giving me a free ride."

Jordan was stunned and felt her face flush. Eric had never talked to her that coldly. She suddenly realized her inheritance *had* intimidated him.

"I'm sorry, Eric," she said calmly. "You're right." She looked at Anna. "I love this man; not only is he bright and good-looking, but he's living proof that chivalry is not yet dead."

Jordan helped Anna get up from the table and the three strode arm in arm out of the café.

When they reached the car, Olivia came barreling out of the café calling after them. She reminded Jordan so much of Myra she had to smile.

"Ms. Maxwell," she said, breathing heavily from running to catch up with them, "I almost forgot to tell you how much everyone is looking forward to your party tonight. My mom has asked me to help in the kitchen, so I guess I'll see you there."

"That's great. I hope no one will be disappointed."

"Oh, no, Ma'am, they won't be disappointed," Olivia assured her.

* * * *

Zeke had been right; Eric loved the lighthouse. The two sat up there all afternoon, gazing out over the water and talking.

"Did you get a chance to look over the articles I sent you about the latest murder?" Jordan asked.

"Yes, I did. Have they gotten any further with the case?"

"No, not that I know of. It hasn't been front page anyhow."

"This is *small-town America*. They aren't accustomed to this kind of thing. Give them some time to check into the girl's background; maybe something will come together then."

"Yeah, maybe so, but why have there been two murders within a month?"

"Could be connected. Didn't you say the first girl was dumped along the water's edge?" Eric asked.

"Yes, not far from here, actually."

"Let's go down there and look around tomorrow."

"I don't know, Eric; it's kind of creepy. It's one thing to read your articles, but dipping into a crime scene, I just don't know."

"Oh, it won't hurt to look around. The body isn't there anymore, Jordan, for heaven's sake."

"There's something else," Jordan said. "It's about Chandler, Mr. Maxwell's son. He went into an asylum after his mother's murder and has never spoken a word since. They say he witnessed the murder and was too frightened to implicate the murderer. Do you think the unsolved murder of Elizabeth Maxwell could have something to do with these cases?"

"Now Jordan, come on. I think you've been living in this oversized castle for a few weeks and now you think you're a super sleuth. Even if they were connected somehow, that was over ten years ago," Eric scoffed.

"I just want to know some more about it. Do you think I should go visit Chandler; after all, I am living in his house?"

"No, you are living in *your house*. If he hasn't spoken in ten years, I don't think you will get much out of him. Why don't we just go to the local library on Monday and pull up some of the old newspaper articles. That would be a start."

"Maybe you're right, Eric. It's all so weird. I want to know more about where I fit into all of this."

"You're the last living relative. Don't overanalyze the hell out of it. Damn, enjoy it. You could be back in that shoebox of an apartment in New York."

"You're right, I'm sorry. It's time for us to get ready for this party that I'm not qualified to host," she said, laughing. "Did you bring a tux?"

"Yes, Ma'am, Ms. Maxwell, I did."

They walked hand in hand back to the house.

"I don't want to talk about the murders in front of Anna," Jordan continued. "She's been through enough. She doesn't need to worry about being killed here."

"Okay, now that's enough about murder. Jesus, I feel like I'm back at work," Eric said.

Chapter 19

Anna tapped on the bedroom door just as Jordan had finished her makeup. She looked lovely in her crème dress and Jordan didn't hesitate to tell her so.

"Wow, don't you look great, Anna? I'm not even dressed yet and I haven't figured out what to do with my hair."

Anna walked over and touched Jordan's hair, pulling it back tight and then twisted it up in a bun. "Let me give it a try. I'll be back in a minute."

Anna returned with a curling iron, a large black barrette, and a bottle of hairspray.

"Are you feeling lucky?" She laughed. "Do you trust me not to give you a beehive?"

"You have to be an improvement over my hairstyling skills, Anna." Jordan laughed. After only five minutes, Anna was ready to show Jordan her new do. She gave her a hand mirror and walked her into the bathroom.

"It looks lovely," Jordan said. "Really, it does."

Anna didn't say so, but she knew Jordan would be the belle of the ball. She had pulled her hair up, and curls were cascading down her back.

"No, you look lovely, Madame. The hair is just an accessory."

"Thanks, Anna. If I haven't told you, I'm glad you came, really, I am."

"Me too. I needed to get away from New York until I could deal with this a little better. Thanks for having me."

The two walked together to Eric's room. As always, he was ready. Jordan could never figure out how men always seemed to be ready long before women. He looked smashing with his black tux and bow tie.

"Wow, I hope you're not taken, Mister," Jordan teased.

"Oh, but I am, Ma'am. Sorry to disappoint you, but I'm here with the most beautiful woman in all of Maine."

"Oh, please, you guys," Anna said. "I'm going to be sick here."

By the time they'd reached the bottom of the stairs, the doorbell was already ringing. Quincy came to answer the door in a black tux. Jordan had to turn around and do a double-take. He was neat, clean, and even had a fresh haircut.

"My, my, but who is this nice-looking gentleman?" Jordan teased.

"Don't get used to it," Quincy said. "I'm a working man. This not fitting for me, but I do it for party."

Jordan smiled at him knowing it was not in his character to be in a tuxedo or to answer the door for business people in the community. Quincy was almost to the door when he turned and said quietly, "So you do something for me, get new car worthy of you, Ms. Maxwell. I have gardening to oversee, no time to fix that piece of junk."

Jordan laughed out loud and winked at him. "We'll see, Mr. Velez; we'll just see about that."

Olivia came by just as Quincy was opening the door. She looked cute in her black dress with the crisp white apron draped over it. She was carrying a tray filled with glasses of white wine. Jordan could tell she was struggling to walk gracefully. She still looked like the young girl that lugged meatloaf specials across the diner.

"I'll take one of those," Jordan whispered. "I think I'll need it by the looks of things. You look very nice, Olivia."

"Oh, Ms. Maxwell, you are the most beautiful thing to ever hit Solomon Cove. I mean it."

"Thank you," Jordan whispered. "Now if you don't mind, I'd appreciate it if you would kind of float by periodically and whisper the names in my ear of who I'm speaking with." Olivia masked a giggle as she walked heavily across the floor.

Quincy lightly touched Jordan's elbow, getting her attention. "Madame Maxwell, this is Mayor Blake of Solomon Cove. Mayor, the honorable Jordan Maxwell." He disappeared as quickly as he'd said it, leaving the two face-to-face.

"Yes, Mayor, we met earlier when I was in town. So glad

you could join us." Jordan felt like someone new had taken over her personality and she was beginning to enjoy it. It wasn't bad being queen of the manor.

"Yes, Ms. Maxwell, nice to see you again. I wouldn't have missed this evening for anything. Please, call me Thomas."

"Call me Jordan."

The staff was all busying themselves in some capacity, either serving wines or hors d'oeuvres. Zeke was standing behind a makeshift bar mixing drinks while a young girl stood beside him with a basket of roses.

"Can we get you a drink, Mayor? I see Zeke has anything you might want."

"Yes, I think I'll take you up on that," Thomas answered, walking toward the bar with Jordan.

She noticed the young girl was not much older than seven or eight and guessed it must be Ruth, Zeke's oldest child. She was in a pretty pink dress with satin ribbons in her hair, and her eyes shone like a child's at a circus.

"And who do we have here?" Jordan asked, bending down to speak to her. "Could your name be Ruth?"

"Yes, Ma'am, it is," she said, showing a tender smile just like her father's. "How did you know?"

"Well, your daddy told me he had the most beautiful daughter in all of the world, and when I saw you, I knew he was right."

Ruth smiled even broader. "Daddy, did you really say that? I thought Mama was the most beautiful girl in the world."

Zeke looked down at her and rubbed his giant hand lightly across her face. "She's the most beautiful wife and you're the most beautiful daughter. I don't know how an ugly old man like me got to be so lucky."

They both laughed as Ruth said, "Oh, Ma'am, you get a rose. All the ladies get a rose."

Jordan bent down beside her again taking a rose out of her basket. "My name's Jordan, Jordan Maxwell. I'm so glad you could come to my party. Make sure that you and your dad take some roses home to your mother when you leave tonight, okay? We can't have the two prettiest girls in Solomon Cove going without flowers."

Ruth's eyes opened wide as she wrapped her thin arms around Jordan's neck.

"Thank you, Ms. Maxwell, thank you very much. Flowers always make my mommy smile."

Jordan stood up and saw the mayor was staring at her. "I haven't met many people in town yet, but I really like it so far. Did you know my great-uncle?"

Thomas looked at her blankly for a moment before answering, "Yes, I knew him. I can't say I knew him well, though. He was a very private person. I'm glad to hear you are adjusting well. Solomon Cove is a great place to live."

"It's certainly a far cry from New York. I guess this is really what I needed right now." Jordan saw Eric walking up and she took the opportunity to snag him.

"Eric, this is Mayor Thomas Blake." She smiled while squeezing his arm enough to let him know she was pissed about him leaving her.

Eric extended his hand. "Nice to meet you, Mayor Blake." He smiled innocently, trying to ignore the pain in his forearm. "Eric Riley."

"Pleasure." Thomas sipped his vodka and tonic.

Fortunately, the bell saved them all as it rang again.

"Excuse me," Jordan said, as she walked toward the kitchen. She passed Olivia on the way and snagged another Chablis. She took a couple of deep breaths as she drank from it.

"You okay?" Anna asked as she walked up beside her.

"I wasn't made for this type of socializing. I'm a nervous wreck."

Anna giggled, then led her by the arm to the bathroom. "You'll be fine. Just slug that wine, and we'll get you another one. After that, you'll just have to make it work."

Jordan downed the Chablis and rubbed her temples. "Just think, Anna, two months ago we only knew each other in passing."

"Let's not look back." She smiled painfully. "Today's a new day."

When Jordan came out of the bathroom, the house had begun to fill with faces she didn't know.

"Don't leave me, Anna," she threatened. "I need you now."

The two women walked from room to room meeting their guests. They were all kind and friendly, and Jordan found herself feeling guilty for dreading the evening. She spotted Eric deep in conversation with the sheriff and mayor and decided to leave well enough alone.

Jordan had made a conscious effort to stand back and observe the staff hard at work. The food was stupendous, and they all looked so professional. She smiled to herself as she watched Cyrus cross the floor with a tray of stuffed shrimp. His hair was slicked down, his clothes were ironed and clean, and his face mirrored the seriousness with which he was taking his job. *I am so lucky,* Jordan thought to herself.

The crowd worked its way throughout the foyer, parlor, and living room. Jordan was thankful they didn't go back toward the library. That was considered her space now and she wasn't anxious to share it. She wound her way through them all before the night was over and was pleasantly surprised at how easy they were to talk to. Jordan now had commitments to the garden club with Sara Crane and bridge with Diane Knox. As promised, Olivia bounced through every so often to whisper names and words of encouragement in her ear.

It was well after 2:00 a.m. when the final guests were leaving and Jordan sank down deep in one of the living room chairs, letting her shoes fall off and hit the floor.

"What a night," she said to her two costars. Anna and

Eric were not as wired as she was and both headed off to bed.

Jordan made one last walk-through before heading to bed herself. The kitchen was winding down with the last of the leftovers being placed in the fridge. Zeke was putting on his coat when Jordan asked about Ruth.

"She's sleeping over with Emma." He smiled, unable to hide his exhaustion. "She fell asleep long ago and Emma let her lay down in her room."

"Good idea." Jordan smiled. "I think I'll turn in myself. It was a lovely party. Thank all of you for your help."

"Good night, Ms. Maxwell," Jordan heard them say as she padded barefoot up to her room.

Chapter 20

Jordan woke as the sunlight flooded into Eric's bedroom. He'd been asleep when she made it up to bed, so she had just climbed in with him. She rolled over and laid her head on his chest, breathing in his masculine scent. Without opening his eyes, he leaned forward and kissed the top of her head.

"So, what do you think of Solomon Cove, so far?" she asked as she reached over and ran her fingers down his muscular biceps.

"Um, not a bad place at all," he said, pulling her on top of him and kissing her lips. Their bodies responded instantly to one another's as they always had. Jordan moaned quietly as Eric made love to her over and over again.

"I love you, Eric Riley, and God, how I've missed you."

He didn't answer. He just held her in his arms and stroked her long, thick hair. They lay together in the position for over an hour when Jordan sat straight up in bed.

"We're late for breakfast. Hurry! Get up and get dressed! Meet me downstairs in fifteen minutes."

"What is this?" Eric asked. "Weren't you enjoying lying in bed together; after all, it's been almost two months?"

"Oh, you don't want to upset Grace, and after you taste breakfast, you'll understand what I mean."

With that, Jordan was gone with the sheet off of his bed wrapped around her, and trailing along behind.

Eric didn't get out of bed right away. He was laughing at Jordan and thinking of how much he'd missed her. New York was not the same without her, and he found himself sinking deeper and deeper into work. Then his mind shifted to the murders. Eric was worried about her safety.

This was a new place to her, a new life, and she really didn't know anyone here. Jordan had always been too trusting, and it left him with an uneasy feeling. *Maybe they did need to go to the library and research Elizabeth Maxwell's murder*, he thought. *Maybe there was something to it.*

Anna was at the table reading the paper when they descended the stairs. "You two won't believe this, but you made the second page of the *Gazette*."

"What?" Jordan asked. "You've got to be kidding?"

"Look for yourself." She passed the paper across the table. "The critics love you."

Anna was right; although the article was small, it was

there, on the second page. Party at Maxwell Mansion a Success

The new owner of the Maxwell Estate, Ms. Jordan Maxwell, hosted an open house get-together among the big names of Solomon Cove last night. They were served expensive wines along with appetizers of stuffed shrimp and caviar, to name a few.

Ms. Maxwell, great-niece to the late James Maxwell, has lived on the estate for only six weeks now, but already has rave reviews about her new hometown. She appears to have no further plans for the place at this time, other than to call it home.

Solomon Cove welcomes you among us, Ms. Maxwell.

"Well, isn't that nice?" Jordan laid the paper back down on the table. "But I wish I'd known I was being critiqued."

"You never do," Eric answered slyly. "That's the way they do it."

"Yeah, I guess you're right."

Grace came through the doors with a tray covered with fresh fruit, bagels, cream cheese, and jellies.

"I didn't expect you to rise early this morning, Ms. Maxwell, so I prepared a cold breakfast. It was a nice party last night; I hope you approved."

"Oh, Grace, it was delightful. We'll have to talk about it all."

"Yes, we will." Grace smiled. "Everyone seemed to enjoy themselves."

With that, she was gone, leaving Jordan amazed at how rested she looked.

"I don't know how she does it," Jordan said quietly to Anna and Eric. "She must be in her seventies and works like a Trojan."

Eric wasn't listening to her as he chewed intently on his bagel. He was thinking of the visit to the library and his conversation with the sheriff. He wanted to kick himself for a minute, thinking he was falling into the web of work, but then decided differently. This wasn't work; he was worried about Jordan.

Fatigue was evident on Anna's face as she sat quietly at the table. "I think I'll go lay down for a while. I'll catch you two later on today." She strode slowly up the stairs leaning heavily on the railing.

"Last night may have been too much for her." Jordan felt guilty she hadn't thought of it before. "Anna still needs time to recover."

"You're right. We need to give her some time to herself. Do you want to go to the library today?"

"You know I do," she said with an enthusiasm he hadn't seen in her in a while.

They were finishing the morning paper when the doorbell rang. Jordan could hear Myra answering it and joyfully meeting the unseen guest. "Oh, I'm so happy to see you," Myra purred. "You look wonderful!"

Jordan tilted her head to the right trying to listen more

intently. "Who do you suppose that is?" she asked Eric.

Before he could answer, they heard Myra calling Grace and Emma, "Guess who's here? It's Cassie, and she looks like a million bucks, even drove herself." Jordan heard everyone scurrying out to the foyer and exchanging pleasantries. Genuine pleasantries. It was the first time they'd all seemed so close, and it warmed her.

"Who's Cassie?" Eric whispered.

"It's Zeke's wife; she must be here to get Ruth. I haven't met her yet."

"She must be something because I haven't seen anyone get that type of reception."

"She has sickle cell anemia and has been very sick. The staff adores her and has helped them out a great deal." Jordan stood up and made her way into the foyer.

"Ms. Maxwell," Myra said, waving her over, "this is Cassie Mullis. Cassie, this is Ms. Maxwell."

Jordan scanned her face and knew instantly why everyone loved her so. Even as thin and sickly as she was, Cassie was still very beautiful. Jordan wished she had known her when her health had been better. Cassie was tiny, not much bigger than Ruth, only a little taller. Her small face was kind like Zeke's, and her black eyes were enormous. Jordan caught herself as she stared into them and shook her head slightly as if to cut off the spell that drew her to them. Cassie extended a frail hand, her smile revealing a set of straight white teeth and a large dimple in each cheek.

"It's a pleasure to meet you, Ms. Maxwell. I've heard so many nice things about you."

"The pleasure is mine." Jordan smiled back. "I have heard so many kind things about you as well." Jordan thought of the contrast between this small woman and her large exuberant husband. Before the two could say anything else, Ruth ran into her mother's arms.

"Hey, Mommy. I got to come to a lovely party and Ms. Maxwell said we could take some roses home to you. They're pink and white."

"Well, how nice of Ms. Maxwell. Did you remember to thank her?"

"Oh, yes, Ma'am, I did," Ruth answered excitedly.

Jordan touched the top of Ruth's head lightly and smiled down at her. "She has been a delight. I don't know of anyone who could've passed out those flowers as well as she did."

Jordan turned to Grace, Myra, and Emma. "Eric and I are going into town today. We'll probably be gone for lunch. I'll see you all this afternoon. Nice to meet you again, Cassie."

"You too, Ms. Maxwell."

Jordan could sense fatigue in her light voice and it made her heart ache. She could see what they all loved about her. As she walked away, Jordan could hear them discussing the next week's plans for a carpool to get her to her dialysis treatments.

She was surprised to hear Cyrus's name mentioned for

one of the afternoons. Jordan smiled to herself, but it was also a smile filled with sadness. *Poor Ruth,* she thought.

Chapter 21

Quincy had pulled the car around before they walked out the front door. Jordan was relieved she didn't have to listen to him reprimand her about it. *He's probably as tired of scolding me as I am of being scolded,* she thought. Eric slid behind the wheel while Jordan sat in the passenger's side.

"Tell me about last night. I know you had to be talking to the sheriff about the murders."

"And what gives you that idea?" Eric asked innocently.

"I know you, Eric Riley, and I know you can't resist digging into a story, especially one that's unsolved."

He laughed heartily as he tapped his thumbs on the steering wheel in beat with the music on the radio.

"They weren't exactly happy to share anything with me, but it helped once I told them about my job with the *Times*. I'm not quite sure, but they may have been a little impressed."

Eric waited for a compliment from her, but Jordan didn't catch he was fishing for one, so he continued. "I gathered they're way out of their league with this thing. You know, small-town police departments, lack of training, staff, and funds, besides the fact they don't see this kind of thing very often. Sheriff Murphy is pretty sharp though, University of New England Grad, Criminal Justice major, lived here all his life, knows the people and the area."

"Oh God, Eric, please tell me you didn't drill the man for his whole life story."

"You know I'm much more discreet than that, Jordan; give me a break. They never saw it coming."

"Jeez, I'm glad I wasn't over there, but tell me everything that was said," Jordan pried.

"They didn't tell me much more than the papers did, but I feel they're tied together somehow, and they don't want it to get out. The mayor is in a knot over it and wants to get to the bottom of it immediately. He asked me several questions about my job and even asked for some input on these cases. He didn't want me to tell the sheriff though. That's interesting. I wonder if he suspects the sheriff or if he just doesn't want him to know he's questioning his expertise?"

"You know how big egos can get, Eric. The mayor has to think of all of that."

"I guess you're right," Eric conceded.

The library was located right outside of town. It was in a small clapboard building but was surprisingly well-stocked. The lady sitting prominently behind the checkout desk was the proverbial, stern-faced librarian that Jordan had run into at every library she'd ever visited. Her heavily sprayed hair was teased perfectly in place and half-moon spectacles clung desperately to the edge of her sharp nose.

Her gray wool cardigan sweater was buttoned to her throat, and her only jewelry was a pair of small pearl earrings. She looked up slowly and feigned a smile before directing Jordan to the computers in a hushed voice.

Jordan quickly pulled up the past fifteen years of the *Solomon Gazette* on the computer and searched for the death of Elizabeth Maxwell.

"This is interesting, Eric," Jordan whispered. "She was found at the base of the cliffs, just below the house. There were questions as to whether she'd been murdered or simply jumped. It was eventually ruled a homicide at James Maxwell's insistence that she would never have taken her own life. It says there's a possibility her young son, Chandler, witnessed her murder. He was treated at a local hospital for shock and released two days later. Police were unable to get any information from him because he was rendered unable to speak due to the trauma of her death." A shiver ran up Jordan's spine as she looked away from the screen. "I didn't know Elizabeth was found on the property. I had no idea. So, that makes three dead women in ten years."

"That may just be a matter of coincidence, Jordan. It's the two girls in a month I'm concerned about. Besides, it sounds as though Elizabeth Maxwell may have taken a plunge. You never know what goes on behind closed doors."

Jordan felt her heart skip a beat. "Oh God, Eric. What if Chandler pushed her? That could answer why Uncle James never had anything else to do with him. Keeping him locked away would cover up the fact his own son could've done it."

"Jordan, dammit, snap out of it. You're taking this and running with it. That never solves a case. As callous as this may sound, she could've jumped, she could've been pushed, but that was ten years ago. Your great-uncle is dead now, Chandler is locked away in some insane asylum, and your life has started anew. The bigger problem at hand now seems to be these latest two murders."

"I guess you're right."

They read all the articles about Jennifer Flemming and Dorian Keller, while Eric made scratchy notes on an old, tattered notepad.

"Who's this Regina Collins? Have you met her?" Eric asked.

"No, I don't believe so."

"She's the journalist who's written all these articles, even the ones about Elizabeth. She's not bad. Maybe I'll talk with her Monday before I leave."

The rest of the day and the following one went well. Eric and Jordan were able to do a little shopping and spend some quality time with each other. They even found a quaint restaurant up the coast that served their favorite Italian dishes.

"I wish you didn't have to leave, Eric. Why don't you stay

and do some of your columns from here? It is possible, you know."

"You know it isn't, Jordan, even as much as I'd love to do it. It is beautiful here and I can't say it's not tempting."

"Then just do it," she said, realizing she was pleading now more than simply suggesting.

"I'll be back soon. We're not that far away, really."

Jordan knew he was right, but as she leaned over to kiss his cheek, she couldn't help but worry that someone else would come along and sweep him off his feet.

As promised, Eric phoned the *Gazette* on Monday morning and asked to speak with Regina Collins.

"May I tell her who's calling?" a nasal voice asked him bluntly over the phone.

"Yes, this is Eric Riley with *The New York Times*."

"One moment."

In less than a minute, Regina Collins was on the other end of the line. "What can I do for you, Mr. Riley, is it?"

"Yes. Eric Riley. I was in town and read your articles about the local murders. I cover a great deal of those in New York and wondered if I might ask you a few questions."

"And why, may I ask, would a journalist from *The New York Times* be interested in a couple of murders in a town— in Maine, no less— that is too small to make it on a map?"

Eric smiled, nodding his head in approval. She was smart to question him. New York definitely had enough unsolved murders of its own.

"Well, my girlfriend recently moved here. I told her I would look into it a little. Besides, I'm smart enough to know if you want the whole brutal truth, you can only get that from a reporter."

Regina sounded pleased with his response and it apparently removed all questions from her mind. "Did you say you are in town or in New York?"

"I'm here, actually, for a couple more days. Do you think you could give me a few minutes?" Eric asked.

"If we don't look out for each other, no one else will," she said with the cynical voice of the media. "Can you meet me in my office at, say, about noon?"

"Sounds good. Where are you located?"

"Two doors down from Knoxes' grocery. Can't miss it. Oh, and don't be late, I have a full calendar." Regina hung up the phone without a good-bye. Eric liked her already.

As they rode into town, Eric agreed with Quincy that Jordan might want to shop for a new car.

"It isn't safe anywhere, Jordan, and you don't want to break down. Let's drive into Anderson while I'm here and look for you another one. It's not like you don't have the money," Eric insisted.

"Maybe you're right," Jordan sighed as she patted the dashboard. "Just so many memories in this old thing. College, moving to New York, and even to Solomon Cove."

"Memories are good, but keep them in perspective. You

can keep it for around the property if you want to. Just get something new for around town," Eric suggested.

They walked into the *Gazette* with ten minutes to spare, but Regina was ready for them.

"Ms. Maxwell," she said, extending her hand, "we haven't had the pleasure of meeting. I'm Regina Collins."

Jordan was surprised she recognized her. "Nice to meet you too."

Regina Collins looked just as she sounded. She was short and stout with an almost masculine demure. She had on a pair of khaki pants and an Izod shirt with a pair of white Keds tennis shoes. Her hair was pulled back into a ponytail and she didn't have on any makeup. For some reason, Jordan could tell this was the way Regina always looked. She was one of those "I'm me, accept me as I am" types. Both Jordan and Eric had grown to respect that quality in people.

Regina gestured for both of them to come back to her office, then slid another chair over in front of the desk.

"Oh, I won't be staying," Jordan interjected. "I have some shopping to do in town. I'll be back in about thirty minutes." She let herself out and stepped into the afternoon sun. Jordan was still enthralled with Solomon Cove. She decided today she would take some time to look into some of the shops she hadn't seen.

After getting a good look at the local shops, Jordan returned to the *Gazette* empty-handed, but she heard Regina yelling from her office.

"Ms. Maxwell, is that you? We're back in my office."

"Yes, it's me," she answered as she made her way back. It was obvious Eric and Regina had hit it off. They had photographs and papers spread all over the desk and floor, and were deep in conversation when she entered.

"Just doing a little research on the victims." Eric barely even looking up. Jordan was used to that. It was how he acted when he was deep into a story, and she was no longer offended.

"Find anything?" Jordan asked, not expecting to get many details from either of them.

"Not really. The only common denominators, if you can even call them that, are both victims resided within about forty-five minutes of each other. They were both young and unmarried; other than that, there isn't a bond." Eric had his glasses on and was rubbing his forehead with his right hand. "I don't know, Regina. What do you think?"

"I'm not sure about anything except for the fact they are intertwined in some way with one another. I intend to find out what it is. I'm conducting my own little investigation. It really pisses the sheriff off, but he knows that I know what I'm doing. He'd never admit it, but Sheriff Murphy appreciates the help. I'm starting with old friends, boyfriends, anyone in this general area. I can't find anything about Jennifer's life before she moved to Somergrove that would suggest any foul play. It must have been someone she knew from Maine. I'll take these pictures to both families, just as the sheriff's deputies are, but maybe between the two of us, we'll come up with different angles."

"Smart," Eric said. "Sounds like you're headed in the right direction." He began stacking photos and documents.

"Don't bother with that." Regina waved him off with her right hand. "You've given me a few leads to take. I'll pick everything up later. Call me before you leave if you think of anything else. I appreciate your help, Mr. Riley."

He scratched Jordan's number down on the same tattered pad and handed the piece of paper to her.

"I'll be leaving Wednesday morning. Take care. Good luck with your investigation."

"Thanks a lot. And, Ms. Maxwell, I hear good things about you from your staff. I hope you like it here in Solomon Cove," Regina said.

"Thank you, I do."

Eric didn't mention any of the meeting, and Jordan did not pry. He would tell her when he was ready. He was rolling it around in his mind and she knew that all too well.

"Regina told me how to get to Anderson." His voice was very noncommittal. "Would you like to go car shopping? It's always better to go with a man, you know."

"So they say," She smiled. "Why not? It'll be fun."

They grabbed a couple of burgers at a drive-thru in Anderson and ate in the car. By the time, they were finished checking out vehicles, they had narrowed their search down to a GMC Yukon.

"It's big enough for Quincy to take into town for things we need at the estate, yet small enough for me to still feel comfortable driving around by myself." Jordan sighed, obviously tired from the effort it had taken to make a final decision. She had decided in the end to trade in her Honda rather than drive it back to Solomon Cove. It had served its purpose well, but she felt a pang of sadness as she got into the driver's side of the Yukon.

"You'll be glad you made this purchase dear, really." Eric struggled to figure out how to use all of the latest gadgets.

"Right now, I'm just ready to see Quincy's face." Jordan laughed, relishing the thought of seeing the excitement on his face.

It had been worth the wait. Quincy was as surprised as she was she had made the purchase.

"I thought you may need to use it sometimes as well." She handed him the keys. "You may want to take her for a little spin before you put her in the garage."

"You sure?" Quincy asked, obviously pleased with the thought of it.

"Oh, yes, it's a family purchase. Just bring her back in one piece."

Quincy didn't say much, but she could tell from the look on his face he approved of her choice.

Anna was up and feeling much better when they walked into the house. She was perched on a stool in the kitchen discussing a recipe in a cookbook with Grace.

"Meringues are next to impossible." Anna sighed. "I quit trying."

"I'll show you how the next time I bake a pie. It just takes practice," Grace said kindly.

"Oh, hello there, you two," Anna said as she spun around to greet them. "How was your day?"

"You won't believe this," Eric mocked, "but Jordan bought a new car. Miracles never cease."

Anna squealed with delight and ran out to see it, barely catching a glimpse as Quincy drove it down the drive.

"Dinner will be ready in an hour." Grace flapped her hands and waved them out of the kitchen. "Find something else to do with yourselves."

"I'm going to grab a book and go up to the lighthouse," Jordan said. "What about you?"

"I need to make a few calls to the office. I'll see you at dinner," Eric answered.

Chapter 22

Billy Crane had taken Dorian Keller's death extremely hard. It still bothered him to close up the bank. Many days, Elias came by just to be company for him after everyone had left for the day.

"I keep remembering her that night, Elias. She was so sad. Maybe I should've done more. I should have *insisted* she ride with me."

"You can't do that to yourself, Billy," Elias said kindly. "You did all you could. You were a good employer to Dorian, and you and Sara were good friends to her. It'll take time before we're all able to accept this."

Billy reached out and laid his hand on his old friend's shoulder. "I know. It just doesn't help much now."

"I was going to see if you and Sara would like to go to dinner Friday night with Alex and me. I thought I'd ask you first."

"Been seeing a lot of her lately, haven't you? Nice-looking lady, she is," Billy said.

"Yeah, she is. We've been leaning on one another."

"You know, Elias, sometimes we forget you need someone to lean on too. Forgive all of us for that. Put Sara and me down for Friday. Maybe it'll do us some good."

Billy didn't look forward to the short ride home alone anymore. It gave him time to reflect which was always painful. It was like those hours in the middle of the night that he couldn't sleep away anymore.

Sara was waiting for him on the living room couch with a larger glass of wine than usual. It was times like this that he wished they'd already started a family.

"Hey, honey, how was your day?" Sara always greeted him with that question, and what he liked about it was she waited patiently for a reply.

"Okay, and yours?" he asked.

"Not anything new. Ms. Keller called today to check on us. She sounded much better than the last time we spoke."

"Good. Good." Billy tried not to think about her now. "Elias wants us to go out to dinner with him and Alex on Friday. Is that all right with you?"

"Sure." Sara sounded more enthused than he'd expected. "It's been so long since we've done something like that. Maybe I'll give Alexandria a call tomorrow."

"That'd be nice." The two sat on the couch for over an hour sipping on their drinks. Sara refused to let them drift apart and reiterated it to herself daily. She was well aware that tragedies like this often took a toll on even good, solid marriages. "I saw Cassie Mullis today at Knox's. Poor thing, she's so small now."

"I know it," Billy responded with genuine sadness. "His mortgage check bounced again. The hospital is garnishing his wages for her medical bills."

"I wonder if Jordan Maxwell knows that."

"I don't know, Sara, but we're not getting involved. It's none of our business."

"Well, maybe it is, maybe it's not," she said stubbornly.

****

Friday night rolled around quicker than expected for the four of them. Alex and Sara had made reservations at Garbo's in Somergrove for seven, forcing Elias and Billy to scramble to get things done by the end of the day.

Alex and Elias were a few minutes early to pick up the Cranes, so they sat down to enjoy a drink. It was a recognized unspoken truce they'd not talk about the deaths in town. They needed and deserved a night away.

The ride to the restaurant was a pleasant one, and the meal even better.

"I have to say tonight was a great idea, Elias," Billy said wholeheartedly.

"Yes, it was," Sara answered as though he were talking to her. "I've needed to sit among friends."

"I think we've needed that." Elias sounded sincere and a little too tired. "How are Ralph and Diane holding up these days? I haven't been by to see them."

"Pretty good," Billy said. "It takes time for things to seem real sometimes."

Chapter 23

Eric had been gone a week and Jordan missed him with the same fervor she had when he'd first walked out the door. He called at least once a day which helped. At least Anna was with her, and getting stronger every day, making Jordan wonder when she'd leave her too.He brushed through her long hair and ran the fuchsia lipstick across her pursed lips. She was running late for her lunch with Sara Crane. Jordan liked

Sara, she was comfortable with her, and for that, she was grateful. Sara had such an easy, uplifting spirit that anyone would be happy to spend time with her.

Jordan wasn't accustomed to having lunch parties with girlfriends, so she was wondering how to conduct herself, deciding, in the end, she'd simply be herself. She was beginning to realize anything else was too exhausting.

Jordan was running down the stairs at top speed when Myra stopped her.

"Here are some roses from the garden. I know Sara would appreciate them."

"How thoughtful of you, Myra." Jordan smiled as she rushed past her, barely taking the time to notice the beautiful vase she'd placed them in. "I'm running late. Please tell Grace I'll be back in a couple of hours." With that, she was out of the door and jumping into the car as Quincy patiently held the door open. "Thanks," she mouthed breathlessly as she pulled away.

Jordan knew she was driving too fast, inwardly scolding herself for not taking the time to bask in the beauty of the scenery around her. Glancing at the clock on the dash, she smiled in relief as she was only ten minutes late.

Maybe this will be considered "fashionably late," she thought, laughing to herself. Who am I kidding about being "fashionably late"? The only luncheons I ever went to were at Lou's Pizza Parlor in college. Somehow, I don't think Sara Crane will have draft beer.

Her thoughts changed quickly when she pulled into the driveway. The house wasn't anywhere near as grand as the estate, but it was beautiful just the same. It was a home, and everything about it reflected that. The gardens were blooming with a variety of flowers, obviously weeded and tended with love.

The large front porch had hanging baskets filled with overflowing ferns and huge pots of geraniums, while begonias made their way up the stairs. There were four large rockers with bright summer cushions and a swing that tempted her to sit in it before she even rang the bell. Jordan was still looking at it when Sara came out of the house.

"Hello, there," Sara said. "How are you today?"

"Oh hi, just fine," Jordan stammered, beginning to feel a little uncomfortable and much less confident than she had in the car. "I was just admiring your swing. It looks so inviting."

"I've spent many hours in that swing." She smiled at Jordan. "Maybe you'll have time for a glass of lemonade in it after lunch."

"I'd love that."

"Please, come in," Sara continued. "I'll show you around."

Jordan was met at the door by the smell of a freshly baked pound cake. The inside of the house was as inviting as the outside, and she felt instantly at home. Everything about the place was so different from the estate and she couldn't help feeling envious. Sara talked nonstop as she led Jordan through the house, ending up in a bright sunroom with blooming plants everywhere.

"This is so lovely, Sara," Jordan said sincerely. "I have to say it's quite different from where I live. It's much homier."

Jordan was walking from picture frame to picture frame enjoying all of the candid shots placed in each of them. Each frame was different and had to do with the theme of the picture. A brown wooden frame with a fishing basket and pole contained a picture of Billy holding an extremely small bass.

"I couldn't resist framing that one." Sara laughed. "My Billy's not a fisherman." Jordan laughed and placed the frame carefully back on the table.

"I don't even know the people in the frames at the estate. I suppose I should research that."

"You'll have to make it your home, Jordan," Sara said kindly. "Everyone needs to make their house reflect themselves. I'm sure Mr. Maxwell would've wanted you to do that."

Jordan stood quiet for a minute and then sat in one of the wicker chairs next to Sara. "Maybe you're right. I've never really thought of it like that. I didn't know my great-uncle well and inheriting the estate doesn't seem quite real to me yet. Maybe with time, it'll seem more like home."

Sara smiled warmly at her, patting her hand as it rested on the arm of the chair. "I'm glad you were able to come today. I think we'll be great friends."

Jordan smiled back at her. "Yes, I think we will, too."

They ate their lunch at the small glass table in the sunroom. Jordan was grateful they weren't having a formal meal at the dining room table. Sara had prepared chicken salad with fresh grapes and walnuts. There was a congealed salad and a warm croissant.

"Hope you have room for some pound cake," she said. "It is fresh out of the oven. That's when it's best."

"I've never turned down a piece of pound cake. It smells wonderful."

The cake was followed by coffee, then the two ladies walked to sit in the swing. The weather was perfect, but the hint of fall was right around the corner. Sara brought out a thin throw blanket for both of them which they wrapped around their shoulders as they talked.

"Have you lived here all your life, Sara?"

"Yes, I have. Billy and I were high school sweethearts. Almost everyone in town has been here most of their lives."

"That's a little intimidating for me." Jordan sighed. "I moved to New York after college, and everyone's a stranger there. I desperately want to fit in here," Jordan said, instantly embarrassed she'd shared it.

"Oh, you will, Jordan. You already do. Solomon Cove is filled with kind people, good people. Before you know it, you'll be family."

The swing creaked lightly as it moved back and forth, almost hypnotizing them as they swung in silence.

"Did you know my great-uncle?" Jordan asked.

"I think everyone knew of him, but few people really knew him well. He was a private person, but Billy always spoke highly of him."

"I can't seem to find anyone who was particularly close to him. I guess the only person who ever seemed to have a lengthy conversation with him was Zeke Mullis."

"Yes. Word has it that Mr. Maxwell was very kind to him and his family. Unfortunately, that's about the only good thing people say about him. Zeke and Cassie were very upset when he passed away."

"I'm sorry to hear that," Jordan said, deciding to change the subject.

"Speaking of Zeke and Cassie," Sara interjected before Jordan was able to say anything else, "they're fine folks. It's a shame things are going so bad for them right now." Sara was aware of what she doing and hoped Jordan would take the bait. Billy would have to be mad at her.

"Yes, I hear Cassie is very ill."

"She has been for so many years. Unfortunately, they also have to struggle with all of those astronomical medical bills too." She paused, looking down at the porch. She could sense Jordan was a caring woman and could hear the sadness in her voice as she spoke.

"They do have insurance, don't they? I was sure Myra told me we offer it to all employees."

"Oh, yes, they do, but I think they still have to fork over a great amount for things that aren't covered. You know how insurance companies are now." Sara was trying to sound nonchalant, but she'd gotten in too deep and Jordan's concern was growing. "What the hell?" Sara said with a small forced laugh. "Billy will kill me, but I'm so concerned about them and those children, that I thought I'd talk to you about it. Billy said their last mortgage check bounced. It seems to be a pattern lately. I just wish there was more we could do."

Jordan sat silent for several moments and the creak of the

swing was almost deafening for Sara.

Maybe I read her wrong, Sara thought. *This really isn't any of my business.* Before she could doubt her motives any further, Jordan spoke.

"You know Sara, I think my great-uncle had planned for this, and just maybe, he wanted me to discover it on my own."

Sara looked up at her, wearing a look of confusion. "I don't understand what you're saying, Jordan."

"I'm still trying to think it all through. Maybe you can help me."

"Count me in, honey, please. Tell me more."

Jordan giggled and reached for Sara's hand. "Yes, we were meant to be friends, Ms. Crane." She paused for another minute, simply to tease Sara. "Okay," Jordan continued, "there are three accounts for the house. One is mine alone and one is for the expenses of the estate. The third one has always puzzled me because it's set aside for repairs, upkeep, and additions to the estate. It only has $250,000 in it, which wouldn't go very far with that enormous place. Besides, there's a ten million-dollar trust for upkeep. We could never surpass that just spending the interest annually."

"I'm not quite following." Sara motioned with her hands for Jordan to spit it out.

"I think it may be time to add a new cottage to the grounds."

"Oh, Jordan!" Sara screamed. "What a wonderful idea. I think I'm going to cry."

"Oh no, you're not," Jordan said quickly. "We have too much to do and I'm going to need your help. I don't know why I didn't think of it before. It makes perfect sense. The other staff will be there to help with the kids and Cassie will be there when they need to take her to doctor's appointments. Sara Crane, you're a genius."

They both laughed, squeezed each other's hands, and swung just a little higher.

Chapter 24

"Let's look through them one more time," Sam said to Mr. and Mrs. Flemming, with more patience than he was feeling. He fanned the pictures out on the table again and gestured for them to look.

"I'm telling you, Sam," Mr. Flemming said bluntly, "we don't see anyone we know. We didn't the first time and we won't this time."

"I'm sorry, Sir." Sam rubbed a handkerchief across his brow. "We just want to find out what happened to your daughter."

Mrs. Flemming looked up at him through the tears forming in her eyes. "I'm sorry, dear, really I am. We feel so helpless, but it isn't your fault."

"I understand." Sam tried not to let his voice mirror the frustration he was feeling. He stacked the photos up, wrapping a thin rubber band around them before putting them in his backpack. He stood slowly extending his hand to Mr. Flemming. "We'll be in touch, Sir."

Once inside his car, Sam was happy to get Rachel's voice

on the phone when he called the station. "What a good sound to hear. The voice of competence again."

Rachel laughed wholeheartedly, but Sam was serious.

"I'm on my way back from Massachusetts. Not any good news to share, unfortunately. Anything happening there?"

"Not a thing. Apparently, the pictures were a bust here too. It's after four now, so I guess we won't see you until in the morning."

"Probably not," he said. "Is the sheriff in?"

"No, he's over at the bank. I'll tell him you called."

"Ten-four, Rach, see you first thing in the morning."

* * * *

The morning rolled around quicker than Sam had imagined, but he was up and dressed earlier than usual. Although he didn't have anything to contribute to the investigation, he wanted to catch up on the latest theories. He poured a cup of coffee, grabbed a stale doughnut off the kitchen counter, and walked out to the car. He had on his short-sleeved summer uniform and made a mental note to pull out his winter ones when he got home that night.

Sam grinned as he pulled up to the station and saw Rachel's car. He couldn't help but worry she might not have as much time for them once the baby came. He was almost to the door when he noticed it was ajar, and just inside was one of Rachel's Dr. Scholl's sandals. Sam stood frozen for a minute, lost in the fear that something had happened to her, then he quickly pushed the door open and ran in. He heard the back door slam shut just as he saw her on the floor. Rachel was unconscious and blood was running across the floor in a small stream from the back of her head. She was face down and her purse lay beside her with its contents spilling out.

"God no, God no!" he heard himself screaming. "Not her, not Rachel!"

He knew he should've run to see who'd left out the back door, but he couldn't bring himself to leave her. Not like this. Sam cradled her head and felt for a pulse. It was weak, but it was there.

"Don't you quit fighting, damn it! You hear me, little girl?" Sam screamed.

He was yelling louder than he realized when Trent came through the door. He hadn't seen Rachel yet and he was wondering what all of the ruckus was about.

"What is it, Sam?" Trent asked.

"Thank God, Trent! Help, it's Rach! I think I came in on the killer. I heard the back-door slam. Call for an ambulance, quick!"

Trent stood over them with his feet glued to the floor, unable to move one way or the other.

"Jesus," he said, tears already flowing down his face.

"Get the phone, Trent! She's still alive; she needs help!"

Trent ran for the phone and Sam could hear him pleading for someone to come. Then he went on the radio, screaming uncontrollably for the sheriff to get to the office.

It took over fifteen minutes for the ambulance to arrive. Rachel was still unconscious, looking like a princess who was sound asleep. Sheriff Murphy was there, holding her in his arms like she was an infant. He was whispering to her through his tears, begging her to come back to him, to all of them.

The paramedics tenderly pried his fingers from her and laid her head back on the floor. There were three of them, all working to save her life, to prolong it if they could, but their solemn faces reflected anything but hope. They lifted her onto the gurney in unison, and then they were gone. Gone, like that, like the whole thing had never happened.

By now, Evan had arrived, and all four men were inconsolable. The mayor walked in looking as though he had just gotten out of bed and was totally speechless. The look in his eyes showed he was searching for just the right thing to say, but it wouldn't come. Blake stood there among them and remained silent.

"That damn son of a bitch!" Elias screamed. "Wait until I get my hands on him, coward, son of a bitch!" He was shaking all over, struggling to get a breath. "I told her not to get here this early anymore. Damn workaholic. What was she thinking? Why weren't you a minute earlier, Sam, or you Trent, Evan? Where the hell were you guys?"

The deputies looked down at the floor, unable to answer. They wished they'd been there for her, and Elias knew it, but it felt better to blame someone.

The mayor reached over and took Elias in his arms and held him. Elias cried like a small child. After a few minutes, he was able to calm down and pulled himself away. He untucked his shirttail and wiped it across his face.

"I'm-I'm-sorry," Elias said.

"Don't, Sheriff," Sam said, touching him on the shoulder. "It's not necessary. We all love her and would go, and will go, to the ends of the earth to find who did this to her." Sam was calming down and realized, that in all the confusion, no one had called Hank. "I'm going to get Hank and I'll meet you all at the hospital. Rachel needs her husband."

"Sheriff," the mayor said, "you need to get on the phone with the ID crew from Anderson. They'll be the closest one to us. Tell them to tear this place apart and get every print there is."

"Don't worry about that, Mayor. I'll be here to see that they do."

* * * *

It was after three in the afternoon when Sheriff Murphy arrived at the hospital. He wasn't taking any chances that the evidence gathered could later be labeled as inadmissible or contaminated. He'd witnessed every move the investigators made. The waiting room was filled with family and friends when he got there. Sam walked over and led him down the hall.

"She's in surgery now. They're removing the shattered fragments from her skull. Their biggest concern is that her brain could start to swell, and they won't be able to stop it."

Elias shook his head in disbelief. "How's Hank?"

"Not too good. They finally gave him a Valium. He's resting in a private waiting room. Rachel's mother is in there with him."

"Do they think she'll make it, Sam?" Elias asked uneasily.

"They hope so. She had one strong blow to the head, It shattered her skull, but they don't believe there's any brain damage. The next twenty-four hours will be critical."

"One of us needs to sit outside of her room when she comes out of surgery. I'll take tonight's shift."

"No, Sheriff, Evan has already planned on it. He went home to get some rest. Maybe you need some too."

"I'll wait until she comes out of surgery. My place is here."

Chapter 25

Word spread quickly throughout Solomon Cove, and the Maxwell Estate was one of the first to hear about it. Jordan came in from the lighthouse to find Myra sobbing in Grace's arms.

"What is it? Are you okay?" Jordan stammered, afraid of what she was about to hear.

Grace shook her head and continued to pat Myra as she rocked back and forth. "There's been another attack. This time it was Rachel Kelley, the young girl at the police department."

"Oh, my goodness." Jordan ran her hand up and down Myra's back in an attempt to soothe her. "You said, 'attack.' Is she still alive?"

"Yes, she's in surgery now. Expecting her first child too, just found out about it," Myra sobbed.

Jordan wasn't sure how to respond. Quincy and Cyrus came through the door slowly, standing at a distance from the two women. It was as close as they got to sharing each other's grief. Their faces bore grave expressions while they both wrung their hands as if they weren't sure what they should be doing with them.

"Let's all sit down in the living room," Jordan said, lightly pushing Grace and Myra in that direction. "I'll be right there." She went down to the wine cellar and grabbed two bottles of Sherry. She put five small shot glasses on a tray and went to the living room. Grace started to object to the drink, but Jordan handed it to her anyway. She took it and they drank in total silence.

Myra was the first to speak. "I don't understand what's happening here. A month and a half ago, we were living in utopia. Now-now," she rambled, "I just don't know."

Cyrus spoke next and his stern words came as a surprise. "Solomon Cove is still our home and it's still a good place to live. We have to hold strong to each other." His words seemed to comfort them more than Jordan could have.

They left one by one as they finished their Sherry, leaving Jordan all alone. She poured herself another drink and sat back on the couch, thinking of all the emotions she'd experienced here. The murders and now the attack, yet she loved this place. Jordan found it odd that it seemed more like a home than she had ever known. She thought of Eric and decided to call him.

Anna had lain down for a nap and she didn't want to startle her with the latest tragedy. Four rings, five, then the answering machine. She almost hung up, then thought better of it.

"It's me," she said, trying not to sound alarmed. "Give me a call when you get in; it doesn't matter how late." She laid the receiver down and finished off her drink.

Chapter 26

The hum of the buffer could barely be heard as it waxed the hospital floors. The television sets were on in the waiting rooms, but they played to an audience of blank faces. Elias was holding a constant vigil along with a handful of Rachel's family and closest friends. They sat in silence among each other with bloodshot eyes and worried looks, holding half cups of cold, stale coffee. Elias stared at the clock heaving small, inaudible sighs of relief with each minute that passed, signaling Rachel was still alive.

The 7 a.m. to 3 p.m. shift started to arrive, a constant flow of nurses and technicians, all in clean uniforms, ready to start their day. Elias looked down at himself and did a quick comparison of his clothes with theirs. His were well over twenty-four hours old now. The wrinkles and rings of sweat were highly visible, and for a minute, he thought about heading home for a shower, then thought better of it.

Hank had finally joined the rest of them in the large waiting room, his emotions a swirl of anger, confusion, and pain. He was a good husband to Rachel. Elias wanted to reach out to him, but selfishly, he was too busy with his own roller coaster of emotions to comfort anyone else.

It was after 9:00 a.m. when a tall man with a fluorescent white lab coat and thick glasses approached the group.

"Good morning," he began in a voice so deep they had to strain to understand him. "I'm Doctor Hamlin. We've made it through the first twenty-four hours; that's a positive sign. However, Rachel is not out of the woods. I don't want to give you any false hope, but she's a fighter, that young lady. She's still in a coma, so we'll have to stand by and wait."

Everyone gasped in large breaths as he spoke, but no one seemed to expel them. They sat there speechless, holding their breaths, scared to ask any questions for fear they'd get an answer they weren't prepared for.

Hank spoke first, "Do you know if there's any brain damage?"

"We are seeing brain activity on the EEG, but we won't know if there will be permanent neurological problems until she wakes up and communicates with us."

The doctor stated it as though he were answering a question about how to tend a garden, void of emotion, and straight to the point. Hank's eyes never left his as he asked, "The baby, is the baby still alive?" His voice quivered on the last two words, and he cast his eyes down as quickly as he'd asked it, afraid to hear the answer.

"The baby appears to be fine at this time, but it's early yet."

No one said anything, afraid the good news would be followed by something bad. Doctor Hamlin stood there for another moment, then turned to walk away, stopping before he got very far. "I'm sorry. Are there any other questions?"

Rachel's mother asked, "Can we see her?"

"Yes, Ma'am, but just immediate family for now. She's in ICU. She will wake when she's ready, so let her get her sleep while she can."

"Thank you, Doctor, we appreciate what you've done for her," Hank responded. Doctor Hamlin nodded and walked back down the hall.

Hank reached for his mother-in-law's hand as she stood.

"We're going to see her now. We appreciate all of your concern, but you should all go home and get some sleep. It doesn't seem things will change quickly. We'll be in touch." Hank walked slowly toward the Intensive Care Unit, each step labored.

Chapter 27

Jordan ate her breakfast while she read the latest article about Rachel. The attack had put fear in the townspeople, and the mood at the estate had grown quiet and sorrowful. She pushed her plate to the center of the table and called for Grace, who was immediately standing by her side.

"Grace, could you get Myra, Cyrus, and Quincy?" Jordan asked, feeling as though she was going to share something happy for the first time in days. "I'd like to meet with the four of you."

Grace would've been concerned, but she could tell Jordan wasn't angered or troubled.

"Yes, Ms. Maxwell, they'll be here right away. Can I get you some more coffee?"

"Yes, please, and enough for everyone else."

Grace was gone leaving Jordan alone with her thoughts. She felt it would be fitting to ask their opinions on the new cottage as they were the ones who played the largest part in maintaining the place. Besides, she wanted them to feel their input was respected.

They were there within five minutes looking as though they were reporting for duty.

"Hello," Jordan said, smiling. "Have a seat."

They sat down as Grace walked around pouring each of them a cup of coffee.

"I called you all here to share an idea with you. I don't feel I should make such a big decision on my own, so I wanted your input. Uncle James left me a policy worth $250,000, specifically to be used for maintenance or additions to the estate. As you know, that wouldn't go very far, and with the trust fund for the property, I couldn't understand why the policy even existed. I think I know where that money needs to go now."

Jordan could tell they were all about to burst with curiosity as they leaned forward in their chairs, their eyes steady on hers. She found herself mischievously wanting to drag it out for a few more minutes, but decided it would be cruel.

Jordan continued, "I haven't any family left, as you probably know. Both of my parents are dead. There were just the three of us. Oh, great-uncle James, of course, but I never knew him well. I see something here that I'm not sure that the rest of you may see. I see a family. I see it every time something happens in the community, I see it every time you pull together for a project, and I see it with Zeke and Cassie."

She studied their faces, but their expressions gave nothing

away. They were staring at her, obviously waiting for her to get to the bottom line.

"Well, I started thinking about that, and I started thinking of how I wanted to be a part of this family too. I'd like to build another cottage on the estate. A cottage for the Mullises."

For a minute, Jordan thought they hadn't heard her, then saw a small tear running down Myra's face, and she waited for a response. She was surprised when Cyrus spoke first.

"Ms. Maxwell, I think that's about the finest idea I've ever heard. What do you think, Quincy?"

He was smiling broadly as he shook his head in agreement. "Good idea," he said, "good idea."

"So, does that mean everyone is in agreement?" Jordan asked. She noticed Grace was crying now too as they all exclaimed their approval of the project.

"Oh, Ms. Maxwell," Myra said, "I'm just speechless. They'll be thrilled beyond belief. When can we tell them? When can we start on it? Who will build it?" Everyone laughed, and the mood changed to one of excitement rather than the sentimental tone it'd carried before.

"I say we get plans for the house from Wilkerson Builders," Quincy said. "Mr. Maxwell would've used them. They are honest people. We can trust them."

"Shouldn't we let Zeke and Cassie choose that?" Myra piped up over her tears.

"Maybe we should get several different plans that would

fit in the price range," Jordan suggested, "and then let them choose."

"That's a great idea," Grace said, sounding much younger than Jordan had ever heard her. "Maybe we should have a dinner for everyone and hit them with the surprise."

"What about a cookout?" Cyrus suggested. "We could do it outside and the kids could play on the grounds. It wouldn't be so formal."

"I think that's a perfect idea," Jordan said. "How soon can you get some plans to choose from, Quincy?"

"Right away, Ma'am. They can be ready by the weekend."

"The weekend it is. Let's say, Saturday afternoon. We'll cook barbecue and enjoy the outdoors. Then we'll surprise them with it. *Mum* is the word." Jordan placed her index finger over her lips. "Don't even tell Cassie. This is our little secret. We'll just say we're having a family picnic before the weather turns too cold."

Grace clapped her wrinkled hands together with the excitement of a child. "Meeting adjourned, folks, see you all Saturday afternoon. Myra, you tell Cassie and Zeke to be here about two."

The group dispersed, still smiling, as Jordan ran back over the meeting in her mind. She was the happiest she'd been since moving here. She tried Eric at the office, only to find out he was at a business luncheon. Jordan laid the receiver down, looked at it, and picked it up again. Today would be the day.

"Information, can I help you?"

"Yes," Jordan answered nervously. "Can I have the number to Milledgeville Hospital, please?"

"One moment," the voice on the other end said flatly. "May I connect you to 207-555-5727?"

Jordan sat silent for a moment, afraid now that she was actually placing the call.

"Ma'am? Ma'am? Are you still there?"

"Yes, I am," Jordan responded nervously. "Please connect me."

The phone rang twice before someone answered. "Milledgeville Hospital, where should I direct your call?"

"I was calling to inquire about a patient," Jordan stammered.

"One moment," the operator said as Jordan heard the phone click over to another extension. "Patient information."

"Yes, hello. I'm calling about a patient I would like to visit. He's a relative."

"Name please, Ma'am."

"Chandler, Chandler Maxwell." There. She'd said it, it was out, and there was no turning back.

"His social worker is Jarvis Ingram, Ma'am. Transferring to his line now."

There went the click again followed by a soothing, deep voice. "Case Management, Jarvis Ingram speaking."

Jordan's mouth opened, but nothing came out. She

would've given anything for a glass of water to soothe her dry, parched throat.

"Hi," she said. "I, I-I-was-calling about one of your patients, Chandler Maxwell."

"Yes," he answered in the same soothing tone. "I'm his social worker. How can I help you?"

"Well," she said, not sure where to begin with the whole sordid tale. "I'm his cousin, well, distant cousin, and I was wondering if I might visit him sometime."

"Has he ever met you, Ms. …?"

"Maxwell, Jordan Maxwell, and no, we've never met."

"I see," he said calmly. "Chandler hasn't spoken in ten years except for a few vital words such as 'water' or 'blankets.' His visitors have been limited, and not to be unkind or callous, but I'm not sure he benefits from them. I just want to be up front with you."

"Oh," Jordan sputtered, trying desperately to find the words she wanted to say.

"Not to discourage you from coming, however," he continued. "Visitors are always welcome. I could talk to him before you come if you'd like?"

"Um, no, don't do that. He wouldn't know me anyway. I would like to come, however. Is tomorrow too soon?"

"That'd be fine. How is eleven? He generally has sessions with the staff after lunch."

"Eleven a.m. it is," she said, unsure if she was relieved or feeling more apprehensive. "Will I meet you?"

"I'll meet with you before your visit. See you tomorrow."

Jordan held the receiver in her hand until she heard the loud repetitive beeps alerting her the phone was disconnected. She laid it carefully on its cradle, but before she could get out of her chair, it rang again. "Hello?"

"Hey, sweetheart, it's me. Sorry I missed your call. I had to make an appearance at a luncheon."

"Hi, Eric. Did you get the fax on the Kelley girl?"

"Yes, I did. Put in a call to Regina as well. She hasn't gotten back with me; I have a feeling she's pretty busy."

"I have so much to talk to you about," Jordan said, before going into the events of the day.

Chapter 28

"Sheriff Murphy," the temp beckoned, "Doctor Chambers is here to see you."

"Send him back," Elias yelled back, too tired to reprimand her again for not using the intercom. He lifted his head off the desk and ran his hands through his hair, trying unsuccessfully to smooth it down.

"You look like hell," Doc Chambers said. "When was the last time you put a razor to that face of yours?"

"Good to see you too, Doc. How's Alex?"

"She's fine, I guess. It's you we're concerned about."

"I'm all right, just tired and worried as hell. Rachel still hasn't come out of the coma."

"I know, I heard. She will, Elias. She's a strong young lady. Any leads on all of this?"

"Not a damn thing. We've got a lot of people on it though, and I feel confident that everything within our power is being done. We're the base for the operation, and here I am without Rachel. The mayor sent *her* over," he said with disdain, pointing toward the front office. "That hasn't been any help at all."

"As a matter-of-fact, that's what I came over for. Thomas was telling me what a time you're having, and I've come to offer my assistance."

"Shit, don't tell me you want to answer my phones. Kind of out of your field, isn't it?"

Doc rolled his eyes, faking a hearty laugh. "Not quite what I had in mind, smart-ass. I thought I'd consider a temporary, and I stress the word *temporary*, switch between Alex and your 'Secretary of the Year' out there. I figure it's only fair, seeing as how my business is slow. Well, almost dead, I guess," he said, unable to stifle a laugh at his own crude joke. "You, on the other hand, are busy as hell. Figured I'd be the bigger man and let you draw the long straw on this one."

"Can't say that I'm not shocked at your generosity, but I'll accept it just the same," Elias said, feeling a little hope for the first time in days. "Am I going to owe you my firstborn or anything?"

He was joking, and Doc knew it. Elias was grateful, and Doc was glad he could ease his burden, if only in a small way.

"No pressure," Elias continued, "but when does this *godsend* happen?"

"First thing in the morning, I guess. Tell your 'ex' that she should report at 8:30 a.m., no later."

"Gladly, Doc."

Elias picked up the phone and dialed Alex at the morgue. She had been so good to him through all of this.

"Solomon Cove Medical Examiner's Office, how can I help you?"

"You could have dinner with me tonight."

"I never turn down a meal with a handsome man, especially if he's the sheriff of the town I'm living in."

"Cute. Did Doc Chambers tell you about his generous idea?"

"Yes, he did. Do you think it's a good idea for us to work together?"

"I most certainly do. I can't think of any face I'd rather see than yours in the morning."

"We'll play it by ear, okay? Any news on Rachel today?"

"She's about the same. Would you mind if we went by the hospital after dinner tonight?"

"Not at all. What time can I expect you?"

"Seven if that's all right," he said.

He walked over and looked at himself in the mirror. Doc was right; he looked rough.

Elias spent the rest of the afternoon coordinating patrol units. Anderson and Somergrove had both sent an ample number of officers, and he was taking advantage of their generosity. He'd doubled the patrol the town was accustomed to and placed one deputy at Rachel's door around the clock. He didn't know if Rachel had seen or heard her attacker, but he wasn't taking any chances with him coming back to finish the job.

Elias grudgingly left the office at 6:00 p.m., just in time to shower, shave, and pick up Alex. He spent twenty minutes in the shower, trying to wake himself from his weariness. He downed a beer before driving over, hoping to calm himself a little. Alex was ready and beautiful as always. He appreciated how he never had to wait on her.

She had on tight black leggings making her legs look even longer. He was instantly excited and had to look away for fear he'd get an erection. She wrapped her arms around his neck and kissed him lightly on the lips. She smelled of expensive perfume.

"I've missed you so much," she said, her breath warm and sweet on his face.

"I've missed you." Elias was unable to control the erection that was filling his pants. He started to pull away and then decided to pull her closer. They kissed until they were breathless, and he pulled her back to her bedroom. Alex walked willingly, then unbuttoned his shirt, slowly, sensually, one by one. He felt he would explode as she slipped out of her sweater.

Her bra was thin and he could see her nipples through it. This time he didn't wait; he cupped her firm breast in his hand and kissed her neck. She slid out of her leggings as he took off his pants and they held each other, breathless until finally, she led him to the bed.

"I've never wanted anyone as much as I want you, Alex; I

swear I haven't."

She didn't answer; she pulled him down on top of her and they made love until they both lay exhausted on the bed.

"That was nice, Elias," Alex whispered. "Where have you been all my life?"

"I'm here now, baby," he whispered back, and they fell asleep in each other's arms.

Chapter 29

Jordan was up at 5:00 a.m., pacing the halls of the estate. If eleven o'clock didn't come soon, she was afraid she'd change her mind.

What should I wear? What should I say to him? Will he want to see me? The questions rolled on and on causing perspiration to bead on her forehead. She finally decided to go ahead and take her shower and dress for the day, realizing sleep was out of the question.

She picked at the large plate of food Grace had placed in front her, unable to force herself to eat it.

"What are you doing up and dressed so early, Ms. Maxwell? Big plans today?"

Jordan wasn't ready to share her decision to visit Chandler with anyone yet, so she danced around the issue. "I guess I'll do some sightseeing, may even go into Somergrove. I heard they have a huge mall."

"And you aren't taking Miss Anna with you? Shame on you," Grace said.

Jordan couldn't tell if Grace was suspicious or if she was

paranoid. At any rate, she felt bad about not telling Anna about her visit.

"I feel like a day to myself," she finally answered. Jordan knew it sounded rude, but they'd have to understand.

The ride into Milledgeville was long, two hours. Jarvis had told her. She stopped right outside of Solomon Cove and typed the address into her GPS to be sure she didn't miss her appointment. She also bought a Coke and a 3 Musketeers bar simply to make herself feel better. It'd worked.

As she pulled into the small town, Jordan followed the large signs with arrows pointing to Milledgeville Hospital. She shuddered at the thought of it. As she'd predicted, it was a huge facility. It looked like a large, cold monument for those that society didn't want to acknowledge or embrace. It was a dark, gloomy, and gray, and there were obviously no efforts made to make it look anything other than generic.

It resembled a prison more than a hospital, and made Jordan wonder how anyone could get well there. She shut off the car and ate the last remnants of her candy bar, feeling dread building up in her stomach. With one last glance at the time, she grabbed her purse and got out of the car. Her feet were heavy now, her mind foggy, causing her to question why she'd even made the trip.

As she made her way to the front of the building, Jordan watched as some of the patients worked aimlessly on the grounds. They looked like trustees at a state pen as they worked at a snail's pace to complete their menial tasks. Blank faces, blank expressions. As she got closer, she noticed their khaki work clothes with their names embroidered across their chests. It failed miserably at giving them an identity.

The young woman cleaning the glass doors, opened them slowly for her, without ever acknowledging her presence. She tried to thank her, her mouth moved, but no sound came out. Jordan moved methodically down the spit-cleaned corridor until she reached an information desk. A middle-aged woman with dyed blonde hair piled high on her head asked if she could help her. She continued entering data into her computer without looking up.

"Yes, Ma'am," Jordan answered almost in a whisper. "I'm here to meet with Jarvis Ingram."

The woman stopped her typing and looked Jordan over from head to toe.

"Take a seat in the room to your left. I'll have him paged."

The typing began again as Jordan walked into the waiting room. The magazines were various types of medical journals, but she picked one up anyway. She thought seriously of changing her mind and nixing the idea altogether. She placed the magazine back onto the rack, put her purse over her shoulder, and was about to make her exit when she heard a man's voice.

"Ms. Maxwell, Jarvis Ingram. Did you have any trouble

finding us?"

"No, not at all." Jordan tried not to appear surprised by his good looks. She estimated him to be about thirty, strong build, medium height, and brown hair that coordinated nicely with hazel eyes.

"Glad to hear it," he said in that soothing voice she remembered from their phone conversation. "Come on back to my office."

Jordan followed him down several long hallways, going through doors that required him to slide his ID card across a keyboard to allow entrance. Noting her concern, he touched her shoulder. "Just precautions, nothing to worry about. We house about 2,500 patients here. It's for their protection, as well as ours, that they're not allowed to move around freely."

"Oh, I see," was all Jordan could think to say.

"We do have different levels of security, however. We treat many different areas here."

They made two more turns before he announced they'd arrived at his office. One more swipe of the card and he pushed the door open. She was relieved to see the small space had some personality. There was a fichus tree, several other plants, and framed photographs of various outdoor sceneries on his desk and walls. They were exceptional shots, and before she sat down, Jordan took a moment to study each of them.

"Just a little hobby of mine." He smiled. "The patients

seem to feel more at ease around them, so I bring them in. Kind of a change from the gray," he continued, with a smile.

"They're fantastic," Jordan said sincerely. "Really, they are." She was obviously intrigued, and he appreciated that. He rarely encountered people who cared one way or the other.

Jordan moved around to the front of his desk and took a seat, wondering where they'd go from here, and if she would meet Chandler in this small room. It would seem odd seeing him up this close.

Jarvis picked up a file folder and opened it on his desk. "So, let's talk a little about Chandler. What brings you here to see him now?"

He asked it in such a kind manner that it didn't offend Jordan. She thought for a moment getting her words together before she answered him. "Well, it's kind of a strange situation. His father, my great-uncle, passed away recently and left his estate to me. It was quite a shock, as I'd only met him a couple of times during my childhood. I wasn't even aware he had a son until I met with the attorney that read the will to me." Jordan stopped for a minute to get her breath, as Jarvis nodded patiently.

"I guess at first I was more curious than anything." She twisted in her chair until she found a more comfortable position. "After living at the estate for the past few months, I guess you could say it seems awkward. I feel as though I'm living in someone else's house and with him being the only

226

living relative I have left, well, it seemed appropriate I meet him."

"I see. Are you aware of why he's here?"

"I know he witnessed his mother's murder and hasn't spoken to anyone since. I understand his father never had any contact with him after that happened."

"Yes, you're right about that—sad story all the way around. I've worked with him the past four years. I think the pain of losing his mother and then the disconnection from his father was too much for him. Chandler has been diagnosed with Post-Traumatic Stress Disorder. It's brought on by a catastrophic event, much like what he witnessed with his mother. There are usually three main symptoms. The patient becomes numb to the world, he relives the trauma over and over in his memory and in dreams, and he experiences extreme anxiety. Chandler fits the mold perfectly. He also harbors a great deal of guilt over the situation, making it impossible for us to break through to him. I don't want to sugarcoat things for you, Ms. Maxwell. I'm not sure how Chandler will react to meeting you. If he should decide he doesn't want to meet with you, I'm afraid we'll have to cancel any future visits. The hospital would consider it detrimental to his recovery. I'm sure you understand."

Jordan nodded in agreement.

"Would you like to meet with him in my office or in the visitation room? Either would be fine with me."

"What do you think would be best? Does he know I'm coming?" Jordan asked.

"Yes, I told him he would receive a visitor today. I felt it better he be prepared for it." Jarvis consulted his files again and continued, "Quincy Velez and um…let's see, Cyrus Hames have been his only visitors through the years. There wasn't any dialogue on Chandler's part, but he appeared to enjoy the visits. He was unresponsive when I told him about you. I think if the two of you meet in the visitation room, there would be less pressure on you. It would just be the two of you in my office."

"Then the visitation room it is." Jordan stood and placed her purse on her shoulder.

"Just follow me," Jarvis motioned, "and I'll walk you over. I'll be available after your visit should you have any questions or need to talk. Please don't hesitate to stop by." He reached his hand out and shook hers firmly.

"Thank you, Jarvis."

They walked a fairly long distance before he led her into a room filled with tables and chairs.

"Pick anywhere you like; I'll be right back."

Jordan walked around them all for a minute unable to decide which one should be witness to their first conversation. *Luckily,* she thought, *no one else is in here.* She heard the door open and watched a large orderly walk in and take his place at a desk across the room. *I guess that's our warden,* Jordan thought sarcastically. *Great.*

It was at least five more minutes before she saw Jarvis. He threw up his hand to her, and smiled as he put his hand on a young man's shoulder, pushing him encouragingly into the room. Chandler stumbled briefly, then stood up straight. He was a tall boy. *Probably six-two,* Jordan thought. Even as a man, he possessed his mother's beauty. His skin was fair, his hair gold, and his eyes, those beautiful electric-blue eyes. His mouth was merely a line, committing to neither a smile nor a frown, and his eyes reflected the years of grief that wouldn't soon be washed away.

Jordan felt the sudden need to run to him, to hold him, to cradle him. His eyes never met hers; he looked at the floor as he walked toward her. Chandler stopped short of his chair, almost as if he wasn't sure what to do, then he slid it out slowly and sat down. He never spoke. Jordan could feel her heart beating in her throat. She tried to hide her struggle to breathe. Her hands unconsciously went to her breasts as if to hold her pounding heart inside her chest.

"Hello, Chandler," she started, sounding like she was introducing herself to a car salesman. "My name is Jordan. I'm your second cousin."

No response.

"I wanted to come and visit you because you're my only other relative. My parents are both gone. There's no one else."

Patiently she waited, no response, no eye contact, no recognition.

Shakily, she continued, "I'm sorry about your parents, Chandler, I've heard about everything. In fact, I'm living at the estate now. It's a big, beautiful place. Everyone tells me how much they miss you and how much life you brought to the place."

Chandler still didn't respond and Jordan felt herself losing what little control she could still muster. She cleared her throat a couple of times and attempted to start fresh.

"I'm glad you agreed to see me. I understand Quincy and Cyrus have visited you some before." She decided to pretend he was responding as she continued with a fervor. "I like them both a lot. They're busy keeping the place up as I'm sure you know. Quincy takes on a great deal of responsibility. He actually rides my case a good bit, and Cyrus, he's doing fine too. Do you remember any of the great meals that Grace used to cook?"

Jordan wasn't sure, but she thought she may have seen a small twinkle of recognition.

"They're as good as ever. I'll tell you one thing: you don't want to be late for a meal."

That time Jordan was sure she'd seen it, not only recognition but a smile, and then, almost a giggle. She didn't dare stop there.

"I was late the first morning, but never again. She may be old, but I bet she could pack a punch."

That brought laughter, but his eyes never met hers.

Jordan knew she couldn't draw much from the laughter,

so she didn't push for any worded response from him. She didn't say anything for a while; she just looked at him. He looked so vulnerable, much younger than his eighteen years, and she could envision the estate being a more pleasant place with him in it. She didn't dare verbalize it for fear of scaring him off. Jordan acted as though she didn't notice when he slowly slid his chair closer to the table. His folded hands and a portion of his forearms rested lightly on the table.

Maybe he likes hearing about the home he lived in as a child, she thought and decided to continue talking about it.

"Myra still works there too. Did you know her daughter Olivia?"

A pause and no response.

"She works at the café in town. I think she's about your age. Pretty girl, funny like her mother too," Jordan said.

And there it was. A nod. Not just a plain nod, but one of recognition. Jordan didn't dare stop talking.

"I eat at the corner café sometimes when I can sneak away from Grace. Good food. Olivia stays busy in there. Did you ever eat there?"

No response this time.

"Chandler, I'm glad that you agreed to see me," she said, finally giving up the façade she was portraying. "I have so many questions and I was hoping we could get to know one another."

Jordan felt her eyes brimming with tears and wasn't able

to stop them from overflowing. She was too exhausted to even try. They rolled down her cheeks in a steady flow as she continued to talk.

"I don't want to pressure you to talk, I don't want to know what happened to your mom or even your father; I just want to get to know you." Jordan let out a high-pitched sob and struggled to regain her composure. "I'm sorry. Really, I am. I didn't realize how much I wanted to share with you until I saw you walk through the doorway. It was a connection, well, one I can't really explain. You're the only hope of what I have left for a family, and I just wanted to reach out to you."

Jordan stopped talking and laid her head down on her folded arms. She knew she'd blown it with him and wished she had prepared more for her visit. She hadn't been prepared for the vulnerable creature in front of her. For a moment, Jordan feared she'd vomit right there on the floor. She wanted to sit back up, but knew she hadn't pulled herself together.

Jordan felt a light tap on her arm, and she raised her head. It was Chandler reaching his hand out to her, and in it was a folded linen handkerchief. She took it and nodded a silent thank-you.

"Can I come back, Chandler? Would you like to see me again?"

She sat and waited, her eyes downcast as his were, then she heard a voice, a quiet, unconfident voice, and it said,

"Yes, Jordan."

She heard herself gasp, and as she looked up, Jordan saw his back as he walked away.

Chapter 30

Regina shuffled her notes back and forth across the desk. She had put in hours of interviewing time and wasn't getting any closer to a prospective murderer. "What am I missing?" she asked herself as the phone rang.

"Regina Collins, *Solomon Cove Gazette*," she answered, pushing her glasses up on her nose.

"Regina, it's Eric Riley. How are you doing?"

"Frustrated as hell, but I'm getting used to it. Did you get anything on Elizabeth Maxwell?"

"As far as I can tell, she really cared about the guy. She had family money of her own, not quite the money James Maxwell had, but she could've led a life of leisure just the same. Can't figure out what she saw in the old geezer though; what was he, twice her age?"

"Damn near it." Regina's forehead wrinkled as she sat deep in thought.

"That's about all I've found out about her from here. Could there have been any affairs?"

"I've looked into that, but she was a beauty, Eric. It

would've been around town if there were any infidelities on either of their parts."

"Well, I guess our theory of these murders being tied together is wrong. Elizabeth Maxwell was squeaky-clean; no one would've wanted to kill her, and I can't see a serial killer waiting ten years for his next victim."

"I don't think it could've been Mr. Maxwell either," Regina continued. "He was too adamant about not having it ruled a suicide. He was devastated."

"So, where do we go from here?" Eric asked.

"I don't know, really. I think I'm going to take these pictures to the school Jennifer Flemming worked for and do some checking there. I'm not sure they checked the boyfriend out too thoroughly."

The line was silent for a few moments as they both pondered different possibilities.

"I'll be back in town in a couple of weeks," Eric said. "I'll see you then."

Regina shuffled the papers around for a few more minutes, then leaned back in her chair. It'd been a long time since she'd reported on a case that had so little to sink her teeth into. It had no rhyme or reason and was making her crazy. She was desperate to find something, *anything* that would tie Jennifer and Dorian together.

She made a call to the school and set up an appointment to share the pictures with the staff. She was surprised to hear the Sheriff's Department hadn't done so.

"I'll see you next Thursday," Regina said to the school secretary. "Thank you for your time."

Chapter 31

The swelling in Rachel Kelley's face was beginning to go down and she was starting to look more like herself again. She still lay deep in her coma despite the fact the swelling was lessening in her brain.

Hank was asleep with his head on her stomach when Elias came in. He walked quietly over and touched her lightly on the cheek. The bruising from her attack was fading a little more, and he hoped and prayed every day would be her last in the coma. Hank stirred, weary-eyed, and looked up at Elias. "Hey, man," he said, rubbing his eyes. "How are you doing?"

"Okay. What about Rach?"

"The same, still the same."

The opening of the door had both of them turning around as Doctor Hamlin walked in followed by a small gaggle of interns. He shook Elias's hand, then Hank's. They all watched in silence as he read the latest notes on her chart and lifted her lifeless eyelids.

"What's going on, Doc?" Hank asked, unable to stay

silent any longer.

"She has cerebral edema, which is swelling of the brain. It's getting better, and I think we're fairly safe in saying it won't increase again. Everyone reacts differently to edema. Some people wake up in a day. Others may take weeks, even months. It's out of our hands now," he continued. "It is up to the man upstairs."

"The baby," Hank started, then appeared to have lost his nerve to continue the question.

"The heartbeat remains strong; we're optimistic."

For the first time throughout the whole ordeal, tears began to roll down Hank Kelley's face. Slowly at first, then they fell with a vengeance. They fell for all the endless hours he'd spent worrying about whether she would live or die, hours of worrying about who could've done this to her, and the hours of feeling the guilt for not being there for her when she'd needed him the most.

"I just don't know what she'd do if she lost the baby," Hank said, his voice cracking several times. "Rachel loves it so much already."

Elias stood beside him squeezing his shoulder, interrupting it with a hard pat or two every few seconds.

"Everything is going to be fine, Hank; we just have to keep our faith."

"What the hell are you talking about, Sheriff? Where the hell were you when she was opening up that damn station by herself? Where was her *big brother* then, Elias?"

Elias opened his mouth but decided not to say anything more. He deserved the hit and took it without rebuttal. He gave Hank's shoulder one more squeeze and walked out of the room and down the hall. The coffee machine was malfunctioning again. After losing eighty-five cents, he decided to call it a day and go home. The ding of the elevator alerted him the doors were about to open, and he shifted his weight to his right leg.

Elias gave everyone time to get off and was stepping in when he saw a group of nurses running loudly down the hall. Stepping back off, he watched as they ran into Rachel's room.

Chapter 32

Everyone was in a better state of mind by the time Saturday rolled around. Grace and Emma were busy making hamburger patties and potato salad while Myra supervised Cyrus and Quincy as they set up the tables and chairs. Two grills were set up in the middle of the tables, along with coolers for the drinks and uncut watermelons.

"It's starting to look like a party." Jordan made her way through the tables. "Do the Mullises suspect anything?"

"Not yet," Cyrus answered. "Zeke is supposed to be here to help set up."

Just as he got the words out of his mouth, they could hear Zeke's truck coming up the drive. Jordan could see his broad shoulders as he stepped out of the truck and watched him as he turned around and lowered two little boys down onto the grass. They were running as soon as their feet hit the ground.

"Uncle Cyrus," they both yelled in unison. "Uncle Cyrus." They were on him in seconds with their little arms wrapped around his waist. Jordan was surprised at their display of affection for him. He hardly seemed the type who'd attract the love of children. Cyrus muttered something to them and rubbed their heads.

"Good boys, you two, good boys," she heard him say.

As quickly as they'd come up to him, they were gone, rolling over the watermelons and chasing each other around the tables.

They were beautiful children, just as Ruth was, and Jordan felt a pang in her chest that she was not yet in a situation to have a family of her own. The Mullis children would have to do for now. Quincy and Myra came up for their hugs from the boys while scolding Zeke a little more than necessary for being late.

"I hope you guys don't mind, but I invited Sara and Billy Crane to join us. Grace said there was plenty of food," Jordan said, still smiling at the rambunctious little boys.

"Not a problem," Quincy said.

The afternoon went according to plan, and the grills were started up at exactly two o'clock. Sara and Billy arrived on time, carrying a pecan pie and a pound cake.

"Yum," Jordan said as she hugged Sara tight. "Something smells good."

She gave Billy a hug too as they went up to join the others at the grill. Quincy passed out sodas to the kids, beers to the men, and wine coolers to the women.

"I think I'll take a beer, Quincy, if it's okay with you," Jordan said.

He shook his head in disbelief but traded her cooler for a Miller Lite. Cassie arrived with Ruth who joined the boys in their kickball game with Quincy and Zeke. It was truly an afternoon to remember, and Jordan soaked it all in.

There was enough food to feed all of Solomon Cove, but the crowd made a large dent in it. Cyrus initiated a seed-spitting contest with the children, but Quincy ended up the winner. As everyone sat down to eat their cake and pie, Jordan made her way to the middle of the tables. Grace winked at her, clapping her hands to get everyone's attention. "Listen up, everybody. I think Ms. Maxwell has something to say."

Zeke waved for the children to continue their seed-spitting further down on the grounds as the small crowd grew quiet. Jordan could see the broad smile on Sara Crane's face, and wanted to go over and hug her.

"Wasn't this a great party?" Jordan asked, listening as everyone agreed.

She looked across at each of the tables and felt a knot rise up in her throat. These past few weeks had been so emotional for her that she feared she would break down. Everyone seemed to be holding their breath for her, sensing her tears were about to start falling. Clearing her throat, Jordan continued.

"As you all know, I don't have any of my own family left. I was frightened to move here because, as crazy as it was, New York had become my home." She could tell they were no longer looking her in the eyes and she shifted her weight from one foot to the other. The last thing she wanted was to embarrass them.

"As soon as I saw this place, I wondered if I'd ever fit in." She laughed a little. "You see, I've never even had a whole set of dishes that matched." Jordan paused to let them laugh. They were being kind to her. "I'll be honest, from the first day I met you all, I knew I'd be happy here.

We're all so different from each other. Grace, you're such a wonderful cook, and you bring such discipline to this place. Myra, you're our backbone, always taking care of what needs to be done, long before we know the problem exists. Emma, you bring youth to keep us all optimistic.

You are so anxious to learn, you're a breath of fresh air." She stopped to take a deep breath and to wipe the tears that were forming despite her efforts to stop them.

"Quincy, you're one in a million. You have cared for me as though I were your own sister, repairing my car, and encouraging me, well, *berating* me, into getting one that's safer for me." That brought a burst of laughter from Quincy as he nodded his head in agreement.

"Cyrus, I learn more about you every day. I think I can sum you up by quoting a famous passage, 'You are truly a success when you have earned the love of little children.' When I see those children wrap their arms around you, I know you have to be a good man."

Jordan rotated her body until she was facing Zeke and

Cassie. She had to stop and reach for a napkin to wipe her eyes. It was becoming too emotional. Jordan could see Sara out of the corner of her eye. She was wiping a tear as well.

"Zeke," she said, struggling to get her voice not to fail her, "you, Cassie, and the kids are the heart of this family. I don't want to make you feel unimportant, but I think it's because you brought these children to us." She was glad to hear laughter from everyone. It helped to keep her composure for a few more minutes.

"I discovered when I met with Billy Crane that I had a problem with the finances of the estate. You see, Uncle James left an account that was to be used for additions, and for so long, I couldn't understand where we could possibly add on to this huge estate. I mean, I certainly don't need any more room. Then it dawned on me. We need another cottage, maybe one that's a little larger, one that could hold up to, um, say three kids." Jordan noticed the shock on Zeke's and Cassie's faces immediately.

"I guess what I'm asking, or rather suggesting, is that we build that cottage. I'd love to have the whole family here together, as much of us as we can, anyway." She lowered her voice and looked directly at Zeke and Cassie. "Would you consider moving on the estate? We have all talked about it, and we'd love to have you here." Cassie jumped up and in between sobs, she hugged Jordan and then Zeke hugged her, and before she knew it, they were all hugging each other. Even Billy Crane was wiping away tears as he looked at his wife suspiciously.

Zeke called for the children and they squealed with delight as they ran off to continue their games. Everyone was talking at once while Quincy brought out several of the floor plans from Anderson.

Chapter 33

Regina hung up the phone feeling positive for the first time in a while. The news that Rachel Kelley had come out of the coma was long overdue. She'd finally be able to print some good news for the people of Solomon Cove. The downside was Rachel didn't have any recollection of who her attacker was, and more than likely, was knocked out before she ever saw him. Square one. Regina was getting accustomed to being there.

She grabbed her briefcase and tossed the funeral photos inside. "I'll be back this afternoon, Angie," she said to her receptionist. "I'm taking my pictures on the road again."

"I'll be here," Angie responded in the nasal voice that grated on Regina's nerves. When she hired her, Regina thought she had a lingering cold, but hadn't been so lucky. Angie was a reliable worker, and Regina knew she was capable of holding down the fort when she was away, but beyond that, they had little more to do with one another.

Regina thought of calling Eric before she left, but thought better of it. *He'll be in town in a couple of days; we'll just get together then,* she thought as she cranked her prized Mustang convertible. She was so deep in thought about the investigation that she was almost in Somergrove before she knew it. The elementary school hadn't been hard to find; small towns were all alike.

Regina walked slowly by the playground, reminiscing about her own youth. There were few cars in the parking lot as the teachers enjoyed their last few days without students. In a week, they'd be filling the halls, bringing the teachers out of their hibernation and back into the real world

Regina sighed with relief she'd scheduled this meeting before the hellions were back in session. She had never been a *kid person* but held the utmost respect for schoolteachers and bus drivers. "Now those have to be the two shittiest jobs on earth," she said aloud for her own benefit.

A big yellow pencil was painted on the wall, pointing to the front office, so she followed it. Regina stepped inside without knocking and looked around at the row of small chairs lining the walls.

"Those are the chairs that hold mad, defiant faces during the school year, not the ideal place to spend your time if you're a student," a middle-aged woman said with a laugh. "Hello, I'm the principal, Ms. Rogers."

Regina had to bite the inside of her mouth to force herself not to ask if she was married to *the* Mister Rogers, but refrained.

Principal Rogers must've sensed what she was thinking

and helped her out, "Unfortunately, no relation." She laughed. "Come on back."

Her office was bright and decorated with huge butterflies made of construction paper, dangling from the ceiling, on clear fishing line. There were two normal-sized chairs in front of her desk, and a small round table with *munchkin chairs* around it.

"Have a seat," she said as she walked around her desk. "I understand you have some photographs you'd like for us to take a look at. We'll be happy to assist you in any way we can. Jennifer was a delight. She was an outstanding teacher, very well-liked. We were devastated to hear about her murder."

"Thank you for taking the time out for this. I'm sure her family will appreciate it." Regina slid a stack of pictures across the desk toward Ms. Rogers, laying the other two stacks to the side.

"There are quite a few here. I'm sure your time is limited. If you could just scan over them, I would appreciate it. These are from another funeral in Solomon Cove. Unfortunately, we had two murders very close together. We'd like to see if you recognize anyone from Jennifer's funeral in these pictures. It's a long shot."

Ms. Rogers thumbed through the stack in relatively short order, not finding anyone who rang a bell with her. Unfortunately, it was what Regina had expected.

"I'm sorry, Ms. Collins. I don't know any of these people.

I wasn't familiar with Jennifer's social life, so unless it was someone from the school, I'm afraid I'm a dead-end."

"Thank you anyway. Is there anyone else I could speak with, maybe Justin Carter?"

"Yes, he's in today; just follow the deer footprints down the hall, and when they turn to bear prints, he'll be the second door on the left."

Regina smiled at the seriousness with which Ms. Rogers gave her directions, then thanked her graciously again.

It would've been difficult to miss Justin Carter's room. A huge polar bear holding a fishing pole was painted on his door greeting everyone to "Mr. Carter's Second-Grade Class". Regina looked through the small window in the door before knocking. She saw him sitting at his desk, cutting out red apples from construction paper. He looked innocent enough. She tapped lightly and he motioned for her to enter.

"Hello, I'm Regina Collins from the *Solomon Cove Gazette*."

"Yes, come in, I'm Justin Carter. Ms. Rogers said you might be coming by."

Regina looked down at his small mountain of apples as he grinned.

"Name tags for the first day. It usually takes a week to learn all of their names."

"I see" Regina was clearly disinterested. "I was wondering if you could look at these photos for me and see if you recognize anyone in them."

She wanted desperately to ask him about his relationship

with Jennifer, but she didn't dare. Sheriff Murphy would have her ass on a platter if he heard of her questioning him in that manner. Regina would have to hope he'd offer up some information.

Justin flipped quickly through the first stack and shook his head. "I'm sorry, really, I am. I was hoping I'd be able to help in some way. Jenny was a great person. I liked her a lot, probably much more than she liked me. We were friends, nothing more."

Regina slid stack two across the desk with little hope of hitting pay dirt. Three pictures into the stack, he stopped, as all of the color left his face. He studied the photo for a full minute before Regina interjected, "Justin," she said slowly and carefully, "Is there someone you've seen before? Someone you may have seen with Jennifer?"

Justin didn't hesitate and his eyes never left the picture. "Yes. I stopped by her apartment one night without calling first. She was leaving with this man. They were going to dinner."

Regina reached across the desk, taking the picture from his hand, and turning it toward her. She felt her blood go cold and could feel her heart pounding rapidly in her chest.

"Justin, are you *sure*? Are you absolutely *sure* you saw this man?"

"No doubt in my mind. I remember that night well. I was terribly embarrassed, well, humiliated. He was older, much more handsome than me. He shook my hand, even looked like he felt sorry for me. That's the man."

Regina's heart was racing so fast she was certain Justin could see it beating in her chest. She grabbed the pictures, stacked them, and threw them in her briefcase.

"I don't believe you're in any danger," she said breathlessly, her mouth so dry it was difficult to speak. "If he thought you could tie him to any of this, you'd be dead by now. Whatever you do, don't mention this to *anyone* until I can get to the proper authorities."

Justin's face was white as a ghost, making his red freckles almost glow. "Do you mean we have Jennifer's killer?"

"Yes, Justin, we do."

Regina ran to the car not even aware of the stares she was getting from the janitorial crew. She looked down at her shaking hands as though they belonged to someone else. The keys jingled as she tried to calm her nerves enough to crank her car.

She was speeding excessively, but she couldn't stop herself. She wasn't even sure where she wanted to go. Her head was swimming and she was grasping at straws.

"Why? Why? It just didn't make any sense. If he was dating Jennifer Flemming, then that would explain his connection to her, but why Dorian Keller? No one will believe this," she kept saying to herself.

Regina pulled into a small gas station and filled up. She was almost on empty and this wouldn't be a good day to run out of gas. She grabbed a single Michelob Light in the bottle and got back into the car. She reached for her cell phone only to discover there wasn't any service.

What a great time for this to happen! She wasn't sure whom she'd call, so it was probably best it didn't work anyway. She needed to gather her thoughts as she drove into town.

She turned on Barry Manilow, let the top down, and unscrewed the top of the beer. She took a long swig from the bottle, before self-consciously looking in the rearview mirror for a cop. Not today. Thank God for small favors. It was a lonely stretch of road, so she lifted her drink again and again until it was gone.

Something flashed in her peripheral vision and then it was gone. Regina looked back just in time to see the shiny fender as it hit the rear bumper of her Mustang. She didn't have time to react, but held it together enough to steer the car in the direction of the skid. It slid onto the shoulder in slow motion, and then, almost as if it were teasing her, the car turned over onto its top, throwing her out, and skidding to a stop.

Regina shook her head back and forth as if trying to awaken from a bad dream. The glaze over her eyes began to fade as the blue sky slowly came into view. Dazed and confused, she reached to brush the hair from her face, but her hands wouldn't move. Panic began to sweep over her as she realized she wasn't able to move her limbs. Regina's body was betraying her, as she lay paralyzed and broken.

"A wreck, I've been in a wreck," she said aloud as though

trying to explain it. "What in the world is going on here?" Regina screamed as she looked around for the careless driver. He was standing above her with an evil grin on his face, watching her, waiting. She turned her head to face him with a combination of fear and disdain. "It was you! You son of a bitch; it was you the whole time!"

"You just couldn't keep your nose out of this one, could you, Ms. Collins? Did you think I'd let you solve this case and go back to share it with the people of Solomon Cove? Come on, Ms. Collins, you have to give me more credit than that."

Regina could feel her anger reaching the breaking point as she struggled to maintain some kind of control. Her jaws were clenched and through her teeth she asked him, "Why? Why did you do it?"

"Oh, it's really very simple. Everyone had to pay, and what a better way than to kill beautiful, young girls? So senseless really. None of it had to happen. They made me do it, and now they're all going to be sorry, just like you, Ms. Collins. Regina with an *R*. Rachel Kelley gets to live now because of you, how thoughtful. Any last words?" His eyes were stone-cold and his mouth was turned up in an evil, grimacing smile as he held the baseball bat up high and brought down his fatal blow.

Regina Collins lay there looking blankly up at the sky as he threw the bat into his trunk onto the blue carpet. *They'll probably find another damn fiber,* he thought.

He didn't bother to remove any of her clothes to throw them off on a motive. She'd never really done much for him anyway.

A little too masculine for his taste.

Chapter 34

Elias walked into the office and wrapped his arms around Alex. "Good morning, beautiful. Things are going to be much better today. Rachel's talking and getting stronger every day, I have a pot of coffee waiting on me, and the most beautiful secretary in the world."

"My goodness." She smiled. "Is this the Elias Murphy that I know or has an alien taken over his body?"

"It's Elias Murphy in the flesh. In fact, it's Elias with a good night's sleep. Beat that!"

Alex swatted him on the behind and pushed him toward his office. "You won't be in a good mood for long." She pointed to the stack of messages on his desk. "Oh, the mayor called a little while ago to remind you about the Rotary Club meeting today. You're going to meet at Corner Café as usual, at noon."

"Okay, just remind me about eleven." He made his way to his desk.

With Rachel better, things seemed to be settling down a bit. He laughed when he saw the message for repairing the potholes in the road had made it back to the top.

"If I get those things fixed, there won't be any need for me anymore."

Elias heard the click of the intercom followed by Alex's voice, "Sheriff, the mayor is here. Do you have a few minutes?"

He pushed his button down in response and told her to send him on back.

"Good morning, Elias," Thomas said as he helped himself to a cup of coffee and a chair. "Did you hear about Regina Collins?"

"No, I haven't. What's up?"

"Somergrove police found her dead this morning. Thrown from her car in an accident. Her secretary just called the office."

"Damn, I hate to hear that," he said. "What caused the accident?"

"Toxicology reports haven't come back yet, but I called the chief and he said they found a beer bottle in the car. That secretary of hers is almost as bad as the one I gave you. She didn't say much about Regina getting killed; she just wanted to know who was going to handle her job at the paper. Pretty cold, huh?"

Elias sat for a minute as he allowed it all to sink in. "Angie isn't exactly Miss Personality," he agreed, "but she does have a point. Who's going to manage the paper?"

"Jesus, Elias! Let's let the body get cold before we worry

about that."

"I came to work in a good mood today too." Elias sounded like a little boy. "Not to change the subject, but did you hear about that Maxwell woman building a home for Zeke Mullis and his family on the estate? I thought it was pretty nice of her."

"I heard something about that…oh yeah, it was from Billy Crane. I don't know, Elias, I've been thinking about Zeke. He spends two nights away at school in Anderson, you know. His wife stays sick, and he has all of those children, financial problems, and…"

"What are you getting at, Thomas?"

"Oh, I don't know, just that this couldn't be a drifter or we'd have noticed, right?"

"Wait a minute here." Elias's voice was getting louder with each syllable. "This isn't the damn South. Just because a young black man has problems, doesn't mean he's going to rape and kill white women. Damn, Thomas, I'm ashamed of you, really!"

"Don't give me that condescending bullshit. As much as we hate to, we've got to admit it could be somebody here in the community. I'm running out of options here, Elias."

"Well, it sure as hell isn't Zeke Mullis!"

"Okay, Jeez. Take it easy." Thomas sipped his coffee and looked around at Elias's desk. "How's it working out with Alex? It looks like your desk could use an overhaul."

"She's great. These are just the daily messages. I can't

complain. Rachel will be back soon, and life can get back to normal."

"Do you think she's safe, Elias? You need to think about that before you bring her back."

Elias looked down at his hands as he tented his fingers.

"I want to *believe* she's safe, but we never really know. One thing for sure, she won't be opening up without one of us here. I guess I could send a deputy to pick her up in the morning and get Hank to pick her up in the afternoon. That sounds like my best bet."

Thomas stood up and tossed his empty cup into the trash. "Just do what you think is best, Sheriff. I'm with you all the way."

Chapter 35

Jordan finished her scrambled eggs, then reached for the phone. She wanted to see Chandler one more time before Eric came for his visit. Three transfers and she heard Jarvis Ingram's voice. She refused to admit that his voice caused her heart to skip a beat. He was a good-looking man, but nothing in comparison to Eric. She shut her eyes as if to erase the thought altogether.

"Jarvis Ingram," he said for the second time. "Can I help you?"

"Yes, hi, Jarvis. It's Jordan Maxwell. I wanted to ask if I could come down today to see Chandler again."

"That shouldn't be a problem, but I'd like to meet with you first, if you have the time. Maybe for lunch, somewhere other than the hospital."

She could tell by the tone of his voice it wasn't intended as a social lunch, so she quickly agreed.

"Meet me at the Seaside Tavern at one. It isn't hard to find. The food is pretty decent, and we shouldn't run into anyone from the institution."

For the first time, Jordan could hear a strangeness in his

voice, and she wasn't sure if it was concern or fear.

"I'll be there at one," she said as she hung up the phone.

That was really weird, she thought as the phone startled her with its ringing.

"Hello," she answered.

"Hey, babe," Eric said, sounding as though he hadn't slept in quite a while. "How's everything in Maine?"

"It's all right. I'm going back to visit Chandler today." Jordan heard him sigh.

"Why do you want to put yourself through that?"

"I just feel that I need to, Eric. I really can't explain it. Are you packing to come my way?"

"Yes, as a matter-of-fact, I am. I called Regina Collins at the *Gazette* and they said she'd been involved in a car accident. She was thrown from the car and killed."

"Oh my God, you're kidding. I haven't heard anything about it. Does this town have bad luck or what?"

"It must have happened last night. The receptionist was kind of in shock herself. I was hoping to meet with Regina as soon as I got there. Terrible tragedy."

"Yeah, I know. It's hard to believe."

"I'm swamped here, so I better get off the phone and finish as much as I can before I head your way. I'll see you tomorrow, probably late afternoon."

"I can't wait," she said, her stomach in a swirl of emotions.

"Jordan," he said sternly, yet softly, "be careful. I don't

know what's going on there, but I don't like it."

* * * *

Jarvis had been right, the restaurant wasn't hard to find, and she made it with fifteen minutes to spare. She was contemplating going inside when he tapped on her window.

"Hello." He grinned. "I respect promptness."

"I'm glad you're impressed," Jordan responded as she got out of the car. She followed him in the restaurant and into a small booth toward the back. They both slid in, and he handed her a menu.

"So, to what do we owe all of the secrecy?" she asked as tactfully as she could.

He smiled before forcing a laugh. "I'm sorry. It's just that Chandler is a special case. I shouldn't be meeting with you outside of the hospital; it isn't ethical."

"'Ethical'?"

"Even social workers have a patient confidentiality agreement. I feel like something is going on here."

"Going on, what do you mean?" Jordan asked, leaning forward in her seat.

"It's Chandler, he's been acting different lately," Jarvis said, hesitating before he continued. "Jittery, nervous, preoccupied." He was about to continue when a waitress showed up for their orders.

"What can I get you to drink?" she asked in a hurried voice.

"I'll take a glass of Chablis." Jordan could feel her hands shaking and hoped the wine might help.

"Make that two. Are you ready to order, Jordan?"

Her mind was going in a hundred different directions. "Can you recommend something?" .

"Sure. Bring us the stuffed lobster tails," Jordan requested, turning to the hurried waitress.

She didn't answer, but wrote it down on her pad and walked away, returning in just a moment with two large glasses of wine.

"Why have you come to see Chandler now, Jordan? Be honest with me."

"I *was* honest with you, Jarvis, really." She looked down at the napkin resting in her lap. "There's something else." Jordan studied his eyes as he waited patiently for her to continue. "Solomon Cove has had two murders and one attempted murder in six weeks. I can't help wondering if they're somehow tied to the murder of Chandler's mother. I wasn't going to ask him about it, honestly, I wasn't."

Jarvis took a large sip of his wine and cleared his throat. "I've been reading about that in the paper. I'm sure Chandler has as well. I'm afraid they're related too."

"What?" Jordan asked, wanting to make sure she'd heard him right.

"I think Chandler knows something, Jordan. It was almost as though he was expecting you to visit. He wasn't surprised at all when I told him about you."

"Well, that simply can't be true," she said, clearly confused now. "How would he know about me?"

"That's what I'm trying to figure out. He won't speak at all about you; he won't even write on my chalkboard, which he normally does."

"God, Jarvis, he knows who the killer is."

"I want to sit in when you visit him today," Jarvis said firmly. "I think it'd be best."

"You can't be serious. Then there'd be no way he'd tell us anything." Her mouth remained open waiting for her next words to form. "Maybe he wants me to know who it is. Maybe he's going to tell me this time."

Jarvis looked uncomfortable and shifted his body restlessly in the booth.

"I'm sorry, but for years I thought his father might have killed his mother. That would've justified the trauma he's been through. Now… now, I have my doubts. I think Chandler knows something that could protect somebody and I think he wants to protect you."

"But how would he even know about me, Jarvis?"

"I'm not sure. Maybe your great-uncle told him about you. He was eight when he left the estate. You have to realize he's not mentally handicapped, Jordan. His IQ is quite high and except for his vocabulary being limited, well, nonexistent at this time, he has developed mentally just as every other eighteen-year-old. When someone doesn't verbalize, we tend to think they don't have the intelligence to do so. That's not the case here."

Jordan finished her wine and held her glass up enough to indicate she wanted another. The wine arrived just as their lobsters did. They ate in nervous silence.

* * * *

Chandler's head was bowed as he entered the visitation room. He walked straight to Jordan's table without making eye contact. She couldn't pinpoint it, but something was different this time. Maybe he was more confident, perhaps he was holding his body a little more upright; she couldn't tell. He sat down lightly and slid the chair forward lacing his two hands together with his fingers.

"Hello, Chandler," Jordan began nervously. "It's nice to see you again."

He sat mute for a few moments before reaching slowly and methodically into the front pocket of his shirt, retrieving a folded piece of paper. As if he were unfolding a priceless piece of history, he took great care as he opened it, then he ran his fingers across it to smooth out the creases that came from being folded. Like a child revealing an art project, he laid it out on the table for her to see, and then he sat back expressionless.

Jordan was surprised to see a crayon drawing that looked indeed, as though it were done by a child. She could make out the estate and the cliffs, then the water. A stick figure stood behind a tree, peering around it to see two other stick

264

figures by the cliff's edge. One of the figures must have been his mother because she had long, heavy strokes of yellow that was undoubtedly her golden hair. She was losing her balance and falling back toward the edge. The other figure was pushing her. For a brief second, Jordan felt faint. She struggled to stay coherent so she could question him. "Chandler, is this your mother?"

She waited for what seemed like hours before she saw a slight nod indicating it was. Jordan wished now she'd allowed Jarvis to come in with her because she wasn't sure what to say next. She didn't want him to feel interrogated, and yet she was anxious to get as much information as he'd give her. She pulled her hair off of her neck and rubbed her hand across the perspiration forming there.

"Did you see who killed her, Chandler?" Jordan asked softly.

The perspiration was rolling down the side of her face, and she could feel the little beads of sweat forming on her upper lip. She dropped her hair, letting it fall over her shoulders, as she looked directly in his eyes. Jordan was surprised to see him lift his eyes to meet hers. She waited as patiently as she could until she feared she'd grab him, shake him, and demand answers from him. Chandler must have sensed her exasperation because he cleared his throat. It was a much deeper sound than she would've expected from him. She braced herself to hear him speak.

"Yes." That was it, a simple yes. A clear confident

answer, but he offered nothing more.

"Chandler, can you tell me who it was?"

Jordan watched as his chin started to quiver and his eyes filled with tears. He shook his head, rubbing his fists against his eyes as though he were trying to wipe away a horrible memory. Tears were rolling furiously down his cheeks, and he shook his head from side to side before whispering, "Can't. Can't say it." Chandler started gasping for air; each gasp seemed to be direr than the last. Before Jordan could even think of what to do, the large orderly was at their side calling for Jarvis on a radio, grabbing Chandler under his arms, and lifting him to his feet.

Before he'd taken two steps, Jarvis came running into the room and started speaking to him in a calm whisper. "It's okay. Everything's okay, Chandler. No one is going to hurt you."

Jarvis was leading him toward the doorway when Chandler turned around and yelled to Jordan, "My sister, my sister is in danger…in danger…my sister." His voice was as frantic as someone pleading for their life, and Jordan ran toward him with a knot in her throat so big she was afraid it would choke her.

"Who is your sister, Chandler? You don't have a sister."

"Sister in danger," he pleaded in between sobs that seemed to rack his entire body.

"Chandler, I'll help, but *who* is in danger? *Who* is your sister?" Jordan pleaded.

Before he disappeared into the hallway, she heard him say, "You are, Jordan, *you* are."

Chapter 36

Jordan vomited twice before she made it to her car. She could feel the dampness under her arms as she struggled to pull her keys out of her purse. The world seemed to be revolving in slow motion, and all she could think about was how much she needed to feel the coolness from the Yukon's air-conditioning. She cranked the car and sat there with her forehead leaning on the steering wheel as she tried to get her breathing back into its normal rhythm.

Jordan tried to organize her thoughts, but none of it made sense. It must be some cruel, sick joke played by some lunatic in an insane asylum. Why in the hell had she even come here? She was just asking for grief; Eric had even told her so.

But the vision of Chandler's eyes and his racking sobs told her differently. He wasn't lying. He had no need to. Her mind swirled, a tempest of emotion. It was all so crazy, so terribly crazy. Chandler couldn't possibly know if she were in danger. She steadied herself in the seat and leaned back against the vehicle's headrest.

Think, she demanded of herself. Calm down and think clearly! Did coming here instigate some killer to come out of hiding, after ten long years? What would be the cause? How could Elizabeth Maxwell be tied to Jennifer Flemming or Dorian Keller? But more importantly, how did she fit into all of this?

Jordan steered the car through the winding driveway and stopped in front of the estate, not quite sure how she'd gotten there. She couldn't hear anything but the beating of her heart as she turned off the ignition and got out. Quincy waved at her from across the lawn and her hand, as if it had a life of its own, waved back at him. She followed her feet as they led her to the one place she thought she might find some answers… the library of James Maxwell.

Jordan pulled the chain on the desktop lamp and stood staring around as though she was seeing the room for the first time. The furniture was recently waxed, the pillows on the couch recently fluffed. She searched for something to help her open the desk and found a silver letter opener. Her hands were shaking furiously as she poured the contents of her purse out on the desk, and as if knowing it was in demand, a bobby pin gleamed among the tubes of lipsticks and a hairbrush. She dropped the pin several times before she was able to stabilize her hands long enough to jiggle the lock. Feeling it finally give, she slid it open with the ease of someone who had just cracked open a safe.

She hadn't heard them coming down the hall and didn't

see them until they were descending upon her at the desk. Their faces wore blank expressions with a mixture of contempt. They were within inches of her before they spoke.

"You won't find anything in there," Grace said. "He was too smart for that."

Jordan gasped both from surprise and fear. "What? What's going on?" she whispered weakly.

Zeke stood firm next to Grace. His large presence looming over Jordan. "What are you doing?" he asked. Before she could answer he continued, "We know where you've been. Chandler shouldn't have told you, but we knew he would."

Jordan felt them move even closer, if it were possible, and she opened her mouth to scream, but nothing would come out. It was fruitless to scream anyway; there was no one to hear. She mustered the strength to jump out of the chair, her voice coming back long enough to scream for them to get away from her. Jordan was within inches of the door when she felt Zeke grab her by her arms and hold her so tight she didn't even attempt to escape. She collapsed in his arms as he laid her gently onto the floor.

Chapter 37

Jordan felt a cool rag on her forehead and saw a piece of paper come and go as it fanned her face. She was wondering where she was when she saw Grace's face.

"It's okay, Jordan. We're not going to hurt you. Calm down, dear."

She turned her face and saw Zeke standing there too with a deep look of concern on his face.

"Ms. Maxwell, Ms. Maxwell," he continued to say. "You're okay, no one is going to harm you."

Jordan rested on her elbows and lifted her head, still somewhat confused about her situation. Looking around, she realized where she was and it all started to come back to her.

"What are you two hiding from me and why?" she asked, the words coming out in little more than a whisper.

Zeke leaned down and picked her up in his arms carrying her to the couch, then turning on the overhead light.

"We didn't think it would ever be necessary to tell you," Grace began, squirming in her seat, obviously uncomfortable. "Zeke and I are the only people who know. We prayed no one else would find out."

"Tell me," Jordan said, no longer concerned about being civil or even pleasant to them. "What's going on? I need to know now!"

Zeke helped her to sit up on the sofa and offered her a glass of water. Jordan drank from it as though she were thirsty, knowing she wasn't.

Grace looked at Zeke, then folded her hands as though she were on trial at the county courthouse.

"My dear," she started. "You could have lived the rest of your life without knowing this, and you would've been no worse for the wear, but it's too late to hide it now." She was so serious that Jordan was braced for the worst.

"Tell me, Grace," she demanded. "Don't try to word it perfectly, just tell me."

Zeke patted her shoulder offering to continue for her, but Grace refused.

"No, dear," she told him. "It is my place." She sat forward on the edge of the couch with her back upright, her hands folded in her lap, and began. "You never had much family, Jordan. The Maxwells were never a large family. Your father was James Maxwell's only nephew and although they were never close, they were blood and that meant a lot to your great-uncle." She reached for Jordan's water and drank deep gulps from it. "Your father wasn't able to have children. They tried for many years without any success.

They were very happy together, Jordan, and they wanted a family very badly. They considered adoption, but your great-uncle would hear nothing of it. Mr. Maxwell was a very lonely man and he had no idea he would ever marry or bear a child of his own. He pleaded with your father to let him father a child, but it was several years before he'd even discuss it with Mr. Maxwell."

Grace reached over and picked up the paper she had used to fan Jordan and began to wave it in front of her own face before she continued, "My cousin was a doctor in Boston. He specialized in artificial insemination. It was far enough away from Solomon Cove that your parents and Mr. Maxwell were confident it would remain confidential. The three agreed you would never know this had occurred. There wasn't any need for you to, really. You'd live your life with a happy family and James Maxwell would have someone to leave his fortune to. Most importantly, you would be a Maxwell by blood."

Jordan tried, but she couldn't even cry. She was so stunned she could do little more than look at the two of them.

Zeke looked at her with one of the kindest expressions Jordan had ever seen. "Ms. Maxwell, your great-uncle told me about this only a couple of years ago. We had become pretty close. I guess as he got older it was weighing on his mind. It was hard for him not to be a father to you. He never thought it would have been, but he struggled with it.

Your parents only brought you by a few times.

I guess they felt uncomfortable. Maybe they worried he would try to be a bigger part of your life. Even after he met Ms. Elizabeth and they had Chandler, he still loved you, and wanted you to have your share."

"I don't understand, I mean, it's so hard to believe," Jordan stammered. She was wringing her hands nervously, but couldn't manage to stop. She folded her arms over her chest, so they couldn't see the pounding of her heart. "How would Chandler know?"

"Mr. Maxwell told him when he turned eight," Zeke said. "It wasn't long before his mother was killed." He drew a deep breath before continuing, "He told Ms. Elizabeth too. He wanted to be honest with them. Mr. Maxwell loved them so much."

"The killings," Jordan whispered, "they're tied together...and Chandler... he knows. He told me I was in danger."

Grace took her hands in hers forcing a smile that wasn't very convincing. "We'll make it through this, child. I know we will. You've brought too much joy to this place for you to be taken from us now." Jordan watched the tears form and glisten in Grace's eyes before she looked away. She couldn't bear any more pain. The day had been too long and too much had happened. She needed her rest.

Chapter 38

Olivia hit the snooze button for the fourth time, rolled over, and pulled the covers up over her head. She muttered under her breath about what a fool she had been to have agreed to come in for Lacy so early in the morning. She wasn't a morning person; it wasn't in her makeup. If the diner were hers, she wouldn't open until noon, and cater to the lunch crowd, but today wasn't her call. She was a waitress, and it was her turn to open up. Her turn to start the coffee brewing, her turn to preheat the ovens, her turn to shower at 5:00 a.m.

The snooze beeped for the fifth time as Olivia threw back the sheets, her bare feet hitting the coolness of the hardwood floor. She strode like a zombie into the bathroom and started the water for her shower.

I've got to marry money one of these days, she said to herself. It's the only way I'll be able to sleep as late as I want to.

She laughed aloud at her thoughts as she stepped into the shower.

Forty minutes later, Olivia was pulling up to the Corner Café. The keys jingled in her hand as she crossed the back-parking lot, her small feet grinding in the gravel. The shower hadn't helped to wake her, and she hoped that turning on all of the lights in the diner would. Olivia fumbled for several seconds with the keys until she found the one that fit. She felt it slide easily into the lock when she heard his voice. "Good morning, Ms. Olivia," he said. "What brings you out this early?"

She was startled for a second and grabbed for her heart in an effort to let him know he'd startled her. "Oh, my God!" she said, exhaling loudly. "What are you doing up this early? I thought only those of us with minimum wage jobs had to rise before the sun."

He laughed politely and offered, with the motion of his hand, to turn the key for her. She handed it to him without a second thought.

They both stepped into the diner, but before Olivia could reach for the light switch, she felt the hairs on the back of her neck stand on end. It was too quiet. He wasn't talking now, even when she was asking direct questions. He had an odd look on his face, not an angry one, but one of indifference.

"Are you okay?" Olivia heard herself ask, knowing all the while something wasn't right. He looked at her with what she almost detected as sympathy, but it washed out of his eyes as quickly as it'd come. She could feel his breath on her

276

back as she tried to ease away from him. She thought of screaming, but decided it would be fruitless this time of day. Her best bet would be to run.

"I hate to get up this early," she said, trying to sound nonchalant. She continued to talk as she made her way toward the front door. She reached for a glass sugar jar and turned to hit him, but he'd anticipated it. He knew she would put up a fight. She was a live wire. He almost hated to have to kill her, but he was running out of options and still had a point to prove.

"Oh, Ms. Olivia," he said as he grabbed her hand with the jar in it. "You should've known that wouldn't work."

She was trembling and struggling to catch her breath. "Why? I don't understand. Why are you doing this to me?"

"It's all part of the game, dear. Didn't your mama ever tell you the world was full of injustice? There are the *haves* and the *have-nots,* and today you're, well, I guess you can figure it out," he said with a wicked grin.

"They'll find me." Her voice was frantic. "You'll never get away with this."

"Oh, I've thought of that," he responded. "They won't find you here because it would mess up my lunch schedule. You know I have to eat here. Dead bodies tend to close a place down for a while."

She only caught a glimpse of the baseball bat before it crashed down on her skull. "Quick and painless. That's the way I like it."

He picked up her small form and threw her over his shoulder. There was still ample time to get her to her car and drive outside of town before anyone else came along.

"This is too simple." He laughed. "Just too damn simple."

He backed her old car out of the parking lot with the ease of someone making a trip into town for some insignificant item. Olivia was in the back seat, her legs folded in an awkward position, almost like a contortionist. He reached into his jacket pocket feeling the nylon ball of panty hose.

He was certain the blow had killed her, but he would strangle her just to make sure. The stretch of highway along the water was abandoned at this hour as he knew it would be. The car slowed, then stopped, as he pulled her limp body from the back seat. Amazingly, there was no blood. He lifted her eyelids, noting one dilated pupil and another enlarged one.

As quickly as he could, he wound the nylons around her young, pale neck and pulled as hard as he could at each end. He stopped when he heard her vocal cords crushing.

"That should do it," he said to the body. "It's all over now." He carried her to the edge of the water and dropped her, ever so lightly, as if not to injure her.

Closing the car door, he drove on, never looking back, his memory almost wiped clean of the horror altogether. He parked her car in an empty lot several miles up the coast. He put on an oversized pair of shoes from a thrift store and walked through the grass to his own vehicle. He'd already checked on his tires.

There were so many of them that no one would consider trying to cast the tracks. It would be too time-consuming and would, more than likely, never yield any results.

It was 6:30 a.m. when he pulled into his driveway, still too early for anyone to be suspicious.

Chapter 39

Eric arrived before lunchtime to find Jordan still in her bed with tear-stained cheeks. He dropped his duffle bag on the floor and sat next to her on the bed.

"I was hoping for a happier reception," he said gently as he bent down to kiss her forehead. "What's wrong, Jordan?"

She could feel the tears coming again, but this time she didn't try to hold them back. "Oh, Eric, everything is so crazy. My life's not what I thought."

She sat up enough for him to hold her as she told him the whole story.

He kicked his shoes off and nudged her over with his hips to give himself enough room to lie beside her. They lay there until she fell asleep, but Eric remained deep in thought.

I've got to get to the Solomon Cove Gazette, he thought. The answers have all got to be there.

Anna tapped lightly on the door before opening it enough to look in. "Hey, there," she whispered. "We weren't expecting you so soon."

Eric held up one finger and slowly eased out from under Jordan, making sure not to wake her. He gave Anna a small peck on her cheek and led her away from the bedroom.

"Can we talk somewhere?" he asked, looking tired and not quite as handsome as Anna had remembered.

"I've been wanting to talk to you," she said, still in a whisper. "Let's go sit out in the garden. No one will overhear us there."

They managed to bypass any of the staff. Eric was grateful not to have to stop and waste time with small talk. The garden was as well-tended as always, but they picked a spot near the water to talk.

"What the hell is going on here?" Eric asked.

Anna smiled nervously, looking like one of those chubby cherubs one would see on greeting cards. "I don't know, Eric." She sounded more serious than he'd ever heard her. "Jordan is having a hard time accepting she's James Maxwell's daughter. It came as quite a blow, especially at her age. She feels deceived."

Eric walked over to the edge of the cliff and looked down, taking in all of its beauty. "You know, Anna, I don't mean to sound uncaring, but I don't think Jordan should feel betrayed. They all loved her, even Mr. Maxwell. Perhaps they should've told her, but she could have lived her entire life without knowing. I guess they were banking on that."

"I understand what you're saying, Eric," Anna said, "but it doesn't make it any less of a surprise now."

They walked over and sat down on a nearby bench.

"You know what concerns me most, Anna, is that this could be tied to the murders. I mean, it has to relate somehow or why would Chandler tell her all that. Why in the world would Jordan be in danger?"

"I haven't figured that out myself. I've never been to a place like this before. The house frightens and soothes me at the same time."

"I know what you mean."

"You're the detective, Eric," Anna said. "What are we missing here?"

"I don't know, but we're going to find out. Can you ride into town with me?"

"You bet."

Chapter 40

Angie was more abrupt than usual as she answered the phones at the *Gazette*. She wasn't paid enough to answer this many calls, nor deal with this much controversy. The mayor had promised he'd send someone else to take Regina's place and had yet to do so.

"Two more days of this, and I'm walking out," Angie had told him.

She didn't bother to change her demeanor when Eric and Anna walked in.

"I already told you about Regina," she said coolly to Eric. "There isn't anyone else here to see."

"Yes, I know." He tried not to sound agitated. "This is Anna Stephens," he said as he put his arm around her shoulders. "She's a friend of mine and Jordan's from New York."

Angie looked at her but did nothing more to acknowledge the introduction. Eric paused just long enough to irritate her a little more.

"I was wondering if we might look in Regina's office. I think we might find some information there that would benefit us."

Angie didn't answer for a couple of seconds and he feared she might call the sheriff for permission first. Finally, she shrugged, pushed her glasses up on her nose, and turned back to the computer.

"Whatever," she said in that nasal voice. "I get off at four o'clock so be finished by then."

Eric and Anna walked back to the office quickly, worried she might change her mind. They found it in the same disarray Regina had left it in. Eric was relieved; it meant she'd still been busy trying to solve the case. There were crime scene photos of both Jennifer and Dorian, along with police and forensic reports. He thumbtacked each of them to the cork bulletin board and sat down behind her desk. His expression slowly turned into a smile as he reached for a spiral bound notebook with handwritten notes in it.

"What is that?" Anna asked.

"Yes," a deep voice boomed from the doorway, "what is that, Mr. Riley?"

Eric and Anna looked up as if they'd been caught with their hands in the cookie jar. "Hello, Sheriff," Eric answered. "I-I-was hoping to find some clues here in Ms. Collins's notes."

Elias entered the room cautiously. "And who let you in

here? If there's any evidence here, I believe the police should be the ones to review it."

"Yes, Sheriff, yes, you're right." Eric felt both intimidated and somewhat accused. "We'll be on our way." Eric stood up motioning for Anna to follow him. "Thanks, Sheriff," he said solemnly. "Have a good day."

Elias let them walk until they'd almost reached the door before he stopped them. "Okay," he said wearily. "Come back in."

They did as Elias asked. He walked behind them and quietly shut the office door. Elias reached his hand out in a gesture to shake Eric's, then turned and did the same for Anna. "Damn, I'm sorry," he said, with a look of genuine regret. "I didn't mean to take it out on you two. I was just surprised to see anyone here."

"We understand, Sheriff," Eric said. "I just got in town this morning. I thought I might find some answers here. Regina and I have been sharing theories."

"I always said she would've made one hell of a detective," Elias said, forcing a smile.

"We could have used her in New York, that's for sure," Eric responded.

The sheriff sat down in one of the folding chairs, put his face in his hands, sighed heavily, and looked up at Eric and Anna. "I think the plot has thickened. I just got a report back from the highway patrol. Regina didn't die in an accident; she was murdered." Elias paused long enough for the information to sink in before continuing, "Blunt force trauma to the head, same damn fibers."

He got up and walked over to the window. "Thunderstorms today," he said, "supposed to be really bad weather." Eric wasn't sure if it was his way of changing the subject or if it were nothing more than a warning.

"Do you mind if we look through her notes?" Eric asked. "We promise to keep everything as it was, and of course, share with you anything that may be of significance."

Elias turned from the window and looked at them. "Yeah, sure, I'm up for any help I can get. I'm fighting a losing battle."

Glancing at his watch, Eric turned to the sheriff. "We have all day. What do you say we grab a bite to eat at that great place on the corner. I've been thinking about that food since I left here last time. Maybe you could catch me up on a few things."

Eric fully expected the sheriff to turn him down and was openly surprised when he accepted.

"Maybe that's not a bad idea."

The lunch crowd had already arrived, and business was booming at the diner. Everyone turned to stare at the sheriff as Lacy sat them down.

"My adoring public," Elias said sarcastically. "Being a public servant isn't all it's cracked up to be."

"They have to blame somebody," Anna said kindly. "It isn't as bad as it seems, really."

Lacy handed them menus without her usual salutations or smile. "Special is baked ham, green beans, mashed potatoes, dinner roll, and apple pie."

"Good afternoon, Lacy," Elias said. "Are you having a bad day or do you just not want to see me?"

She forced an unconvincing smile. "I'm sorry, dear. It's just a bad day. I was supposed to be visiting my sister in Somergrove today, but Olivia didn't show up to cover for me. It's not really like her, but she's been excited about starting college. The diner hasn't been foremost on her mind."

"Oh, I see. Did you call Myra?"

"Yeah, I did. I hated to tell on Olivia; I was a little worried. Myra said she might have spent the night with a friend. She's been getting in late these days; you know how kids are when they're ready to fly from the nest."

Elias laughed. "Yes, I do. Unfortunately, I was a kid myself once."

Lacy wrote their orders on her tablet and walked away.

"She's lived here all of her life," Elias said. "One of the best women I know."

"That's one thing I don't understand." Eric unfolded his paper napkin and placed it in his lap. "This is such a close-knit community. You would think this would be the last place for a string of murders to occur."

Lacy returned with their tea. Eric sipped from it before he continued, "Things like this are not only common in

New York, but they're expected. I have to admit, I don't have a clue."

"The only thing I know is they were all killed by the same hand. Beyond that, we have nothing. No motive, no murder weapon, no suspects."

Anna looked at Eric and nudged him under the table. "Tell him about Jordan," she whispered.

"I do need to share something with you," Eric said. "It's about Jordan Maxwell. We've heard she may be in danger."

"And where did you hear that from?"

"Chandler Maxwell."

Elias looked up at Eric and laughed. "You're kidding, right?"

Chapter 41

Grace knocked on Jordan's bedroom door, then let herself in. She could tell Jordan was in a fitful sleep and decided to wake her. She shook her lightly on her shoulder and leaned down to speak her name softly in her ear. "Jordan, sweetheart, wake up. It's me, Grace."

Jordan sat up and rubbed her fingers across her eyes. "Yes, Grace, I'm sorry, did I miss breakfast?"

"Yes, dear, and lunch as well. You need to get up and eat. Zeke and Cassie will be here in thirty minutes to talk with you. Why don't you take a quick shower and come down for a bite?"

"Grace," Jordan said with an exhausted whine, "I don't feel up to visiting with anyone today. For God's sake, can't you all just let me drown in my sorrows for a couple of days?"

Grace reached for one of Jordan's hands and held it in both of her own. "No, dear, we can't, we love you too much. Now get up and shower, you'll feel better."

When Jordan stepped out of the shower, she saw a pair of panties, a bra, and a clean, peach colored sweat suit laid out on the bed.

Sweet Grace, she thought.

She dressed, slid into a pair of sneakers, and pulled her wet hair into a ponytail. *I draw the line with makeup today. It's just not going to happen.*

She stopped by Anna's room before she went downstairs. She wasn't there, but Jordan went inside anyway. The room sparkled, like the rest of the estate, but somehow this room was different. It reflected Anna now; she didn't exactly know why. There were very few personal items, but it fit her so well.

She walked over and sat on the bed, picking up a pale-yellow pillow and wrapping her arms around it. She loved having Anna around and was afraid that any day she'd announce her departure. She made a mental note to spend more time with her in the next few days. After laying the pillow back in its place, she made her way down the stairway.

Quincy walked by and nodded to her, obviously unaware of the unraveling of events from the day before. "Mornin'. Daylilies are somethin' else today. Better enjoy them while they are here."

"I'll do that, Quincy." She turned to walk into the dining room and thought better of it. "How are things going with you?" Jordan asked.

Quincy gave her a confused look and shrugged his shoulders. "Everything good, I guess."

Jordan smiled. She liked him. He was a man of few words, but she liked him.

The dining room was well lit, with large bowls of flowers everywhere. It was an effort to make her feel better, and she appreciated the gesture. Jordan sat down and reached for the paper, but before her fingertips could touch it, Grace was placing a large plate in front of her. It was a huge hot ham and cheese sandwich melted on sourdough bread with a pile of French fries large enough for a family.

"Yum." Jordan took time to breathe in the aroma. "I guess you were right, Grace." She smiled. "I do need to eat."

Grace smiled and walked back into the kitchen leaving her alone with her meal. Jordan slowly took her first bite and then ate with a vigor normally reserved for holiday meals. As she wiped the last fry across a pool of ketchup, she sat back and put both hands on her stomach. "I can't believe I ate all of that," she said aloud.

"And neither can I," Grace said as she walked in with a tray of cookies and lemonade. "Does the world look a little brighter now?"

"Yes, Grace," Jordan admitted. "It does."

The ding of the doorbell brought Myra dashing across the foyer with a look of anticipation on her face.

"Hello, Ms. Maxwell," she said as she raced by. "I need to

see my babies; it's been a while." Myra was undoubtedly speaking of Zeke and Cassie's children and before she could respond, she heard their footsteps beating across the foyer.

Jordan smiled and let her mind wander back to when she was a kid. She'd had a great childhood; there was no denying that. It wasn't right for her to be angry with any of them, not even Uncle James. They'd done what they thought was right and they'd done it out of love. She had been wanted, and she had been loved.

"Good afternoon, Ms. Maxwell," Cassie said, bringing her out of her thoughts.

"Good to see you, Cassie." Jordan stood and wrapped her arms around the fragile, young woman and kissed her lightly on the cheek.

"Hello, Ms. Maxwell," Zeke said. "Sorry to bother you today, but Grace insisted we come."

"Zeke," Jordan said, her voice faltering, "I needed a visitor today, and I wasn't aware of how much, until you two came through the door." She walked over and took his hands in hers. Giving him a knowing smile, she motioned for them to join her at the table.

They could hear Myra's laughter as she walked briskly through the dining room to the kitchen. Both Taylor and Danny were attached to her apron with both hands, and the grins on their faces told Jordan they were headed to the kitchen.

"I think I smell fresh cupcakes," Jordan said.

"Do you smell frosting too?" Danny asked as everyone laughed.

"There is frosting, indeed," Myra said, "but I didn't have time to frost the cupcakes, so I guess you two will have to do it for me."

"Yeah!" they both squealed.

Zeke and Cassie sat down at the table and Jordan poured everyone a glass of lemonade.

"Ms. Maxwell, I think we've settled on a floor plan," Zeke said. "We'd like for you to take a look at it."

"Great, I'd love to see it," she said as they spread it out on the table. "This is lovely," she added. "Do you think there's enough room?"

"Oh, yes, Ma'am," Cassie said. "It's twice the room we have now."

Jordan furrowed her brow and looked a little closer. "I only see three bedrooms."

"We thought the boys could share a room," Zeke replied. "They're used to that now."

Jordan held her chin in her right hand and closed her eyes for a minute. "Do you mind if we ask Quincy to come in for a few minutes?"

"No, Ma'am," Zeke answered. "He knows a lot more about this kind of thing than I do."

She went into the kitchen to have Grace call Quincy and returned with three very *carefully* decorated cupcakes. "I think they finger-painted these," she said as she laughed.

293

"But we better take our chances anyway."

The three sipped from their lemonades and nibbled on their cupcakes until Quincy stepped through the door.

"Do you have a few minutes to sit with us?" Jordan asked.

Quincy walked slowly to the table and sat down. "Got all the time in the world. What can I do for you?"

Jordan pointed toward the floor plan and took another bite of her cake. "This is the plan that Zeke and Cassie would like. Do you think you could talk the builders into adding one more bedroom? That is if the Mullises wouldn't mind."

"We're asking too much already," Zeke interrupted. "Really, we couldn't ask for anything more."

"Shouldn't be a problem," Quincy said. "Mind if I take care of it, Zeke?"

"No, Sir, not at all. Thank you both for everything."

"Don't thank us, you two deserve it. We'll do whatever we can to get this project underway as soon as possible. In the meantime, Myra and I took it upon ourselves to settle up with Mr. Crane for the next six months of your mortgage. I figured if you were going to be living here, may as well start that benefit now."

Jordan was trying to make it sound as insignificant as she could, and her attempt to quickly change the subject was shot down.

"Ms. Maxwell," Cassie said, "we cannot accept all of this.

It's far too generous."

"Cassie," Jordan answered, "Quincy and Cyrus have been living here for years, and it's only fair that you two should enjoy the same privilege. Mr. Maxwell meant for you to have it just as sure as he meant for me to have my inheritance. Now, let's not talk about it anymore. We have a house to build, and a location to choose. Let's go outside and look around."

It was obvious how excited they were as they smiled at each other.

"Please, Lord," Jordan prayed, "give them many more years together."

Chapter 42

Elias walked back to Regina's office with Eric and Anna and sat back down in the folded chair.

"Eric, I wish I could come up with an answer to all of this, but I don't think Chandler Maxwell is going to solve it for us. He's had ten years to do that. Hell, I wouldn't be surprised if he were playing a part in this somehow."

Maybe he killed his own mother, Elias thought but didn't dare to say it out loud.

As if reading his mind, Eric said, "You think he's guilty of murder himself, don't you?"

"I don't know. The whole ordeal was just a little too strange for me: his father shipping him off, him refusing to finger the murderer, just weird."

"Things like that happen, you know. Especially with 'children of privilege,' like Chandler."

"Guess I wouldn't know too much about that. I never had much of anything, including a father."

Eric looked over at him, realizing how tired and weary he looked. "Have you been sleeping, Sheriff? No offense, but you look like you've missed a few nights' sleep and a few meals too."

"I'm doing the best I can. Let's see what we can find in all this mess. She sure wasn't *Miss Organization,* was she?"

"We journalists never are."

They all took a different area of the office and started reading through all the material. Most of it was doodles on a pad, an abbreviation, or single words. It was hard to make anything out of it. Just when Elias was ready to walk back to his own office, he heard Eric's panicked voice.

"Oh, Jesus, no," he said as he looked at the papers spread evenly across the floor. "Damn you, whoever the hell you are," he continued, getting more emotional than either Anna or the sheriff had ever seen him.

"What is it? Tell us for Christ's sake!" Elias demanded.

Eric's head dropped, his chin resting on his chest. "Olivia is dead. He's killed her too."

"What? What are you looking at that we aren't?" Elias was yelling now and unaware of it.

"Jennifer, Olivia, Regina, Dorian, the son of a bitch is spelling out 'Jordan.'"

Elias stood up and then sank back to the floor. His back was heaving up and down in sync with his sobs. Eric's shock turned into embarrassment for Elias, and then, panic for Jordan. He grabbed the back of the sheriff's shirt and pulled him up with such force it startled them all.

"Listen to me, damn it, pull yourself together! I'm sorry about the girl, God knows I am, but there are still people who need to be protected, starting with Jordan Maxwell, Sheriff. Then we need to protect the next victim." His mouth dropped open, and for a minute, he didn't say anything; he only struggled to breathe. "I'm sorry, but Anna, you could be next."

Anna was so stunned by the previous information that her reaction wasn't any different to her own potential for danger. Her face had gone white, and she held onto the desk as she made her way to a chair. Elias had stopped crying, but he was hyperventilating and pacing like a wild animal.

"Alex, dear God, she could be next!" he screamed.

"Call your deputies in now, Sheriff," Eric demanded. "We've got to get someone to the estate and someone to stay with Alex."

Elias did as he asked, trying to sound calm over the radio, but failing miserably. "Sam, Trent, meet me at the *Gazette*, ASAP," he said, breathing heavily into the radio. "Evan, go by the office and get Alex. Guard her with your life!" They responded one by one with a "Ten-Four."

While they waited for them to arrive, Eric called Jordan and told her to lock the house and only open it for one of the deputies. Then he sat down and started to come up with a motive.

"Maybe there's someone who didn't want to see Jordan

inherit the estate, maybe someone thought they should get it, or maybe his employees liked things the way they had been."

Eric was running his fingers through his hair, and for a minute, he felt like pulling it out. He'd solved murders for most of his adult life, but he'd never felt like the clock was winding down on him. There was no way of knowing who else was in danger.

"Hell," Eric said, "for all we know, Chandler Maxwell could be in danger as well."

"Rachel, oh thank God she survived," Elias was saying over and over again. "I've got to send somebody over to her apartment."

"You're right," Eric agreed. "We need to cover all the bases. We can protect the people we believe are in danger, but we need to find the killer. We've got to get to Chandler Maxwell; he's the only one who holds the key. We've got to find a way to break through to him. It's our only hope."

Chapter 43

Jordan put the phone back on the receiver and stood dazed and confused.

"Who would want to hurt her? What could she have possibly done to warrant all this?"

She started up the stairs to her room, then stopped dead in her tracks.

"The answer is somewhere in this house," she said, turning to walk back into the parlor. Jordan was so frightened by the revelation that someone wanted to kill her, that the room couldn't scare her anymore. She flipped the light switch and was relieved to find it much brighter since Zeke had replaced the bulbs. The room was still dreary and uninviting, but she tried to look at it differently now. Uncle James, her… *Damn! I hate the thought*, her… birth father had loved this place. He'd felt comfortable here. It was a far cry from the bright, beautiful bedroom she loved so much, but everyone had their own tastes. Maybe in its own way, this room was serene. Maybe it made him feel powerful and important. Whatever it was, she was grateful he'd had it.

Jordan made her way around the room, taking note of the dark, heavy window treatments, the dark mahogany end tables, and the exquisite Chinese urns that sat at each end of the mantle. She was determined to look at it all in a different light now. It wasn't a room for someone to lounge around in; it was far too elaborate for that, too stuffy, too reserved. Maybe that's what he'd liked about it.

James Maxwell was not like the father she had known, not like him at all. She couldn't envision him acting out a story from a child's book or playing hopscotch on a chalked sidewalk, not as her own father had done. But she knew he had to have his own good qualities. Elizabeth had fallen in love with him for a reason.

Jordan carefully slid the drawers open on the end tables and found nothing inside. The rest of the room netted no other clues.

That's odd, she thought. He has to have some personal papers somewhere. If they're not located in here or the office, they have to be somewhere in the attic. Jordan got up to start her search just as the doorbell rang. It was one of the deputies. Myra let him in and called for Jordan.

"Good afternoon, Ms. Maxwell," Trent said. "Sorry to intrude on you, but Sheriff Murphy thought I needed to be here with you. Some really strange things are going on."

"So, I hear." Jordan tried to sound friendly and not as

irritated as she felt. She wasn't worried about her safety at the house even though she knew it wasn't wise not to be. She simply wanted some time by herself to nose around, to find some clue that was bound to be there.

"Ms. Maxwell," Emma said as she leaned her head around the corner, "there's a call for you. It's Mr. Riley. He says that it's urgent."

"Thank you, Emma. I'll take it in the parlor. Trent, make yourself at home. Grace is preparing lunch for you."

"Thank you, Ma'am."

Jordan felt odd taking the call in the parlor, perhaps even hypocritical, but she knew no one would bother her there.

"Hello, this is Jordan Maxwell."

"Hey, babe, it's me," he said, sounding out of breath. "Has the deputy arrived yet?"

"Yeah, he's here. Did you find that necessary?"

"Yes, it's necessary, Jordan. Don't be naïve and don't rule out anyone as the culprit of this whole thing. Someone is after you just like they were after Elizabeth. I don't know why yet, but I intend to find out. The sheriff and I are going to the courthouse to see if we can find any clues, any wills, or unknown descendants, something along that line."

Jordan felt her blood run cold as panic quickly set in. She placed her hands on her chest as if to hold in her beating heart. "What about Chandler? Is he safe?" She felt like an overprotective mother. It was a strange feeling for her. She'd never had a brother or even anyone to protect. It was a helpless feeling.

"We're going to make a trip to the institution, Jordan, and we're going to need you to go along. Probably, first thing in the morning. Right now, we have no reason to believe he's in any danger. Chandler is probably in a safer place than any of us."

"Oh please, Lord, let that be true. There has to be something here that'll help us, Eric. I'm going to look around. When will you be home?"

"I don't know, but be careful and don't even go into another room without Trent. I don't mean to scare you, but it could be someone on the staff."

A shiver ran up Jordan's spine as she considered it. She'd never even thought about it before. Her mind started racing down the list: Quincy, Cyrus, Zeke, Grace, Emma, Myra…no, she wouldn't allow herself to think that way. She couldn't.

"I'll be there as soon as I can," Eric continued. "Sam is bringing Anna home."

"I love you, Eric."

"I love you too. Now, don't leave the room without Trent!"

Jordan sat in the chair holding the phone to her chest until the automated message came on telling her to please place a call or hang up. She laid it on the receiver and rested her head on the back of the wing chair. Her mind whirled with possibilities, none of which she'd care to imagine.

I've got to get to the attic, she thought.

Jordan walked stealthily from the parlor and up the stairs, listening all the way to Trent complimenting Grace on her cooking. With a glance over her shoulder, she made her way down the hallway. She reached the closed door leading to the stairway that'd take her to the attic. She could see her footprints in the dust indicating no one had been up there in quite some time. That was comforting. Feeling her way up the stairs, she stifled back a cough as she breathed in the stagnant, dusty air. She waited until she reached the top before she dared to turn on a light.

The attic was a massive room with stacks of boxes everywhere. She noticed an empty baby crib, a red tricycle that must've been Chandler's, and several large wooden trunks. She maneuvered her way around the room, careful to brush away the cobwebs as she went. This place hadn't seen any visitors recently.

Jordan stopped to read the labels on the cardboard boxes, many of which read "out of season clothes," others were toys, and many more were books. Nothing on the outside of the boxes roused her curiosity. Jordan turned her focus to the trunks, noting the heavy round locks.

She looked around for something to open them with and decided on a lightweight hammer. Now was not the time to worry about covering up her intrusions. Bigger things were at stake now, her life being one of them.

With two quick thrusts, she was into the first trunk. A

thin, white blanket covered its contents. She removed it carefully as if something would jump out and attack her if she moved too fast.

"Oh," she whispered as she lifted the white wedding gown out of its resting place. It was the loveliest dress she had ever seen. Made of French silk, it flowed like a cloud as she continued to pull it out. Thousands of tiny pearls were sewn all over it, leading down to the dramatic train. "This had to be Elizabeth's," she said as she placed it carefully back in the trunk. Her mind raced instantly back to Chandler, her brother and her blood. Jordan thought of the life he'd had with his parents and their dreams of the future, cut short by some selfish, deranged person. Her spine stiffened as she thought of it, and she closed the trunk with a thud.

The next two trunks were filled with photographs and trinkets. Jordan quickly scanned over them moving on to the next. As the hammer crashed across the lock, she knew this one would be different. She saw newspaper clippings of Elizabeth Chandler's murder and letters from the hospital concerning Chandler. There were receipts for payment of his medical bills, even for the mortuary that had embalmed Elizabeth's body. Jordan sifted through as quickly as she could without overlooking anything of significance. And then, there it was—an envelope from a detective agency in Portland addressed to her great-uncle.

Ripping into it, she wasn't concerned about tearing

anything, so she had to sit back on the floor and gather her thoughts. Her hands shook so badly she struggled to hold the envelope. Jordan closed her eyes and inhaled deeply.

It seemed to help. She slid the papers from the envelope and walked over by the window. They were from a detective agency that was working for Uncle James. They regretted to inform him throughout most of the correspondence that they'd not reached a conclusion on his wife's murder. More and more bills followed, along with stamped receipts for payment.

Beyond that, she couldn't find a thing. She dug through the trunk for over an hour until she found a letter addressed to the agency that hadn't been mailed. Opening it, she felt an eerie presence, but she continued to read. It was a request for them to talk with Lauren Blake. Below the letter, she saw a newspaper clipping of Lauren's death from a car accident. *That's strange,* she thought, as she stuffed the letter into her pocket.

Looking at her watch, she realized she'd been gone over an hour now. She knew she had better get back downstairs. Anna would be back and she was sure Eric would have called by now. Turning off the light and making her way back to the stairs, she made a silent promise.

"Uncle James, everything is going to be all right. We'll find out who murdered your wife and we'll bring your son back ."

Chapter 44

Jordan collided with Eric as she made her way down the stairs to the foyer. His face was red with anger and deep concern. "Where have you been, Jordan?" he demanded, not waiting for an answer. "This is not some silly child's game. You're in danger; what part of that don't you understand?"

"I was in the attic…" she started saying before he grabbed her arm and almost dragged her down the remaining stairs. Eric continued to pull her until they'd reached the living room where they joined Trent, Sam, and Sheriff Murphy. Sleep deprivation had clearly taken its toll on all of them.

"I found her," Eric said angrily almost as though Jordan weren't even in the room. "Where do we go from here?"

Sheriff Murphy stood with a glazed look in his eyes and twisted his head around in slow circles. He let out a deep breath asking the deputies to excuse themselves.

"Ms. Maxwell," Elias began. "We're going to have to make a visit to Chandler. I think he holds the key to all of this. Will you agree to go with us?"

"I'll do whatever we need to do," Jordan answered without hesitation, "but he's not going to talk to you two. I'll go in by myself; it's our only shot."

"Jordan," Eric said with a little more tenderness now, "I-I…"

"No, Eric," Jordan countered. "I have to see him alone. You can wait outside, but he won't talk to you. I'm making progress with him; don't take that from me."

Elias threw up his hands in disgust and excused himself to call the mayor.

"Can you be ready in ten minutes?" Eric asked Jordan.

"Yes, just let me call Jarvis Ingram before we leave."

The sheriff drove the unmarked car around the curves as fast as he could without being reckless. Jordan clenched the door with both hands as the oversized automobile rolled through the turns like an unsteady boat. Her thoughts went back to the letter folded in her pocket. She shared her findings with Eric and the sheriff, saving the letter for last.

"What does that mean to you, Sheriff?" Eric asked, not knowing enough about the death of Lauren Blake to draw any conclusions himself. Elias remained silent for what seemed like minutes, a confused look once again taking over his face.

"I can't see how any of this is related to Elizabeth Maxwell. Lauren was married to Thomas Blake, and she too died not long after Elizabeth. It was a horrible tragedy," he said, his face reflecting genuine sadness. "She was speeding excessively along the coast and had been drinking a great deal. Her young son, Connor, was in the car with her."

Elias paused briefly as though to rest his nerves and assemble his thoughts. "I'll never forget that night or the days that followed, for as long as I live. Still dream about it, actually." Another moment of silence before he continued. "Funny thing, there weren't any skid marks. The rains were so heavy that night, she probably never even realized she'd left the road. The car fell over a hundred feet and was demolished—worst scene I've ever come upon."

The look in his eyes told Eric and Jordan he was reliving the event as horribly today, as when it'd happened.

"Lord, may I never have to see anything like it again," Elias said as he looked up toward the heavens. "I had to tell Thomas. He took it hard, real hard, never has been the same. It changed him into a cold, hard person, and only the death of these young girls has begun to bring him back to the land of the feeling. Thomas denied she would've been speeding, even that she had been drinking, but there was no denying the evidence. Lauren's blood alcohol level was well above the legal limit. For years, he pressured me to find her killer, saying someone had drugged her and cut her brake lines. But there wasn't any truth to that. God knows I would've investigated it if I'd thought so."

"Was there anything in Lauren's past that would've tied her to the Maxwells?" Eric asked.

"Oh, hell no, not Lauren." Elias started to say more, then thought better of it. "I'm not one to talk about folks, especially when they're dead. She was a good person."

"What are you holding back, Sheriff?" Eric asked, pounding for more answers and not caring how it sounded anymore. "She's dead. If there's something that might help us, now would be the time."

Elias looked beaten, his lips drawn into a tight line that only suggested a frown. "She...she wasn't really like us, she was, well, kind of lower class, *white trash* a lot of the kids called her. Her mother was the town tramp. They never had anything to speak of and to say she was ridiculed as a child is an understatement. Her mother went from man to man, getting whatever she could." He beat his thumbs on the steering wheel with nervous repetition.

"She grew into a beautiful girl though, smart too. Yep, she was a looker. She couldn't wait to get out of Solomon Cove. Lauren studied hard and counted the minutes. She left when she graduated from high school and went away to college, University of Georgia, I believe. Did pretty good for herself. In fact, we lost track of her for a while."

He rubbed his forehead and asked Jordan for a Tylenol, which he swallowed without any water. "Her mother never changed her ways and eventually drank herself to death. When Lauren came back for the funeral, she ran into Thomas Blake and never left again. They married soon after. Happy as hell, those two. What a shame."

"So why would Uncle James want her investigated?" Jordan asked, more confused now than ever.

"Can't tell you," Elias continued. "She never ran in the same circles as Elizabeth Maxwell, that's for sure."

"I say we contact that detective agency as soon as we can."

"I suggest we do that first thing in the morning. It's always better to show up in person. They're more apt to give us information then."

"My thoughts exactly," Eric agreed.

Chapter 45

Jarvis couldn't hide his nervousness as he escorted Jordan to his office. "Chandler wants to meet with you in here today," he told her, his hand shaking as he swiped his security tag. "I'll be right outside, of course, and there's a radio on my desk that will alert me immediately if there's a problem."

Jordan sat down in one of the chairs and waited for him to return with Chandler. Some of the pictures on his desk had changed, along with the season. *He's a kind man*, she thought, and the pictures were his effort to bring the world inside to them. The wait was longer than she'd expected, so she paced back and forth what little she could in the confines of the small office. Just when she thought she couldn't stand it any longer, Jordan heard the faint swish of Jarvis's ID card going across the security pad.

One look at Chandler and Jordan wanted to hold him tight, tighter than she'd ever held anyone before. She took his arm and led him to the empty chair, sitting down simultaneously as he did.

"Chandler," she started, praying for God to give her the strength she needed so badly. "Chandler," Jordan started again. "I'm afraid. Things are getting crazy and I don't know how to stop them." She gave him a couple of seconds to speak, and when he didn't, she continued. "People are getting hurt, killed, Chandler, and all because of me. I can't understand why. A young girl that was in her first year of teaching elementary school; Dorian Keller at the bank, she's about your age; Regina Collins at the *Gazette*; and now Olivia Yates is missing and presumed dead."

The sound of Olivia's name brought a flash of panic to his eyes, a moment of recognition. Jordan jumped on that opportunity. "She was to open up the diner early and never made it. Her car is missing too. I want to help and I think you do too."

Chandler swallowed hard and looked down at his hands. It looked as though he was struggling to speak, but his mouth wouldn't open. Jordan reached over and took his hand in hers. He instantly curled his fingers around hers.

"I'm sorry, Chandler, that this is how we met. I'd have wanted it to be different." He shook his head and squeezed her hand painfully hard.

Jordan reached into her pocket and pulled out the letter from his father. "I found this in the attic. Your father, um, our father, wanted a detective agency to investigate Lauren Blake. Do you know why?"

Jordan could feel his grip instantly tighten as he leaned

forward and the pain almost caused her to yelp. "Do you know why, Chandler? If you do, please, dear God, tell me."

He stood up and started hyperventilating, grabbing his chest, and swaying back and forth.

"Chandler," Jordan screamed. "Oh my God, are you all right? Please, be all right. I didn't mean to scare you, I love you." They were holding each other and sobbing.

Jarvis was in the room in an instant, pulling them apart, trying to calm them.

"You've got to go, Ms. Maxwell," Jarvis commanded. "This is too much for my patient. Please, you have to leave."

Jordan tried to pull herself together. She watched as Jarvis strained to pull Chandler out of the room. He broke away from Jarvis just short of the doorway and ran back to Jordan grabbing her arms tightly. "She can't have the mansion; don't let her get the mansion. It's not rightfully hers."

"Who are you talking about, Chandler? Lauren Blake is dead; she can't get the estate."

"Don't let her get it, Jordan, please."

Jarvis was still tugging at him and their arms seemed to be flailing everywhere in the small, cramped space.

"Wait, Jarvis, please," Jordan pleaded. "He's not making any sense. Please let him stay." She was crying hard and pleading like a child.

Jarvis jerked one last time on Chandler and pulled him free of his grasp on Jordan.

"Come with me now, Chandler," Jarvis demanded. "Ms.

Maxwell, you're making him ill. I refuse to be a party to it any longer. Now step away or I'll have you forcibly removed from the premises, automatically expelling you from any future visits."

Jordan's sobs were uncontrollable as her legs gave way, leaving her sitting on the cold, polished floor. "Go now, Chandler," she was finally able to say. "I'll be back. I love you."

Chapter 46

The large orderly helped Jordan get back to the car, almost having to carry her. Before they could reach the police cruiser, Eric and Elias had both jumped out and run to meet them. Jordan's tears had dried, but she continued to struggle for breath.

"Thanks, man," Eric said, taking over from the orderly. "We appreciate it, but we'll take her from here." The man nodded, then turned to walk away.

"Jordan, sweetheart, are you okay? I'm sorry we sent you in there. God, I feel like such an ass," Eric stammered, continuing to curse his decision for the meeting.

They made it into the car, putting her in the front seat this time. She laid her face in her hands and cried while both men stood by helplessly. It seemed like hours before she lifted her face again, but when she did, she seemed to be much more under control.

"He talked to me," she said calmly. "He actually talked to me."

Eric was pushing forward softly so as not to send her

back into tears. "What did he say, sweetheart?"

"It's weird, real weird," she said, her voice trembling. She shook her head slowly as if to clear it and continued, "Chandler said not to let Lauren get the estate, that it isn't rightfully hers."

Eric looked over at Elias who looked equally confused.

"I don't understand," Elias said. "Does he know she's dead?"

"I told him she was. He got so hysterical, so out of control." Her eyes looked far away for a second and then she was back. "His case manager came in and took him back to his room. He wouldn't allow us to talk any further. He said the situation was making Chandler ill."

Eric lifted Jordan's legs and put them in the car, lightly closing the door. "Elias, we've got a lot to do. Let's get out of here."

They rode several miles before anyone spoke. Elias broke the silence. "I need to call Alex at the station. She can get in touch with vital statistics and pull birth and death certificates from Lauren and her mother, as well as the boy, Connor. Then I'll have her call that detective agency in Portland and make an appointment for us."

"I'm worried about the detective agency," Eric interrupted. "Chances are they don't know anything if they never received Mr. Maxwell's request."

"Didn't think of that," Elias said, "but it's worth a try." He reached into the console and felt around for his cell phone, pulling it out from under an array of papers. He punched in the number quickly. It was difficult not to detect the shaking of his hands. "Alex," he said calmly, "I need you to do a couple of things for me."

"Shoot." She poised her pencil above a sheet of paper.

"Get in touch with vital records in Augusta. You'll have to fax a letter to them from the department with a request for birth and death certificates for Mae Clark," he said, continuing slowly so that she could write it all down, "and for Lauren and Connor Blake; her maiden name was Clark as well." Elias waited a couple of seconds before he spoke again. "Let them know we need them faxed over immediately, but do it in a way that strokes their egos. They're cocky little bastards over there and they won't send it until they're ready to."

"Okay, I've got it," Alex answered. "I've got a contact over there from dealing with them through the morgue. Shouldn't be a problem."

"You're a charm," he said flatly, but she knew he meant it wholeheartedly.

"Oh, and Elias," she said, urgency in her voice, "A, um, Justin Carter called from Jennifer Flemming's school. He heard about the death of Regina Collins and said he needs to speak with someone in law enforcement right away. He said he met with her the day she was killed. He sounded really frightened."

"Got a contact number handy?"

"Yes, said he'd be there all day."

"Thanks. And Alex, don't let the mayor know we're pulling those records. It would send him over the edge. I don't have time to babysit right now."

"Be careful out there," Alex warned gravely.

"Don't worry about me," he said, "but there's one more thing I need you to do. Contact the Hartman Detective Agency in Portland and set up an appointment with Wilson Hartman as soon as possible. I want to drive down and see him." He held the phone out, locating and pressing the end button firmly.

"I think we may have something, guys." Elias told them about Justin Carter as he called the number, causing the big car to swerve over the middle line. Unconcerned about it, he asked for Justin Carter telling the secretary it was an urgent call.

After two full minutes of silence, Justin picked up the phone. "Hello, this is Justin Carter."

"Mr. Carter," Elias said in a staunch, firm voice. "This is Sheriff Murphy from the Solomon Cove Sheriff's Department. I understand you may have some information for us."

"Yes, Sir, I do," he whispered into the phone. "I need to see someone right away."

"Can you fill me in a little here?" Elias asked. "We're in the middle of a murder investigation."

"I met with her, Ms. Collins, on the day she died. She

brought some photos for me to look at, of a funeral, not Jennifer Flemming's."

"Yes, I'm aware of those," Elias said, losing patience and struggling to hear the quiet whispers. "It was the funeral of Dorian Keller."

"Yes, that's it," Justin said. "Anyway, I saw someone I recognized. It pretty much flipped Ms. Collins out. She asked me over and over again if it was the same person and I was sure of it. I saw him at Jennifer's apartment to take her on a date."

"What?" Elias screamed. "Why in the hell haven't you called me? This is serious shit here. It may have caused another young girl her life!"

Justin began crying softly and his whispers were almost inaudible. "I'm sorry, I swear I am. Where can I meet you?"

Elias squeezed the top of his head with his right hand. "Stand right by the phone!" he demanded loudly. "I'll call you back in five minutes."

"What is it?" Eric asked, leaning over into the front seat. "Tell us, damn it!"

"It's Jennifer Flemming's boyfriend. He noticed someone in the photos. He has our killer. I don't know where to meet him. I don't think he's safe coming into Solomon Cove. I need to reroute him somewhere."

"Have him come to the estate," Jordan said. "Trent and Evan are there with Anna. We can be there almost as soon as he can."

Elias sat silently, then asked for more Tylenol. "Maybe you're right "Would you mind calling him back and giving him directions? My head hurts like hell."

It took Jordan five minutes to give Justin the directions. He was so nervous she wasn't sure he'd even find the place. As soon as she hung up the phone, it was ringing again.

"Sheriff," Elias answered.

"It's me," Alex said. "Got some bad news. Your detective was killed in a car accident a few years ago. Thrown from the car."

Chapter 47

A deputy from Anderson found Olivia Yates's abandoned car and called the sheriff's office.

"Hello, Ma'am," he said to Alex. "Sheriff Murphy told us to be on the lookout for a girl missing in your area. Believe we found the car."

"Olivia Yates?"

"Yes, it is. Locked up and appears to be okay, found it in a lot that isn't used very much anymore."

"Hmmm," Alex said. "I'll check with her mother and see if there's a reason for it being there. Thanks a lot. I'm sure the sheriff will appreciate it."

She turned to Sam who was walking into the room. "Olivia Yates's car was found in Anderson. She didn't show up for work this morning. We're very concerned."

"Anything out of the ordinary with the vehicle?" he asked.

"No, nothing to be concerned about; it was found in an

unused parking lot. I'm going to give Myra a call."

Myra had been confused and worried when she spoke with Alex. "I can't imagine where she'd be going," she said. "She has friends in Anderson, but she wouldn't park in an abandoned lot."

"Let's not get worried yet." Alex tried to mask her own fears. "Call us if you hear from her."

Alex immediately relayed the information to Sam who agreed to be on the lookout for her. "I'm sure it's nothing," he said, thinking he should take a look along the coast to be on the safe side.

* * * *

Jordan walked into the estate and sensed, right away, the tension in the air. Anna was a mess, her cheerfulness long gone. She was sitting in the living room with Trent and Evan and they were all fighting off nervous energy.

"It's all going to be okay," Jordan heard herself saying, wondering if it ever would be again. Elias sat down heavily on the velour couch and started recapping the events of the day. Emma came in and motioned for Jordan.

"I'm sorry to interrupt you," she said, looking nervous and a little scared, "but Cyrus is on the phone for you. He says he needs to speak with you right away."

Jordan stepped out of the room and grabbed an extension in the long hallway. "Cyrus, it's Jordan, what's going on? Now is like the absolute worst time to call me."

"I know, Ma'am." Cyrus's speech sounded slurred and thick. "I have to see you right away. Bring Sheriff Murphy and no one else. Meet me in the lighthouse, right away, *please*."

"What's this about, Cyrus? We could be in danger and for all we know right now, Olivia is already dead."

"Trust me, Ms. Maxwell," he said. "I must see you now; bring the sheriff and come immediately!"

Jordan hung up the phone and walked over to the nearest window. It was getting dark outside and the clouds suggested thunderstorms. *Why couldn't he come to the house?* she thought, feeling more than a little suspicious.

Walking to the door of the living room, she motioned for Elias to come out, interrupting him in mid-sentence. Eric stood up and Jordan waved for him to stay there.

"What is it now?" he asked almost rudely.

"It's Cyrus. He called and wants to meet us at the lighthouse right away, said it couldn't wait."

"Did you tell him what we're dealing with in there?" he asked, motioning wildly toward the room filled with his deputies, Anna, and Eric.

"Yes. I think he may be intoxicated."

"Jeez, let's go. Grab an umbrella."

They walked out the back door rather than answer any questions from the others. The thunder boomed as they walked across the lawn, so Jordan opened the umbrella in case they needed it. The light was off atop the lighthouse making Jordan feel uneasy. Zeke had fixed the door, and it now opened with ease. They called softly for Cyrus.

"I'm up here. You two need to come up. I'm really afraid."

"What in the hell are you doing?" Elias barked, not in the mood to climb the seventy-five stairs.

Jordan flipped on the dim light that covered the staircase, cursing herself for not getting Zeke to put in bulbs with a higher wattage. They reached the top to find Cyrus sitting on the floor in the corner with a half-empty bottle of Jack Daniel's.

"I need to tell you both something. Something I should've told you years before."

"Look, Cyrus, come out with it," Elias demanded. "I don't have the time to pry it out of you."

"It's about the night Lauren was killed. It was all my fault," he said, beginning to cry.

Elias attempted to be a little more sympathetic. "Why was it your fault, Cyrus? Talk to me…now, please."

"Lauren was here that night. She was arguing with Mr. Maxwell. I could hear them through the door."

He paused to take a big swig of his whiskey, rolling it around in his mouth before swallowing it. "I listened, I couldn't help it. She was telling him she'd make him pay for making her grow up as white trash when she was an heir to the Maxwell fortune. She shoved her young son in front of him and demanded he tell the boy he was his grandfather.

Mr. Maxwell was stunned, to say the least. He demanded Lauren explain herself.

She told him her mother had told her he had fathered her and all of these years, she'd lived in poverty while he hid behind the fact she was his child. Mr. Maxwell was astounded because he'd never slept with her mother. He was a gentleman, a man who took family very seriously. He lost his temper with her, calling her a tramp, and a gold digger, like her mother. He demanded she leave right away." Cyrus took another big swallow of liquor and wiped his eyes.

"Go on," Elias said impatiently.

"I went into the room without even knocking. It angered Mr. Maxwell, but I had to do it. I opened a bottle of whiskey and started to tell Lauren the truth. She was my child. I loved her even though I was never allowed to know her. Her mother would hang around the estate, first trying to get a job, and then trying to seduce Mr. Maxwell. He knew what she was and he cast aside all of her advances. I was drunk one night and she shared a bottle with me. I ended up bedding her."

Another swallow followed by a heaving sob. "I knew Lauren was mine. I wanted to do the right thing by her, but I had nothin' and Mr. Maxwell would've never allowed Mae to move onto the grounds. I didn't have nothing to offer her, nothing. She wouldn't let me be a father, even told me she'd kill me if I ever said it was true. Mae worked all the men in town and somehow raised that beautiful daughter of ours. Hurt like hell, it did."

Cyrus sobbed aloud and his thin shoulders shook so badly that Elias sat beside him and put his arm around him.

"It's not your fault, Cyrus. You wanted to do the right thing."

"I finally told Lauren the truth right in front of Mr. Maxwell. She was so angry, she grabbed the bottle and drank long and hard from it. Said she wasn't trash and demanded to be made legitimate. Hit me, she did, right across the face. Hurt inside more than out. She grabbed the boy and left in a rage, killing them both before they could reach her destination."

The air was thick and silent until they heard the sound of clapping, applause actually. "That was great, Mr. Hames," Mayor Blake said. "Great performance!"

Everyone turned around in surprise. The silver of a small handgun gleamed as he pulled it from the back waistband of his pants.

"Drop your weapon down the stairs, friend," he said to Elias, who was shocked enough by the whole incident to do so.

"I knew where to find you. Trent said he saw you coming up this way with Ms. Maxwell. I figure they'll be up here soon. I think that houseguest of yours, Anna, recognized my voice. She'll get over the shock in a minute and they'll storm the place."

"What?" Elias asked. "What are you talking about?"

Thomas ignored Elias altogether and turned to face Jordan. "You should've died in New York. I thought Anna was you because she parked in your place that night in the parking lot. It would have been so nice and clean if you'd just died then. You would've saved a lot of heartbreak here in Solomon Cove, you know. Hey, did you figure out I was spelling out your name? Pretty clever, huh?" Thomas bared his teeth as he sneered at her.

"Why? Why did you do it?" Jordan asked nervously.

"You thought you'd just walk in and get this place, didn't you? Thought it belonged to you when it never rightfully belonged to anyone but my wife. Lauren lived through years of torment because of that bastard. Fathered her and let her live with the town whore. Then, oh, and then, he thought he'd make things right by having a legitimate child with that bitch, Elizabeth. Oh, no, it doesn't work like that, Ms. Maxwell. I would never have known until Lauren told me, two years after we were married."

Jordan could see Elias's shoulders rise and fall as though his heart was beating out of his chest. Thomas was as calm as anyone she'd ever seen and it made her sick to her stomach.

"Yep, Elias," Thomas continued, "always thought she was too beautiful to be white trash, didn't you? She had money in her blood; so did Connor."

"Did you kill Elizabeth Maxwell?" Elias asked, his eyes clear and transfixed on Thomas.

"Had to. Confident bitch, wasn't she? Refused to believe that her dear husband could've been party to such a travesty. She didn't deserve this place and neither did that Chandler fuck-up. Elizabeth made me push her; she just wouldn't shut up."

Thomas Blake laughed a hard, cruel laugh that seemed to last for eternity. "I told Chandler I'd kill his father in the same way if he ever told it."

"You cruel bastard!" Jordan screamed jumping up to hit him.

Thomas raised his gun toward her. "If my Lauren didn't get this place, then neither will you!"

"NO!" Cyrus yelled, jumping up and pushing Thomas out the doorway and onto the balcony of the lighthouse. "No more pain, no more lies, Thomas!"

Thomas Blake laughed again and raised the pistol with such force that Jordan could only hold her breath. Just as it fired, Cyrus gave him one final push and Thomas toppled, slowly at first, looking like a stuntman falling from a building in a movie. His mouth was open but silent, and his eyes, wide and disbelieving.

Jordan heard a loud grotesque thump as he hit the rocks below, the same rocks that killed Elizabeth Maxwell. The killer now dead at the hands of a good man, a man that wanted to make everything right from the beginning.

Jordan could hear screams from Anna, the deputies, and Eric as they ran full speed across the lawn. She looked past them and saw the glimmer of Olivia Yates's blonde hair floating on the water.

Epilogue

Two Years Later

Very little of the estate remained the same and that's how Jordan had wanted it. The old lighthouse was torn down to make room for a playground for the Mullises' children, Ryan Knox, and Whitley Kelley, Hank and Rachel's daughter. Along with the playground came sufficient fencing to keep them away from the cliffs.

The estate itself had gone through a dramatic transformation, looking more like the home of Jordan and Chandler Maxwell than a dark museum. The only room that remained the same was the parlor. It was all they had left of their father. They used it for morning coffee and nightcaps of bourbon or wine.

The music played softly in the background as the bridesmaids walked down the white carpet leading to the minister, Sara Crane, Alex Cannon-Murphy, Cassie Mullis, and the maid-of-honor, Anna Stephens. The ushers followed in behind—Cyrus Hames, Quincy Velez, Zeke

Mullis, and the best man, Elias Murphy.

The crowd rose from their seats as Ruth scattered rose petals from her basket and Danny and Taylor walked down with their satin pillows.

Chandler lifted the veil of his sister's headpiece and kissed her lightly on the cheek. "My mother would've been so proud to see you in that gown. She would've wanted you to wear it."

"She *can* see me, Chandler, and she's so proud of *both* of us," Jordan said as she started down the aisle to marry Eric Riley.

About the Author

Kim Carter is an author of contemporary mystery, suspense, and thrillers. She has won the 2017 Readers' Choice Award for Murder Among The Tombstones. This is the first book in her Clara and Iris Mystery series. Her other titles include: When Dawn Never Comes, Deadly Odds, No Second Chances, And The Forecast Called For Rain, and Sweet Dreams, Baby Belle.

Kim has been writing mysteries for some time and has a large reader fan base that she enjoys interacting and engaging with. One of her favorite things about writing mysteries is the research and traveling she does to bring her novels to life. Her research has taken her to places such as morgues, death row, and midnight cemetery visits.

Kim and her husband have raised three successful grown

children. They now spend their time in Atlanta with their three retired greyhounds.

She is a college graduate of Saint Leo University, has a Bachelor Degree of Arts in Sociology, and now has become a career writer and author. Between reading and traveling, she will continue to write mysteries.

Get In Touch With Kim Carter:

Website: https://www.kimcarterauthor.com/